THE BAYOU BULLETIN

Harry's Hotline

The buzz around the shedrows has Beau Delacroix's Hot Shot and Ma Chere as the fillies to watch. Track aficionados will get a look at Ma Chere in the upcoming stakes race when Beau puts her up against Philip Delacroix's Camptown Racer. Insiders predict Ma Chere will bring home the trophy, but this race will be close.

Recently the Delacroix stables have been plagued by a series of unusual mishaps and that doesn't bode well for Ma Chere or Beau's trophy shelf. The Delacroix stables have a top-notch reputation for quality breeding and training, but small mishaps have a way of turning into big mishaps. Don't bet your paycheck that Delacroix will stamp out the recent spate of brushfires before Ma Chere enters the gate.

Harry's tip: Buy a win ticket on both Ma Chere and Camptown Racer. This one's too close to call.

Margaret St. George is acknowledged
as the author of this work.

ISBN 0-373-82569-2

FOR THE LOVE OF BEAU

Copyright © 1997 by Harlequin Books S.A.

This edition published by arrangement with Harlequin Books S.A.

® and TM are trademarks of the publisher. Trademarks indicated with ® are registered in the United States Patent and Trademark Office, the Canadian Trade Marks Office and in other countries.

Printed in U.S.A.

DELTA JUSTICE

For the Love of Beau

MARGARET
ST. GEORGE

Harlequin Books

x

TORONTO • NEW YORK • LONDON
AMSTERDAM • PARIS • SYDNEY • HAMBURG
STOCKHOLM • ATHENS • TOKYO • MILAN
MADRID • WARSAW • BUDAPEST • AUCKLAND

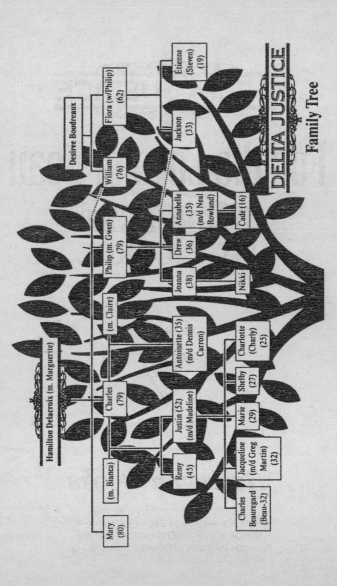

DELTA JUSTICE
Family Tree

Hamilton Delacroix (m. Marguerite)

Desire Boudreaux

Mary (80)

(m. Bianca)

Charles (79)

(m. Claire)

Philip (m. Gwen) (79)

William (76)

Flora (w/Philip) (62)

Remy (45)

Justin (52) (m/d Madeline)

Antoinette (35) (m/d Dennis Carron)

Joanna (38)

Drew (36)

Annabelle (35) (m/d Neal Rowland)

Jackson (33)

Etienne (Steven) (19)

Charles Beauregard (Beau–32)

Jacqueline (m/d Greg Martin) (32)

Marie (29)

Shelby (27)

Charlotte (Charty) (25)

Nikki

Cade (16)

CAST OF CHARACTERS

Beau Delacroix—runs the Delacroix stables, and doesn't want a wife or a family of his own until he achieves his lifelong dream. But someone is determined to destroy him.

Dr. Holly Gibson—a newcomer to Bayou Beltane, seeking hidden knowledge. She discovers the price of forbidden knowledge might be her life, or the life of the man she loves.

Philip Delacroix—Beau's great-uncle and his arch rival in the racing world.

Jackson Boudreaux—a desperate man. The loan sharks are after him, his father won't acknowledge him, and somehow Beau Delacroix will have to pay.

Desiree Boudreaux—formerly a great voodoo queen, she is seeking a successor to carry on the traditions of an ancient belief system. When her daughter fails her, she turns to Holly Gibson.

Flora Boudreaux—Desiree's daughter. She jealously guards her powers, real or imagined. When Holly and Beau threaten her small empire, she decides they must be punished.

Dear Reader,

For years my husband drove eighty miles to Denver every Friday to the stables where he boarded his two Arabians and his pack mule. Two years ago, his dream came true when he brought his horses home to our new house and twenty-one acres of good pasture in the heart of the Colorado mountains. I was thrilled for him, but not quite so thrilled for me.

As a child, I was thrown from a horse and have been apprehensive about the animals ever since. I never knew much about the care and feeding of horses in any case, and my ignorance has caused us a few problems. During our first summer with the horses, I'd look out my office window and my heart would stop. Bold was dead. Lying on his side, stone dead. I'd gasp and feel so sorry for my husband, knowing he was going to be devastated by this news. About the time I'd get him on the phone, Bold was alive again, but now the mule was dead. One of the three horses was dead every time I looked out my window. After I called the vet twice to come out and haul off the dead horses before my husband got home, George took me aside and told me that I should write books and he would deal with the dead horses.

I've learned a lot since then. Now I check with the binoculars to see if they're breathing before I call the vet. I can feed them carrots without fearing they'll bite off my fingers. When they rub against me I don't fall down in a faint. I actually love to ride. George would very much like me to accompany him on pack trips into the wilderness, but I'm afraid that isn't going to happen until he finds a twenty-mile-long extension cord so I can take along an electric blanket and my hair dryer.

I've made enough progress with these huge gentle animals that it was a pleasure to write about the Delacroix horses. Although ours are not race horses, I've come to love and respect all breeds. There's no greater pleasure than to look up from my keyboard and see Bob, Bold and Rebecca running across a spring field, their manes tossing and their tails flying. I especially like it when they're all alive.

Margaret St. George

CHAPTER ONE

AT SIX-THIRTY IN the morning, the air in the woods was cool and laced with wisps of ground fog, not as hot or as oppressively humid as it would be later in the August day.

Holly Gibson hadn't expected many things in Louisiana to remind her of Wyoming, but the towering pines that framed the riding trail permeated the air with a fresh scent that made her remember a camping trip in the Tetons. The pines here were a different type, and Wyoming didn't have the thick, tangled underbrush that encroached on the wooded path. Still, inhaling the fragrance of pine needles and feeling the horse beneath her body reminded her of home.

She leaned forward to stroke the neck of the sleek gelding Beau Delacroix had chosen for her to ride. Homesickness wasn't a problem, but she did feel the slight discomfort of being an outsider, a feeling that six months in the Louisiana town of Bayou Beltane had done little to diminish. It wasn't that Southern hospitality was a myth; Holly had discovered the opposite to be true. The problem was more that the South was so different from the West. In addition to widely divergent topography and a rich cultural mix, attitudes and mannerisms differed in the South. And unlike the West, where most people came from somewhere else, Southern roots sank deep and spread in tangled branches that first charmed, then bewildered and mystified a newcomer.

Releasing an unconscious sigh, Holly suspected she could live the rest of her life in Bayou Beltane and still fail to penetrate the subtleties and nuances of relationships formed by events that had taken place in distant generations. Evidence of long-standing feuds and grudges surfaced almost daily in her family counseling practice and never failed to surprise her. It was relatively easy to understand resentments resulting from a recent slight; harder to grasp why a lovesick Du Bois could not marry an equally lovesick Guillary because their grandfathers had fallen out with each other fifty years ago.

"What?" she asked, realizing that Beau had ridden up beside her and said something. "I'm sorry, I guess I was daydreaming."

"This is a perfect place for daydreams." He gave her a smile that made her heart stop, then thunder forward. "At this time of morning, the woods have an otherworldly quality, don't they?"

That's what she had been thinking, but she hadn't expected Beau to view the landscape in those terms. Not for the first time, she decided that Beau Delacroix was an interesting man. He seemed to have an instinct for saying exactly the right thing, and he was capable of charming surprises.

"While you were daydreaming, I was praising your riding skills. Where did you learn to ride so well?"

Holly laughed. "Thanks for the compliment, but I'm no equestrian, not like you and your sisters." She smiled at Shelby Delacroix, who rode in front of them. "I learned about horses and riding on a Wyoming ranch. Believe me, that's very different from dressage." Her gaze traveled over the Thoroughbred Beau rode so well. "As different as cow ponies and show horses." She hesitated a minute. "Shelby keeps looking over her shoulder...I think she'd like to talk to you."

Beau met her eyes and smiled, flashing white teeth against a tanned face. "Don't go away," he said softly, before he touched his boot heels to the flank of his horse.

Holly watched through ribbons of fog as he rode up beside his sister, and it occurred to her that the Delacroix confirmed the observations she had made in her practice. Beau's family was large, and in keeping with Southern tradition, most of them still lived in the same area as their grandfathers and great-grandfathers had. At first glance, the powerful and wealthy Delacroix family appeared charming, cordial and amiable. But Holly had sensed dark currents running beneath the surface. When she'd counseled Beau's teenage niece, Nikki, who'd recently been acquitted of a murder charge, she had discovered that, far from being united, the Delacroix family was split into feuding factions. Like Louisiana itself, they had secrets and hidden areas of darkness and mystery. She might have dismissed this perception as fanciful, or persuaded herself that she was merely romanticizing an old-line aristocratic family, if she hadn't gotten so personally involved with the family while counseling Nikki. And if she hadn't started seeing Beau Delacroix.

A light flush heated her cheeks as she studied his relaxed posture and the dark hair that curled away from the back of his collar. Watching him, she could glimpse where the idea of centaurs had sprung from. Beau didn't just ride a horse, he appeared to blend with the horse. They seemed to anticipate each other and move as one entity, a pleasure to observe.

But Beau Delacroix was a pleasure to watch in any circumstance, Holly admitted with another sigh. All of the Delacroix were good-looking, and Beau was no exception. Like most of the family, he had dark hair and gray eyes that appeared silver in some lights and smoky in others. His trim, muscled body reflected an active life largely lived outdoors. Beau was knock-'em-dead handsome, but Holly's degree in psychology had taught her to look beyond physical attributes. What attracted her most was his easy charm and the obvious fact that he genuinely liked women, a trait she found especially appealing.

The problem was that she was *very* attracted. This was a complication she hadn't anticipated. Biting her lip, she frowned at his profile as he leaned toward his sister and said something that Holly couldn't hear. Soon she would have to decide, as would Beau, where their budding friendship was going. So far, they had been circling each other cautiously, usually, like today, in the company of at least one other person. But the moment was approaching when one or the other of them would decide to step forward or step away.

She was thinking about that, frowning slightly at the wisps of fog, when two gunshots exploded in rapid succession. Almost like an echo, she heard the *chunk* of bullets striking the trunk of a pine terrifyingly close to Beau and Shelby.

Then her horse reared and pawed the air, and for the next few minutes she had her hands full trying to retain her seat and prevent the startled gelding from bolting. When she had him under control, she leaned forward to stroke his quivering neck, murmuring soothing sounds deep in her throat, and she cast a frantic glance toward Beau and Shelby, who were doing the same thing, struggling to calm their mounts.

Once she confirmed that neither was injured, Holly swung her gaze toward the dense underbrush beneath the pines. Gripping the reins, she tried to peer through streamers of fog hanging in the still air like smoky threads. She wasn't certain where the gunshots had originated, could see nothing in the thick foggy leaves and brush. But gooseflesh rose on her skin and she felt as if someone was watching them. Someone with a gun.

Beau shouted back at her. "Holly! Are you all right?"

"Yes." A shudder rippled down her spine. She felt exposed and vulnerable to whoever had fired at them.

"Back to the barn!" Leaning over, Beau slapped the flank of Shelby's horse and a white-faced Shelby flew past Holly.

Heart pounding, Holly touched her heels to the gelding's sides and galloped back down the trail, hearing the hoofbeats of Beau's horse behind her. Minutes ago, the fog had seemed pleasantly cool and picturesque. Now it felt imbued with a sinister quality, a veil hiding someone with a gun. She didn't relax until they broke out of the woods and into the sunshine, until she could see Delacroix Farms spread out in the distance.

As if they had planned it, the three of them reined in and silently gazed back at the woods. Beau was first to speak.

"The woods are full of poachers," he said after a minute. "It was a careless accident."

"Was it?" Shelby asked, her voice angry. "I'm not so sure. Peculiar things have been happening since the files on the old Perdido case showed up." She shoved a hand through a tumble of dark hair. "I suspect someone doesn't want me to discover the truth!" She hesitated. "You know I've been reading Great-granddad's notes and I'm..."

"Poking your nose into matters that are making some people very uneasy," Beau said, finishing her sentence with a humorless smile. "Haven't you heard that curiosity killed the cat?"

They all shifted in their saddles and looked back at the dark woods. Holly cleared her throat and wished her hands would stop trembling.

"The whole thing is driving me crazy," Shelby said, shaking her head. "I tried to talk to Aunt Mary but she begged me not to pursue this. Then I tried Grandfather, but the instant I mentioned the case, he clammed up so fast you'd think he'd forgotten how to talk. And he'd probably *never* talk to me again if he found out we know he was one of the murder suspects."

Beau shook his head. "Shelby, honey, you're just making things rough on yourself. Some members of the family are saying that raking up family skeletons led to Aunt Mary's heart attack. If you start in on Grandfather Charles and get him upset..."

Shelby let her head fall back and gazed at the sky for a moment. "I'm getting close to the truth, I must be. Why else would someone take a shot at me?"

Holly's eyes widened with shock, and she looked from sister to brother then back again. "Shelby, do you really believe that you were the target?"

Beau frowned, letting his horse dance a little away from them. "My sister is getting paranoid about something that happened at least sixty years ago. Come on, honey. Get a life." It was the kind of no-nonsense comment only a brother could get away with.

"You're wrong." Shelby stared at him. "Someone is warning me to drop my investigation."

"Or maybe a disgruntled ex-employee is sending me a message." Beau shrugged broad shoulders. His frown deepened. "It could even have been one of Uncle Philip's minions. I know Philip doesn't want me to run Ma Chere against his entry in the Delta Stakes race. He might figure he needs to make a point." He gazed at Holly, his eyes betraying deeper turbulence than his voice revealed. "Most likely it was an accident, as I suggested before."

Suddenly Shelby laughed, giving in to an irrepressible sense of humor. "Do you realize we've just come up with three possible reasons to explain why someone might shoot at us, all of them deliberate?" She grinned at Holly. "If I were you, I'd run away from this family—" she slid a mischievous look toward Beau "—as fast as I could."

"This time you've gone too far," Beau said, lowering his eyebrows in a mock glare. "It's one thing to muck around in an ancient murder case, quite another to mess with your favorite brother's love life. That can't be tolerated."

"My only brother," Shelby said, laughing, "not necessarily my favorite brother."

Holly cast him a quick look at the mention of his "love life" and felt her heart turn over in her chest. Then good sense prevailed. He was only teasing Shelby. The comment didn't mean anything. She listened to the easy banter as they rode toward the paddocks behind the barn, and she envied the affection in Beau's and Shelby's voices, the way they unconsciously helped each other move past the unsettling incident in the woods. Whatever problems plagued the Delacroix family, the resentments seemed to have skipped Beau and his four sisters.

When they neared the paddocks, Shelby reined to a halt and turned a serious face to Beau. "Should I tell Dad about the shots?"

Beau hesitated. "I'll tell him. But let's do a little investigation first. There's no sense alarming Dad if it was merely an accident."

"Mr. Delacroix!"

They all turned to look at one of the assistant trainers running toward them.

Instantly, Beau straightened in the saddle, all business. "What is it, Jim?"

"Hot Shot is colicky. Miss Jax and Mr. Taggart are at that horse show in Shreveport." He spread his hands. "Bear is working with Hot Shot, and we sent word to old Desiree. She just arrived a minute ago." His eyes widened. "There were marks in the barn."

Beau frowned, swore under his breath, then cantered forward. He jumped from his horse and handed the reins to Jim before he ran toward the barn.

"Hot Shot is Beau's baby—his best hope for the Derby," Shelby said softly, pulling the reins through her palms. "Well," she said after a minute, smiling at Holly, "I need to shower and change and drive to work. It was good to see you again. Maybe next time we'll actually be able to visit a little.''

They made loose plans to meet soon for lunch, then rode into the paddock and gave their horses to a waiting groom. Shelby waved and glanced at the barn before she strode toward the big house.

Removing her hat, Holly shook out a tumble of reddish brown hair, letting it fall to her shoulders, then walked toward the stables in time to see Beau leading a filly outside. She stayed out of the way of the commotion, watching the trainers, assistants and grooms pass before she entered the barn, intending to wait for Beau in his upstairs office.

But movement along the row of stalls caught her eye. When she saw who it was, Holly drew a quick breath. She recognized Desiree Boudreaux from Nikki's trial. It was her grandson that Nikki had been accused of murdering. But Desiree's name had also turned up again and again in the preliminary research Holly was doing for a book she planned to write. She studied the slight, elderly woman frowning at the ground in front of Hot Shot's stall. Gray tendrils escaped from a bandanna wrapping the woman's hair. Beneath a blue apron with bulging pockets she wore a faded dress that reached almost to the tops of heavy swamp boots.

This was too tempting an opportunity to ignore.

Holly reached her as Desiree rubbed her boot across a symbol drawn in the packed earth of the aisle. She wished she had arrived in time to study the marking. Trying not to show her disappointment, Holly extended her hand. "Hi. I'm Dr. Holly Gibson, and you must be Desiree Boudreaux.''

Immediately she wondered if the reports of Desiree's great age were exaggerated. Surely this woman was not in her nineties. Judging by her straight spine and clear dark eyes, Holly would have guessed her closer to seventy. Her skin, the creamy color of café au lait, was finely wrinkled by time, and remnants of a stunning beauty remained in high cheekbones and classic features.

Eyes on the ground, her brow furrowed, Desiree reached for Holly's hand in what was clearly an automatic and distracted response. But the instant her fingers closed around Holly's palm, her head snapped up and she peered through the dim light, her eyes sharp on Holly's face.

The unusual heat generated by their hand clasp puzzled Holly, and Desiree's intense scrutiny unsettled her. Whatever she had hoped for from meeting Desiree Boudreaux, it hadn't been this strange charged sense of connection. That was a surprise. Yet she felt as if something had passed between them the instant they touched.

Wetting her lips, she waited to speak until Desiree released her hand. "I've been wanting to meet you," she said finally, rattled enough by the handshake that she was glad they were alone.

"Yes," the old woman said, nodding slowly. She examined Holly's eyes another full minute, then turned away and stepped to the doorway of Hot Shot's stall. Standing very still, she closed her eyes and tilted her head to one side.

The fresh scent of hay and wood shavings filled Holly's nostrils, along with the fragrance of mingled herbs that seemed to emanate from Desiree's apron. Fascinated, Holly watched the old woman draw a deep breath and frown as if she were listening to an inner voice.

There were so many questions Holly wanted to ask that it required great willpower to stand silently and merely observe.

A minute passed and then another before Desiree opened her eyes and walked directly to the back of Hot Shot's stall. Kneeling, she dug her fingers into the bedding and made a grunt of satisfaction as she pulled forth a length of rope twisted into a knot. "Uh-huh."

"A gris-gris," Holly commented softly. She had studied fetishes, but this was the first one she had actually seen. They could be elaborate or as simple as this knotted piece of rope. Fascinated, she noticed strands of horsehair woven into the knot as Desiree carried the rope past her and back into the aisle. Bending, the old woman removed a lighter from her pocket and set one end of the rope on fire, watching the flame climb toward her fingers.

Frowning, Holly cast a quick glance toward the men working with Hot Shot outside the barn doors. "Is it a good idea to burn the rope in here?" she asked uncomfortably. Fire was the disaster most feared by stable owners and workers. She'd noticed a couple of the grooms looking into the shedrow and expected one of them to dash inside and insist that Desiree's small fire be extinguished at once. But no one did.

Desiree didn't look up at her. "It must be done here."

The brief explanation suggested that further conversation wouldn't be intrusive. Holly cleared her throat, watching the flame consume the rope. "I have a serious interest in vodun," she began.

"Yes," Desiree said, placing the burning rope on the ground.

It was disconcerting the way the old woman said yes, as if confirming Holly's remark. "I've been informed that I could learn a great deal from you. You see, I hope to write a book, a scientific analysis of religions outside the mainstream. I'd greatly appreciate it if you would be willing to speak to me and perhaps teach me more about vodun."

When the twisted rope had been reduced to ash, Desiree pushed to her feet and spread the ashes with the toe of her swamp boot. After she was satisfied that the ashes covered the area of the symbol she had rubbed out, she rummaged in her pocket and counted out nine horseshoe nails. Another pocket produced a jackknife, and she carefully cut two notches in each nail. "You will find a hammer in the tack room," she said to Holly. "Would you fetch it, please?"

"Oh. Of course." Amused and pleased that she had been pressed into service, Holly walked toward the door of the tack room, which she had passed when she entered the barn.

Inside, the long, dim room smelled of leather and oil and was crowded with saddles, bridles and all the accoutrements of training, racing and riding. Holly found a hammer on a Peg-Board with other tools and carried it back to Desiree.

Desiree drove the nine notched horseshoe nails into the door frame of the stall, then stood back and gazed at them before she nodded. Next, she overturned a bucket, stepped on top of it and nailed a horseshoe above the entrance to the stall.

If Holly hadn't studied vodun, she might have smiled. But this horseshoe was not intended as a good-luck piece; she knew it was a protective talisman. So much of vodun required one to see beyond the ordinary, to see from a different perspective.

"The trick is ended," Desiree murmured, dusting her hands together.

"Turned back on the trickster?"

Desiree gazed at her again, and Holly saw a flicker of curiosity in her eyes. "No."

She would have liked to inquire why Desiree had not turned the spell back on the one who placed it. She wanted to ask what the notches in the nails meant and what Desiree had done while Holly fetched the hammer. But the dignity of the old woman's bearing erected a barrier that would be breached only when and if she wished it to be.

Still, Holly's curiosity was strong enough that she might have risked a question if Beau hadn't strode into the barn. "Will Hot Shot recover?" she asked as he walked up to them.

"Yes," he said in a relieved voice. "The crisis is over, but the grooms will keep walking her." He smiled at Holly before he placed a hand on Desiree's shoulder. "Thank you for coming."

There was long-standing affection in the gesture, but his voice was politely expressionless, Holly noticed. At once she understood that Beau Delacroix considered Desiree's ministrations useless nonsense, and sensed that Desiree understood this, also.

"I'll consider your request," Desiree said to Holly, examining her face. "When the time is right, you'll know my decision." To Beau, she added, "Your little one is protected. This won't happen again."

"I appreciate your coming by. Bear will take care of your fee."

Desiree squared her shoulders. "There won't be a fee." She nodded to Beau, looked long at Holly, then walked away from them, her spine as straight as the pines in the woods.

"What a morning," Beau said, rolling his head on his shoulders. Turning to Holly, he took her hand in his. "Come upstairs to my office. You must be as ready for a cup of hot coffee as I am."

"Sounds good." She tilted her head and smiled, liking the feel of his hard, callused hand around hers almost as much as she liked the look of him dressed in tight riding pants and boots. "Unless it's chicory."

Beau grinned. "You know something? I don't like chicory in my coffee, either."

"How do you feel about crawfish?" Holly asked, preceding him up the staircase.

"Now, crawfish I like. Doesn't everyone?"

Holly laughed, stepping into his large, comfortable office. "I can't get past the idea of eating insects."

"Crawfish are crustaceans," he said, rolling his eyes, "not insects."

While Beau poured coffee, Holly examined his office, admiring the rustic appeal. The walls were made of wood planking like the rest of the barn, and covered with framed photographs of horses, awards and rows of ribbons. Many of the photographs depicted Beau's twin sister, Jax, standing beside a hunter-jumper, holding a trophy. Others pictured Beau beaming inside a winner's circle next to various flower-bedecked Thoroughbreds.

Trade magazines were strewn across a comfortable-looking, old leather sofa. A bridle and a pair of boots had been left beneath a side table. Otherwise, the office contained what Holly would have expected, all the equipment—computer, fax—that Beau required to operate the horse farm plus manage the financial investments for his side of the Delacroix family.

When he sat down behind a massive antique desk, Holly took the chair across from him. "Good coffee," she murmured after the first sip. "Do you have that much paperwork every day?" she asked, nodding at the stacks of paper covering the surface of his desk.

"Just about. These are breeding reports," he said, touching one stack. "These are track times. This pile is payroll information." He drew a line down the center of the desk with the edge of his hand. "The other side is for family business."

"I thought Delacroix Farms was a family business."

"Perceptive lady," he said, giving her a smile that released butterflies in her stomach. "It is, but I think of the farm as mine. I guess I always have. From the time we were kids, Jax and I were horse crazy. Neither of us outgrew it. While the rest of the family was dreaming about law degrees and precedent-setting cases, Jax and I were dreaming about gold medals and Kentucky Derbies." His gaze moved to the photograph on the wall. "Jax brought home Olympic gold, but I have yet to post the blue."

"Excuse me?"

He laughed. "Win the Derby. But I will someday. Hot Shot's coming along. She has the right gee-gee." When Holly lifted an eyebrow, he grinned. "She has the heart to be successful."

"Thanks for the translation." She considered him a minute. "Beau, may I ask you something?"

"Of course."

"You don't believe for an instant that Desiree Boudreaux had anything to do with Hot Shot's recovery. Do you?"

If she hadn't been watching for it, she would have missed the wariness that came into his eyes. "Hot Shot recovered because my trainer, Bear, kept her up and walking, and Bear administered a paste wormer immediately. Tonight Hot Shot will have bran mash with a small amount of salt and mineral oil, and Matt Taggart, the vet—Jax's husband—will check her out when he and Jax return from Shreveport."

Holly noticed that he hadn't answered her question, not exactly. "Yet you thanked Desiree and offered to pay her."

Leaning forward, Beau cupped his hands around his coffee mug. "Jim said there were voodoo markings in the aisle. If Desiree hadn't come to deal with the signs, most of my employees wouldn't show up for work tomorrow."

"Your employees believe that a spell caused Hot Shot to colic?" Holly asked, recalling the length of twisted rope. There was no doubt in her mind that someone had believed they were working a trick on Beau's horse.

"I'm sure a few of them do," Beau said cautiously. He lifted one dark eyebrow. "It's my turn to ask a question. What did Desiree mean when she said she would consider your request? What request?"

Frowning slightly, Holly inspected the surface of her coffee. So far, this subject had not come up between them and she wished it hadn't, because now she glimpsed how Beau felt about vodun. His attitude didn't surprise her, not really. For two centuries,

Louisianians had been uneasily trying to deal with this ancient religion, trying to decide what to do about it and how to regard it.

In the early days, slave owners had attempted to obliterate what they considered to be pagan animal and ancestor worship by forcing Catholicism on their slaves. When that effort failed to eradicate vodun, concern turned to fear and dread. As a consequence of rigorous suppression, the religion went underground for a time before it strongly resurfaced in the mid-1800s. Following the death of the great voodoo queens, vodun once again appeared to die out. Having passed through repression, fear and dread, denying or ignoring its own history, Louisiana now treated vodun as an amusement for tourists. An ancient religion had become something to smile about and exploit.

"I'm not evading an answer, I'm just running late enough to suggest we discuss Desiree another time." Holly glanced at her wristwatch, then set down her coffee cup and stood. "I'll have to hurry to be on time for work. Thanks for the ride. It was...interesting."

Beau stood when she did. "I apologize for the excitement. I hope Shelby and I didn't frighten you by making it sound as if half the parish has a reason to take a shot at us."

It suddenly occurred to her that they were alone, and that hadn't happened often. At the same moment, she realized Beau's eyes had taken on a speculative smoky hue and his shoulders had tightened as if he, too, had realized they were by themselves.

"You were great out there," he said in a husky voice, looking at her. "A less experienced rider would have lost control."

"Thank you," she whispered, gazing into his eyes. And all at once, she knew they would become lovers. Somehow, the gunshots in the woods had marked the beginning of a new and deeper phase. They would move toward each other, not away. Looking at his handsome face, her mouth dry with anticipation, Holly felt a moment of panic. She wasn't impulsive when it came to relationships, and she suspected Beau wasn't, either. When they took the next step, they would both understand they were making a commitment of sorts. Or was she imagining what she saw in his eyes?

Annoyed with herself for reacting to something that fell into the realm of a hunch, Holly moved toward the door. She had a doctorate degree in psychology and an analytical mind; surely she had outgrown hunches and feelings she couldn't explain.

"Holly?"

When she looked over her shoulder, Beau was running a slow glance over her riding pants and crisp white shirt. His eyes were slightly narrowed and his lips curved in a sexy half smile that sent shivers of excitement up her spine.

"Are you free for dinner this evening? I know a wonderful place in New Orleans...."

Occasionally one recognized a crossroads and knew with absolute certainty that the future could be altered with a single word. This was such a moment.

"Yes," Holly said softly. Then she smiled. "I'd love to have dinner with you."

AFTER HOLLY LEFT, Beau leaned back in his chair and gazed at a point in space, idly tapping a pencil against his cluttered desktop.

He would take her to the Colonel's, a private establishment off Royal Street where the lights were low, the music soft and the ambience decidedly romantic. It wasn't a place he took casual dates.

A frown drew his eyebrows and he bounced the pencil off his desk before he dragged a hand through his hair.

Dr. Holly Gibson, with her slim, curvaceous figure and calm, intelligent eyes, had arrived in his life at absolutely the wrong time. He should have met her ten years ago, before his parents divorced and his belief in marriage soured, or he should have met her a few years from now, after he'd won the Derby, accomplished his goals and perhaps was ready to risk a serious relationship.

The danger with living a planned life was that fate didn't always cooperate. Fate had yet to send him to Louisville, which had become an ongoing frustration. Now fate had placed a very special woman in his path who was not from the South, who didn't share his background. He definitely was not ready for a woman like Dr. Holly Gibson.

After hesitating a moment, he sighed, then reached for the telephone and made reservations at the Colonel's. Next he dialed Jake Trahan, the chief of police, and told Jake about the gunshots in the woods.

"You think it was just poachers?" Jake asked after he'd heard about the incident.

"That seems the most likely explanation," Beau answered, speaking slowly. He couldn't recall any ex-employee with a grudge, and he couldn't bring himself to believe that his great-uncle Philip would risk the lives of a niece or a nephew. Philip might have the morals of a swamp rat, but Beau couldn't visualize him turning a gun on another Delacroix. Finally, if Philip wanted to stop Beau from competing against his own entry in the Delta Stakes, he would have been more direct. He wouldn't have sent a warning that was open to misinterpretation.

That left Shelby's investigation into the old murder case.

"I'd be obliged if you'd check it out, Jake. Discreetly, of course. The ground was damp, there may be tracks."

"You're looking to confirm or rule out an ambush?" Having spelled out Beau's concern, Jake lapsed into silence for a moment. "I have a feeling you aren't being entirely forthcoming about this. You want to explain why someone might want to ambush you or Shelby?"

"There's no sense getting anyone riled up unless there's something to be riled about," Beau said. "Let's take this one step at a time." Old habits died hard. He trusted Jake's integrity, but Jake had married Philip's youngest daughter not long ago. After a lifetime of mistrusting Philip's side of the family, and usually with good reason, it was difficult now to think of Jake without remembering who his father-in-law was. Difficult to relinquish the habit of withholding personal information from Philip's side of the family.

After going outside to check on Hot Shot, Beau returned to the pile of paperwork on his desk and cleared most of it by midafternoon. Here he *did* see the slippery hand of his uncle Philip. It was no accident that the IRS had taken an inexplicable interest in Delacroix Farms, a nuisance that promised to take a lot of time and aggravation before Beau proved nothing was amiss. Philip had tried to use the IRS for his own ends in the past, and Beau suspected the current investigation had begun with a phone call from Philip's office. Several frivolous suits had also recently been filed against companies owned by his side of the family. Beau would have bet Hot Shot's promising future that all these incidents could be tracked back to Philip if he wanted to spend the time, energy and money to find out.

He made a note to discuss the recent flurry of pinpricks with his father. If Justin wanted him to investigate further, Beau would be happy to oblige. More likely, considering his father's recent and strange state of melancholy, Justin would advise him to deal with Philip's petty schemes without a confrontation.

Finally, at the end of the day, Beau leaned back in his chair and let his thoughts drift over the morning's events. He considered speaking to Bear about sending for Desiree when Hot Shot colicked, then decided against it. Bear had done the right thing. Ten minutes after Jim spotted the veve drawn in front of Hot Shot's stall, everyone on the farm would have heard that a spell had been placed on her. If Bear hadn't sent for Desiree, he would have had a hell of a time finding anyone willing to work with the horse.

A lot of that kind of nonsense had been showing up lately, Beau thought with a frown, remembering a suspiciously similar incident that had occurred with King Lear, one of Jax's prize horses. There had been a gris-gris then, too, and the animal had colicked. There had been talk that Flora Boudreaux, Desiree's daughter, was responsible for Lear's colic, but nothing had been proved. And nothing would be proved this time, either. Trying to pin down the source of spells and hexes was likely to be as successful as trying to catch the wind.

Standing, he turned off his computer, and collected the mail to put in the box. For a contemplative moment, he stood behind his desk, tapping the envelopes against his palm.

Could the voodoo stuff be some half-baked scheme of Philip's to unnerve Beau's employees? Could Philip believe that a nervous staff at Delacroix farms might give him an edge in the Delta

Stakes? If so, then why not hire someone to hex Ma Chere, who was running in that race, instead of Hot Shot?

Suddenly he laughed out loud. What was he doing, seriously considering voodoo spells and hexes? The gunshots must have rattled him more than he'd thought.

Still, someone had targeted Hot Shot—and by extension, him—for trouble. Someone had slipped into the barn and drawn the veve in the loose dirt in the stall aisle. And Desiree had found a gris-gris.

It occurred to him that Holly was exactly what he needed right now. The company of a cool, rational psychologist would chase the boogeymen away. The last thing he needed was to fall prey to foolish superstitions. The only lesson to be learned here was to stay on top of the grooms assigned to keep the shedrow clean. And strangers out.

Whistling to improve his mood, he closed his office door and clattered down the staircase, headed toward the main house, Riverwood, where he would have a quick drink with his father before he returned to his cottage to grab a shower and change clothes.

Already his thoughts had moved ahead, past dinner, to the moment when he would finally take Holly into his arms It felt as if he had waited a lifetime to kiss her.

CHAPTER TWO

A WAITER WEARING tuxedo slacks and a brightly patterned shirt with an open collar led Holly and Beau to a candlelit table in the corner of a wrought-iron balcony overlooking Royal Street. He seated Holly and flicked a linen napkin across her lap, then took their drink orders.

"This is lovely," Holly murmured, smiling.

"So are you," Beau noted in a low, appreciative voice.

After a great deal of indecision, she had chosen an emerald-colored silk sheath and a light paisley shawl. On a whim she had added long earrings that picked up the gold and green in the shawl, and a pair of sling-back evening sandals that she'd been saving for a special occasion.

Feeling the heat in her cheeks raised by his compliment, she turned her head and watched a horse-drawn carriage pass in the street below them. "I love the Quarter, don't you? I never come here without sensing New Orleans's history all around me."

Beau waited until the waiter served their drinks before he spoke. "You've studied Louisiana's history?"

That quickly, they were into a subject that Holly had hoped to avoid tonight, and she hesitated a moment, not wanting to spoil what Beau clearly intended to be a romantic evening. But relationships didn't have a chance unless they were based on open communication. She of all people understood that. Hardly a day went by in her counseling practice that she didn't urge people to talk to each other, to be open about their interests and feelings.

"Yes," she said, drawing a breath. "I wrote my doctoral thesis on the mind-altering effects of cult religions. One of the cults I studied extensively was vodun. As you undoubtedly know, voodoo societies can be found in all major cities, but the point of origin is strongest here in Louisiana, particularly in New Orleans." When Beau's silence became uncomfortable, she gestured toward the street signs below them. "Did you know that the greatest voodoo queen, Marie Laveau, lived on St. Ann Street? Some claim her house is still there, others swear the house was pulled down years ago and insist that the place pointed out to tourists never belonged to her."

"Frankly, I'm surprised by your interest," Beau said at last, his handsome face carefully expressionless. "You don't impress me as the type of person who would take ignorant superstitions seriously."

Despite wishing that they hadn't gotten into this subject, Holly couldn't let his statement go unchallenged. Leaning forward, she warmed to the subject. "What's interesting about vodun is its dependency on a layered belief system. All religions are grounded in faith in the unknowable, of course. But voodoo demands belief in manifestations outside the core philosophy."

"And that's interesting to you?"

"Of course. Anything involving the workings of the mind is interesting to a psychologist." The skepticism in his expression made her smile. "Consider this. If you believe, truly believe, that I can cast a spell on you and I believe that I can cast a spell on you...then it's very likely that a spell cast on you will be successful. Not because a mixture of herbs and incantations can cause you to fall ill or fall in love or whatever, but because the power of the mind is so strong."

Beau tasted his drink, watching her above the rim of the glass. "All right," he conceded slowly, "put that way, I can see how hoodoo might interest you."

Holly gazed across the table, watching flickers of candlelight play across his strong features. The desire to touch him was so strong that she almost reached a hand across the table, wanting to discover if his cheek was as smoothly shaven as it appeared. Swallowing hard, she forced her thoughts back to the conversation.

"I can't imagine that you're unaware that hoodoo and voodoo are not the same thing," she said after a minute. "Hoodoo truly is a collection of folk superstitions. Voodoo is the evolution of a body of ancient African religious beliefs.''

At least Beau had the grace to look uncomfortable, confirming her guess that he was making light of her interest, but his expression remained set in lines of disapproval. ''It's all nonsense, if you ask me.''

''Really?'' She arched one eyebrow, interested in the conversation despite his obvious distaste for the topic. ''Then how do you explain what happened to Hot Shot this morning?''

''Holly, come on. We talked about this. Colic happens in stables everywhere. It's a frightening emergency, but it's not uncommon.''

''All right, I can buy that. But do you really think it's totally coincidental that a veve was drawn outside Hot Shot's stall and a gris-gris left inside her stall, and then—out of all the dozens of horses at Delacroix Farms—Hot Shot is the horse that colics?''

''Of course it's coincidental. What else could it be?'' He smiled. ''You can't seriously be claiming that a mark in the dirt and a piece of twisted rope caused Hot Shot to colic. Are you?''

''I'm not claiming anything. I'm merely suggesting that it's rather remarkable that someone places a spell, or a trick, as it's called, on Hot Shot and then Hot Shot is the horse that colics. Not one of a dozen others. That strikes me as an interesting coincidence, for want of a better description.''

''It *is* a coincidence, that's all it can be.'' Studying her in the candlelight, his gaze lingering momentarily on her lips, he leaned forward. ''By the way, you never answered my question about Desiree.''

She'd hoped that he had forgotten, because she sensed he would strongly disapprove of her plan. Turning her head, she looked down at the narrow street. She wished they hadn't gotten into this. On the other hand, the subject would undoubtedly have arisen at some point. Perhaps it was best to talk about areas of disagreement now, before either of them had their emotions fully on the line.

''I asked Desiree Boudreaux if she would be willing to discuss vodun with me, and possibly teach me more about it.'' Knowing she would see disapproval, she forced herself to look at him again and meet his gaze head-on.

But it was shock that darkened his eyes to a charcoal color. "Holly, that's crazy! It's just..." He halted, and she recognized that it was an effort for him not to castigate her further. "May I ask why you want to do this?" he said finally.

"I'd like to expand my doctoral thesis into a book. That's why I came to Louisiana, Beau, to learn about vodun firsthand. Louisiana's official stance is that voodoo died out decades ago. But evidence suggests it went underground, instead. I'm not talking about the theatrics arranged for the tourists or the hoodoo superstitions in the rural areas. I'm talking about the veneration of animals and ancestors that forms the core belief of true vodun. I'm talking about the respect paid to a pantheon of loas and the belief that these loas can possess a devotee. Vodun still exists. It's out there." She leaned forward, unaware that she did so. "Beau, vodun is unique in that it was and is an evolving faith system. Instead of being vanquished by Catholicism, it absorbed elements of Catholicism and continued stronger than before. What other belief system has it absorbed? How else has the religion evolved? Or has it reverted to a purer form? Is it still a strong, if hidden, presence? These are some of the questions I'm interested in for my book, and Desiree Boudreaux may be able to provide some answers."

Beau stared at her until, self-conscious, she eased back in her chair and took a bite of her salad. "I had no idea that's why you came here."

"That was one of the reasons, but not the only one," she replied with a smile. "The clinic's offer was very attractive." To lighten the moment, she let her voice assume a teasing note. "Have I shocked you?"

"Truthfully? Yes." He gave her a humorless smile. "I didn't think you hard-headed Westerners could be taken in by a lot of mumbo jumbo. Especially not you."

"Oh?" she asked, trying not to take offense. "Why not me?"

"I can accept that an uneducated groom might be superstitious enough to place some kind of credence in hexes and spells. But you're a bright, educated woman."

"Beau, wait. Let's be clear on this. My interest is strictly intellectual—scientific, if you will." She drew a deep breath in frustration, feeing that she wasn't expressing herself well. "Vodun is as complex as a root system. In addition to ancestor worship, there is a belief in good and evil, and..." She waved a hand. It was too complicated to explain without sounding as if she were lecturing. "Look. I've been told that Desiree Boudreaux is a manbo, one of those trying to keep the pure faith alive. If that's true, then Desiree may be in possession of a body of knowledge that will die when she does. I'd hate to see that happen."

"Who told you about Desiree?"

She hesitated while the waiter served their entrées, then spread her hands. "The proprietors of the tourist voodoo shops sell a lot of frivolous doodads. But many of the shops also sell more serious items out of their back rooms. Once these people understood that my interest was scientific and not based on mere curiosity, a few were willing to admit that the area supports a large number of genuine believers. Desiree's name surfaced time and again, the implication being that without her imprimatur, any discussion could go only so far, but no further."

Leaning forward, Beau reached across the table and took her hand. It was exactly the right gesture to lighten what had become a serious conversation. "I've known Desiree all of my life, Holly." Clearly, he chose his words with care. "I believe she's a good woman with the best intentions." He paused. "I also think she absolutely believes in the spells she thinks she casts."

"That's my point!"

"Here's my point. If you believe spells are possible, then you fit the example you gave earlier, and pursuing this could be dangerous. As you said yourself, belief makes you vulnerable to the effects of a spell. Conversely, if you don't believe spells are possible, then you're wasting your time. Aren't you?"

She blinked, and then laughed. "You're no intellectual slouch, Beau Delacroix."

"Well?" he asked, grinning at her. "So why pursue Desiree?"

"For the book I want to write. It isn't a question of belief, in my case. I don't have to believe in vodun to treat it seriously in an analytical study. But I do need access to a genuine believer and practitioner.''

Beau contemplated her in somber silence before he spoke. ''Seriously, Holly. I don't want you to go any further with this.''

Instantly the smile vanished from her lips and she bristled, withdrawing her hand from his. ''Beau,'' she said slowly. ''This isn't going to sound like it has any bearing on the present topic, but it does.'' She pressed her lips together and gazed down at the blackened fish cooling on her plate. ''My father was a major in the air force until he retired eight years ago. Imagine every autocratic stereotype you've ever heard about the rigid, by-the-book military man, and you have an instant thumbnail sketch of Harlan Gibson. My father didn't ask or explain—he gave orders.'' Lifting her head, she met Beau's steady gaze. ''Consequently, the surest way to make certain that I do something is to tell me not to do it. Do you understand what I'm saying?''

He nodded slowly, then his wide, sexy mouth curved upward. ''Holly Gibson,'' he said gruffly, ''I order you not to kiss me. I insist that you do not put your lips on mine. In fact, I forbid you to wrap your arms around my neck and press your body close to mine.''

Holly stared at him, then burst into laughter. ''That is shameless manipulation! I've revealed a weak point and you're using it against me.''

He grinned, looking impossibly handsome in the candlelight. ''Is it working? Can I hope that you'll throw yourself in my arms and kiss me passionately to prove that you don't take orders?''

''You can hope,'' she said, still laughing as Beau raised his wineglass to her.

While they ate, Holly thought about Beau's considerable charm. He had sensed when their conversation was heading toward a potentially explosive disagreement and had known exactly how to defuse the moment with humor. Holly had seen him do the same thing with his sisters and his employees. And now with her.

He had saved the moment, but he hadn't solved the problem, she thought, frowning slightly. She was in Louisiana to study vodun, and she would definitely interview Desiree Boudreaux if

Desiree agreed. Beau's disapproval wouldn't change either situation. In fact, his resistance strengthened her resolve.

"It's odd how family circumstances continue to dictate our behavior, isn't it? Even when we're old enough to think and act for ourselves."

Beau lifted an eyebrow and gazed at her mouth, which made her suddenly feel self-conscious. "Is that a reference to your father, the retired major? Tell me about him."

"I'd rather talk about you," she said, waving a hand. "We've talked too much about me already." Before he could protest, she gave him a smile. "Tell me more about your sisters."

"Shelby chose law, but the rest of us didn't," he said, looking away from her. "Charly was in pre-law then changed to law enforcement, Jax trains our jumpers, and Marie..." He smiled. "Marie is into something called aromatherapy."

"It must have disappointed your father when you didn't follow in his footsteps," Holly said gently. "Especially since you're his only son."

He gazed at her for a long moment. "Holly, are you trying to psychoanalyze me?"

At some point in every relationship this issue arose. "Let me explain something. I don't work twenty-four hours a day. I don't try to analyze friends, relatives or acquaintances. Believe me, I'm not sitting here taking mental notes along the lines of father complex or mother complex or this or that. I'm just having a get-acquainted talk with someone I'd like to know better."

"I can recognize a racehorse whether I'm working or not...."

"And I can recognize full-blown psychosis whether I'm working or not. I concede your point," she said crisply. "And if you exhibited any obvious deviant psychology, I wouldn't be here tonight. Fortunately, you don't." She smiled at him. "Look, Beau. Normal people exist with normal problems. I see them every day in my office. As far as I've seen, you and I fall in the normal range." Her expression sobered. "But if you're going to interpret every question as an analytical probe..."

For a moment he was silent, then he laughed. "Is there really such a thing as 'normal'?"

"There's a condition called 'close enough'," she said, returning his smile.

"Well then...yes. Of course my father was disappointed when I didn't study law. He's delighted that Shelby is following in the family tradition, but he would have liked it if all his children had become attorneys." After the waiter removed their plates, he continued. "Law was never really an option for me. From the time I was knee-high to a tadpole I knew I wanted to build my life around horses. Somewhere along the line, I also discovered a talent for business." He shrugged. "Dad and I worked out our differences long ago. We're both happy that I'm handling the family business. How about you?" he asked curiously. "Did you and your father work things out?"

Holly looked down at her after-dinner coffee. "Not really. To a large extent, I'm still rebelling against authority." She thought a minute, then laughed. "Still letting Dad pull my strings."

"Makes sense to me," Beau said smoothly. "I won't feel entirely comfortable about turning my back on a law practice until I win the Kentucky Derby. Then I'll feel as if I've proved to my father that I made the right choice."

"There are other issues, too," she said, wondering how far she should take this. Truly getting acquainted, particularly with someone who could be important, meant looking at situations in one's life that were painful. "The truth is, things would have been better in our family if my parents had divorced. But they didn't."

Curiosity and sympathy filled his smoke-colored eyes. "It's hard to accept that things could be better with divorced parents. Based on experience, I'd say the jury's still out on that question."

"It's seldom better for the children involved," she agreed tactfully. "Then again, sometimes it is. I grew up in a home where my parents fought constantly. Even as a child I used to wonder why they stayed married." She didn't talk about this often, and it was difficult now. "My parents have very little in common. That means they can argue fiercely about something as small as which television program to watch or how brown the toast should be. When it comes to larger issues, like where to spend the holidays, with which set of in-laws, or how much to spend on what item, the fights can go on for weeks."

As a child, Holly had never brought friends home, and after she started dating, she met her dates outside the house. What she remembered most about growing up was the loneliness and waking up at night to the sound of her parents arguing with each other.

"Did your parents fight and argue a lot before they divorced?" she asked curiously.

Beau turned his head toward the street. "If they did, it wasn't in front of us. Which made it all the more shocking and upsetting when they announced they were divorcing." After a minute, he added, "That was ten years ago. I wasn't a child when it happened, I was twenty-two, fresh out of college. Still, the news of my parents' divorce rocked my world. I came away from it believing that if my parents' marriage could disintegrate, then no marriage is safe."

"Interesting," Holly murmured, watching him. "You learned to mistrust marriage because your parents divorced...and I learned to mistrust marriage because my parents didn't divorce."

Beau smiled. "So where does that leave us, Doctor?"

"Rhetorical question or real?"

"Maybe a little of both."

"On the professional side, I'd say there are some issues to be resolved." She smiled. "On the personal side, I'd say neither of us is a good candidate for marriage. At least not at the moment."

"That being the case, how do y'all feel about a good old-fashioned affaire?" Beau drawled, winking at her.

Holly burst into laughter. When she caught her breath, she smiled across the flickering candle. "You have a wonderful way of turning serious and possibly depressing moments into something warm and funny. It's a nice quality."

His gaze traveled slowly along the scooped neck of her green silk sheath. "Did you think I was making a joke?" he asked in a husky voice, raising his eyes to meet hers.

She might have given him a coy answer, but she'd never been a sexual tease. Her earlier intuition that they would become lovers had not wavered during the discussion of difficult topics. It would happen. Despite a deepening certainty that they had areas of serious disagreement, Holly knew they would end in each other's arms. The attraction between them was too strong not to be explored. She saw his desire for her every time he looked at her, felt her own desire fluttering in the pit of her stomach.

"I haven't frightened you away by talking about voodoo and admitting to a stubborn streak?" she asked, wetting her lips, which were suddenly dry.

"If you can overlook getting shot at, I guess I can overlook a stubborn streak and an interest in the Twilight Zone," he said with a smile that didn't touch the speculation in his gaze. Although he kept his eyes firmly fixed on her face, Holly had the distinct impression that he was visualizing them in bed together. Trying to imagine what he might be imagining impressed her as rather an adolescent thing to do, but she couldn't help it, couldn't help feeling a ripple of pleasurable tension flow down her spine.

"Let's get out of here," he said gruffly, standing. Walking around the table, he helped pull back her chair and let his hands brush the nape of her neck, the curling ends of her hair.

Goose bumps of anticipation rose on Holly's skin, and for an instant she couldn't move. Then she stood and wrapped her paisley shawl around her shoulders, tying it in a careless knot before she smiled up at him. The solid heat of his body enveloped her, and she realized she could stand under his chin, which made her smile as it called to mind the phrase, "tall, dark and handsome."

It was still early and the evening was warm when they emerged from the Colonel's. Beau took her arm and they strolled along the narrow streets of the Quarter, looking into shop windows and commenting on the showcased items.

"At last," Beau teased, "something we can agree on. We both like antiques and art." He hugged her arm close to his body.

"There may be shops like these in Wyoming, but I've never seen them." Holly gazed through the window at a bedroom suite from the Napoleonic era. "Is Riverwood furnished in antiques?" she asked curiously, trying not to think about the muscles pressing against her arm.

"Some of the items have been in the family for a couple of generations. Other furnishings were purchased by my mother before the divorce, very likely from some of the shops along this street."

At the corner, Beau gazed toward Bourbon Street, and Holly knew by a slight stiffening exactly when he spotted the garishly lit voodoo boutique.

"That shop is strictly for tourists," she said, amused by his frown. "We can stroll past it without fearing any dire consequences."

He studied her for a moment, then firmly turned her in the opposite direction. "Let's walk up to the levee."

At night, the Mississippi River was as dark as the velvety sky, reflecting the lights of slow-moving barges and the fairy-tale glitter of the riverboats. Arm in arm, they meandered along the Riverwalk, enjoying the warm evening and the beauty of the river and its myriad reflections, enjoying the tension building between them.

He would kiss her, they both knew it. The delicious question was when. And would it be as wonderful and as exciting as Holly guessed it would be? And what would happen next? Every action carried a consequence. Like a stone tossed into a pond, their kiss would reverberate in ways they couldn't yet foresee. That was part of the excitement heating her skin and tightening her stomach.

Pausing beside the railing separating the Riverwalk from the broad, dark Mississippi, they watched a riverboat decorated with strings of lights as it drifted away from the dock.

"There's a lot of controversy about the riverboats," Beau murmured, turning her to face him. "Are you a gambler, Holly?"

She knew his question didn't refer to riverboat gaming. "Occasionally," she whispered, dropping her gaze to his lips, feeling his strong hands on her shoulders.

"So am I," he said in a voice husky with desire.

For a long moment they looked into each other's eyes, drawing out the moment. Then Beau's hand slid from her shoulder to the small of her back and he drew her against his body, molding her pliant form against his hips and torso.

"Your hair feels like silk," he murmured, cupping her head in his hand.

Holly couldn't speak. Her lips parted and her eyelids fluttered shut. She slid her palms up his chest, then circled his neck. After a brief hesitation, she gently guided his mouth to hers.

He didn't kiss her passionately; it was too soon for that. The river at night was romantic, but it was also public, and neither of them would have been comfortable making a spectacle of themselves.

They kissed softly, exploring their first contact with gentle deliberation, discovering the taste and touch of each other. Curious to learn if expectations would be met. Wondering if their chemistry would mesh and be as powerful a force as long looks and accidental touches had promised.

For Holly, all doubt vanished the instant Beau's lips brushed hers. It was as if a bolt of electricity traveled instantaneously from his mouth to her chest and then radiated through her body, leaving her shaken and trembling. If she had believed less in willpower and more in fate, she might have believed that Beau's kisses revealed her destiny.

Oddly, the moment reminded her of shaking Desiree Boudreaux's hand. She leaned into Beau's body, surrendered her lips to his kiss, and experienced the same hot tingle of connection that she had felt when Desiree gripped her hand. The same sense of more to come, a recognition that a handshake or a kiss could change the course of one's life. And the passion. She felt that, too, an explosive cauldron of desire bubbling just below the surface, seeking to break past their efforts at control.

"Good heavens," she said, leaning back in his arms and raising her fingertips to her lips. "Suddenly I'm thinking like a moonstruck teenager."

"You, too?" Smiling, Beau kissed the tip of her nose, then held her in a loose embrace and rested his chin on top of her head.

Holly pressed her cheek against his shoulder and relaxed in his arms, feeling safe and protected. That surprised her. Until now, she hadn't realized that part of her had been searching for safety. But this was an insight to consider at a later time when her thoughts were less heated and more rational, when the scent of his cologne didn't make her head reel and the touch of his body didn't kindle flames in the bottom of her stomach.

"I think we've started something," Beau murmured, bending his head near her ear.

Oh, yes, she thought, smiling against his chest. Tonight was the first step toward something more. Something deeper and profound. Something that could end in joy. Or pain. Beau knew it, too. That's why he had asked if she was a gambler.

"Beginnings are always exciting, aren't they?" she whispered against his jacket, not wanting to step out of his embrace, but knowing it was growing late and they had at least a thirty-minute drive back to Bayou Beltane.

"This one certainly is," he said, laughing softly. He gave her a moment to straighten her shawl and smooth her hair, then he tucked her arm around his and they walked toward the steps leading down from the levee, passing through pools of light cast by picturesque lampposts. "Exciting enough that I've completely forgotten where I parked the car."

Holly smiled, liking him for letting her see that he was as dazzled as she. "I can lead you right to it," she said, trailing her fingertips over the muscles beneath the sleeve of his jacket. "I have a memory for things like that."

"I'm glad one of us retained their senses."

She stopped and looked up at him. "Beau? I don't know where tonight will lead, but I want it to happen."

Instead of answering, he pulled her into the shadows and kissed her deeply, powerfully, giving them both a glimpse of the passion boiling between them.

When he released her, they were breathing heavily and staring at each other in wonder.

"I think we're in trouble," Holly whispered, her hands framing his face. "After that kiss, I can't remember where the car is, either."

"Honey, after that kiss, I can't remember my name."

Holding hands and laughing, they ran through the streets of the Quarter looking for a sleek green Porsche.

JACKSON BOUDREAUX was sitting in his police car, exploring his back teeth with a frayed toothpick, when he spotted the green

Porsche sweeping down the causeway ramp. Instantly a frown tugged at his heavy eyebrows. Beau Delacroix.

If Beau was driving the Porsche tonight, it meant the bastard had a hot date. Women loved those low-to-the-ground foreign cars. Loved the power under the hood and the money cars like that represented. Sure enough, he caught a glimpse of a woman's profile as the Porsche glided past him.

Now, that was interesting. As far as he knew, Beau hadn't thought about anything lately except finishing in the blue. Whoever the woman was, she was important enough to bring out the Porsche, important enough to impress with dinner in the Big Easy, special enough to drag Beau away from his precious horses.

Jackson tossed the toothpick out the window, reached for the ignition and guided the car off the shoulder and onto the road. He wanted a look-see at the woman, wanted to find out who had taken Beau's mind off track times and winner's circles.

Before he hit the switch for his flasher, he waited to see if Beau would take his date back to his cottage at the farm. And he smiled when the Porsche turned down Main instead of taking the road out toward Riverwood. It did his heart good to know that old Beau wasn't going to score tonight.

The instant the Porsche signaled a right turn, Jackson hit his flasher. He didn't want to stop Beau on a side street. He wanted to stop him on Main, where passing cars would slow to take a look and he could enjoy Beau's discomfort to the fullest.

When the Porsche pulled over, he stopped behind it and stepped out, sliding his baton out of the belt loop and swinging it against his thigh. As he walked past the rear of Beau's expensive foreign car, he tapped the taillight with his baton hard enough to crack the shield but not hard enough to shatter it. Practice makes perfect, he thought, pleased with himself.

"'Lo there, Beau," he said, leaning to look inside the car. Well, well. If it wasn't Dr. Holly Gibson. She'd been Nikki's counselor during the trial, before the kid skated on the murder charge. And didn't she look dewy-eyed, all flushed and her lipstick gone like it'd been kissed off.

"Evening, Jackson. What's the problem?"

The problem was that Beau was an acknowledged Delacroix

and Jackson was not. The problem was that Beau Delacroix was rolling in dough and owned a green Porsche and a string of polo ponies. Beau wasn't working tonight. *He* had a beautiful woman at his side. *He* didn't have a handful of menacing loan sharks breathing down his neck. *He* wasn't worried about his job or where he was going to come up with thirty thousand dollars.

"This is just a courtesy stop," he said in an even tone. "Were you aware that your taillight is cracked?"

Holly Gibson was a beauty, all right. Creamy skin framed by a tumble of reddish brown hair that curled on her shoulders. Jackson had seen her from a distance and knew she was petite and delicate-boned, but she was also one of those women who seemed to be all breasts and legs. Shake and bakes, that's what they called such women over at the truck stop. But they probably wouldn't have called Holly Gibson a shake and bake; she looked too elegant and untouchable. She had class written all over her.

"Damn," Beau said. "Thanks for bringing it to my attention. I'll drop the car off at Elroy's shop tomorrow."

"Don't put off getting it fixed," he warned, staring at Holly Gibson's shapely legs. "If I have to stop you again I'll have to give you a ticket."

"First thing tomorrow, I'll take care of it."

He had dated a few good-looking women, but none as classy or as beautiful as Holly Gibson. He wondered what it would feel like to walk into a joint with a woman like that on his arm, knowing every man in the place envied him. Unless some big changes were made, he'd never find out.

"I heard on the grapevine that you've been breezing Ma Chere," he said to Beau, sneaking looks at Holly's legs. "Mind if I come out some morning and watch?"

Just as Jackson figured, Beau hesitated but he didn't refuse permission, not with Holly Gibson hanging on his every word.

"She's scheduled for the training track next Tuesday, early." Beau shrugged and then he grinned, the arrogant bastard. "Sure. Come on out and take a look. I think you'll be impressed."

"She'll have to be fast to beat Philip's Camptown Racer. Camptown's the favorite for the Delta Stakes."

"Camptown's the one to beat," Beau agreed pleasantly, turning the key in the ignition. The Porsche sprang to life with a low rumble. If money could make a noise, Jackson decided, it would sound like the purring rumble of a Porsche. Beau lifted a hand, then pulled away from the curb and turned onto Magnolia Street.

Jackson stood on Main and watched the cracked taillight recede. He should have given Beau a ticket instead of a warning. Would have served him right.

Walking back to his car, he wondered if Philip knew that Beau was seeing the same psychologist who had counseled his granddaughter, Nikki. Probably. Hell, Philip had spies all over the state feeding him tidbits of information, some of it as small and insignificant as who was cheating with who's wife, and some of it as potentially profitable as where the next multimillion-dollar development project was slated to be built.

Still, considering how obsessive Philip was about winning, knowing the competition's track time ought to be worth a little something in the pocket. Ma Chere's track time probably wasn't worth thirty thousand dollars, but it should earn him something.

A sick feeling built in the center of his chest whenever he thought about the thirty thousand. He needed more time. That kind of money didn't grow on trees. He didn't own a fancy green Porsche that he could slap a loan on whenever he needed some quick cash. He wasn't in charge of a portfolio of family holdings that he could tap if he wanted to.

After opening a tube of antacid tablets with his thumbnail, he popped one into his mouth. Lately he'd been chewing the tabs like they were M&M's.

He'd talk to Huey. Ask for an extension. Huey could be reasonable when he wanted to be. Huey knew that Jackson was tight with Philip Delacroix, and that counted in these parts.

And it wasn't totally out of the question that Philip might loan him the thirty thousand. He'd been doing Philip's dirty work for several years; Philip owed him. It was time he paid a little something on account.

Feeling better, Jackson let his thoughts drift back to Beau, wondering how he was coping with the IRS audit and what was happening on the lawsuit filed against the Royal Street Art Gallery. He was particularly proud of that one. It had been a setup all the way. A masterful art forgery had been sold to the gallery, who then sold it to the Louis family at a price that would make a preacher weep. Claiming a tip-off, Jackson then informed old man Louis that he'd purchased a stunningly expensive fake. Outraged, Louis went to the New Orleans *Picayune*, which picked up the story and revealed that the Royal Street Art Gallery was owned by the Delacroix family. Louis then slapped a humongous lawsuit on the gallery, exactly as Philip had predicted, claiming the gallery sold art forgeries as a matter of course. That news also made it onto the pages of the *Picayune*.

Laughing, Jackson cruised down Main. Philip—he didn't dare call Philip Dad, not even in his thoughts—was a sly old bastard, he had to give him that. The art gallery was such an insignificant part of the Delacroix holdings that Jackson doubted most of the family even knew they owned it until they read about the lawsuit in the newspaper. But Jackson had found out. And Philip had used the information to embarrass and harass his twin brother Charles's side of the family.

Now it was Philip's turn to give *him* something.

CHAPTER THREE

HOLLY BOLTED UP IN BED, drenched in sweat, her heart pounding.

It was the fire dream again, so real that she extended her shaking arms and stared at them, searching for evidence of burns. As her mind gradually cleared and she realized she was uninjured, sitting in her own bed, she covered her face with her hands and drew several deep, shuddering breaths.

The dream always began the same way. She was in a car, wearing her nightgown, driving toward a blazing structure. She could see huge fingers of flame leaping toward a dawn sky, could hear the terrible crackle and snapping sounds of fire. Then she was outside the car, smiling dreamily and walking toward the flames. Walking into the burning structure. She could feel intense heat on her face and on her skin, and she looked at sparks and bits of ash as they fell on her nightgown. Her lips curved in a vacant, trancelike smile as the sparks burned her bare arms, but she didn't feel any pain. Aside from the lack of pain, the dream was so real that she could smell sparks scorching her hair, could see the fiery ash burning her skin.

There were other people in the dream, but she didn't know who they were. They were black silhouettes against the fiery red and orange of the flames, shouting and running all around her. And there were screams. High-pitched, unearthly screams, shrieking at her from every direction, clawing her senses through the smoke and flames.

The most terrifying part was her fascination with the flames, their deadly attraction. She couldn't stop herself from moving toward the blaze, feeling the flames licking at her, wanting to touch them. It was as if she were trapped inside her own body, aware of the strange sleepwalker's smile on her lips, aware that she was in terrible danger, but unable to break through the enchantment that drew her deeper into the burning building. That was the worst. Being caged inside herself, comprehending her danger and feeling the terror of it, but helpless to control her body or awaken from the deadly fascination with the blaze.

At the moment when she fully understood that she was doomed, that it was too late to escape and save herself...that's when she always awoke, choking and trembling violently.

Giving her head a shake, Holly pushed back a wave of tangled hair and glanced at the pale light pressing against her bedroom window. The clock confirmed it was early, not yet six o'clock. But she knew she wouldn't go back to sleep.

Swinging her legs out of bed, she pushed her feet into a pair of white terry slippers and reached for the matching robe, tying it at her waist. Still disturbed, she went to the kitchen of her rented house and plugged in the coffeepot, standing at the sink and looking outside as she waited for the coffee to brew.

Recurrent dreams were nothing new; she'd had them off and on for most of her life. As a child, she had believed such dreams offered glimpses into the future, and occasionally bits or pieces of her dreams had indeed seemed to occur in actual life, although usually in a slightly different form. As a psychologist, she knew the dreams were merely her subconscious dealing with issues her conscious mind had not yet resolved. At least, that was one theory.

An entire field of study was devoted to dreams and dream interpretation. One could say, for instance, that the fire represented her attraction to Beau Delacroix. The dream was saying, You could get burned if you go further. It could also be telling her to listen to her inner voice, to awaken and recognize the danger in a hot, passionate relationship.

A humorless smile touched her lips. She had colleagues who could have written an entire book analyzing her fire dream. They would have written a chapter discussing the nightgown she wore in the dream, signaling a sexual connection or possibly the vulnerability of feeling exposed. Another chapter might address the meaning behind her arriving at the fire driving a car. There were enough elements and symbols in the dream to gladden the heart of any serious dream scholar.

But instinct insisted that any symbolic interpretation would be wrong. The dream had something to do with Beau. She didn't dispute that because she felt it so strongly, and yet she didn't really see how the dream could refer to Beau since it had begun shortly after she arrived in Bayou Beltane, weeks before she had met him or even known his existence.

Dropping her head, she rubbed her temples and wondered why she had chosen such a subjective profession. There were times, and this was one of them, when she wished she were in a profession that offered straightforward, black-and-white answers.

Sighing, she poured a cup of coffee and carried it out to the front porch. This was a lovely time of morning, quiet and still cool. The damp scent of dew clung to the grass and leaves. If a car hadn't passed in the street, she might have remained standing on the front porch, drinking her coffee and breathing deeply of the fresh morning air. Instead, she picked up the newspaper and carried it back to the kitchen, thinking that she needed to mow the lawn.

Yard work was the downside of renting a house instead of an apartment, but she didn't regret her decision. She liked living in a neighborhood that mixed ages and backgrounds, enjoyed the privacy of a house versus the thin walls of an apartment building.

She especially liked it that her small rented house was not the structure she had seen burning in her dream. The building blazing in her dream was distorted, and she sensed it was vaguely familiar. However, she couldn't identify it. Perhaps she didn't want to.

Frowning, she popped some raisin bread into the toaster, then poured Frosted Flakes into a bowl and opened the fridge, looking for milk.

And she fervently hoped the dream would evaporate with the dew and not sit at the back of her mind all day as it occasionally did.

"HI. DID I CATCH YOU between appointments?"

"Your timing is perfect," Holly said into the telephone, leaning back from her desk. "Your cousin Joanna just left, and I have a few minutes before my next appointment."

"I didn't realize you were still working with Joanna and Nikki," Beau commented, surprise deepening his tone.

She loved the sound of his sexy voice. It was like smooth, dark honey pouring into her ear. "It wasn't an official visit. Joanna and I became friends while I was counseling Nikki, and we've kept in touch. She dropped by today to tell me that she's pregnant."

Joanna had been so radiant and excited by her news that for a moment Holly had felt a twinge of envy. At age twenty-seven, her biological clock was ticking so softly that she seldom noticed it, but occasionally a light buzzing occurred when she spent time with a woman as happily pregnant as Joanna. Then, a niggling question rose in her mind about her decision never to marry.

"Joanna's pregnant? That's good news," Beau said, sounding genuinely happy. "I'll call her and Logan tonight and congratulate them. How do the girls feel about a new baby?"

"She said that Nikki and Shari are delighted, and Logan is absolutely over the moon about the baby. The only person who isn't happy is her father, your uncle Philip. But I'm sure you're aware there are several issues on that front. Joanna is hoping everything will work out eventually."

"Frankly, I'd rather not talk about Uncle Philip. I've been working all morning assembling three years' worth of records for an IRS auditor who's scheduled to arrive in about an hour. I'd bet the barn that Uncle Philip sicced them on me." An annoyed sigh sounded in Holly's ear.

"Do you anticipate a problem?"

"Not at all. The next week or so is going to be a waste of time for the auditor and for me. I've already lost several days preparing for this." Exasperation roughened his voice. "But I didn't call to complain about Philip. I called to ask if you're free for dinner tonight? I thought we'd grab a pizza at PJ's, then wander over to the Music Festival if you'd like. They've closed off Azalea Street for the event. There'll be jazz and country music. Dancing."

"Sounds like fun," she said, staring out her window at an ancient moss-backed live oak. The oak would be a wonderful climbing tree for children, she thought, then smiled. Joanna's visit was still on her mind.

"Also...tomorrow morning Bear and I are going to breeze Hot Shot. Would you like to see her strut her stuff?"

Holly hesitated. After a late night at the Music Festival, wouldn't it make sense to stay overnight at Beau's cottage since they would be getting up early to watch Hot Shot on the training track? Was that where his invitation was leading, or was she jumping to a wrong conclusion? She wasn't sure they were ready for an overnight yet. The passion was there, no doubt about that, and she knew they would explore their desire for each other. But she didn't want it to happen casually or as a matter of convenience.

"I'd love to see what Hot Shot can do," she said after a minute. "But I thought you told Jackson Boudreaux that you weren't going to put her on the track until Tuesday."

"That was Ma Chere. We'll breeze Ma Chere next Tuesday and I can guarantee she won't set any records while Jackson is watching." A grim tone tightened his voice. "I suspect Jackson is a conduit to Philip, and I'd prefer that Philip didn't learn just how stiff his competition is going to be in the Stakes race. I'd like to save that surprise for the actual race."

Glancing up, Holly looked at the door of her office as the receptionist rapped lightly, then stepped inside, bringing her a cup of coffee. She indicated the corner of her desk and mouthed the words "thank you." The receptionist pointed to her watch and whispered, "Your next appointment is here. Mr and Mrs. Deland."

Holly checked the wall clock, then covered the mouthpiece on the telephone. "Give me five minutes to get off the phone with this client, then show them in."

"I heard that," Beau said with a laugh. "So I'm a client, huh? Suspicions confirmed. You *are* analyzing me."

"I couldn't possibly," she said, teasing him after the receptionist had closed the door behind her. "You defy analysis. You're a hopeless case." She smiled when he laughed again. "Sorry. I'd rather not tell the receptionist that I'm talking to my..." She paused, wondering what to call him. *Boyfriend* seemed too adolescent. *Lover* wasn't yet true. So, how did she refer to him?

"To your friend," Beau said, finishing for her. "I'm your friend first. You know that, don't you, Holly?" When she didn't answer immediately, he continued. "Looks like I've got five minutes to spell this out." He cleared his throat with a sound that mixed amusement with something more serious. "A man doesn't grow up with four sisters without learning something, and one of the things I learned, thank heaven, is that relationships based on friendship work best. Would you agree?"

"Definitely." She saw the truth of what he was saying every day in her practice, and she'd observed it in her own life.

"So, at great sacrifice to the male in this couple, you and I are going to take things slowly and build our relationship on a firm foundation. Agreed?"

Smiling, she doodled a heart on her scratch pad. "There's a bit of sacrifice involved on the female side, too."

"I'm delighted to hear it," he said, and she heard the grin in his voice. "When the moment's right to end our great mutual sacrifice, we'll both know it. But, Holly? Most important, I want us to be friends."

"So do I," she whispered, liking everything about him. She wondered if he knew how special he was, or how difficult it was to find a man who could be sensitive and considerate without losing any of his masculinity. "I owe you an apology, Beau. I figured you wanted me to spend the night at your cottage and that's why you invited me to watch Hot Shot run tomorrow morning."

"Believe me, I'd love to have you spend the night. I can hardly think about anything else." He paused. "But I don't think either of us wants to rush this. Right?"

"Right," she answered softly.

"Too bad," he said with a deep sigh. "If you'd insisted, I was willing to make this a brief sacrifice."

Holly laughed and drew a circle around the heart she had drawn. "Hang up, will you? I have to go to work and you have to dazzle an IRS auditor."

They decided what time Beau would pick her up, talked for

another minute, then they broke the connection. After glancing at the clock again, Holly returned her gaze to the live oak outside the window.

Beau Delacroix would be so easy to love.

The thought came winging in out of the blue, shocking her. Annoyed, she reminded herself that she wasn't looking for love and she didn't want that kind of complication in her life. What she wanted was exactly what Beau was offering. Friendship. Friendship that would accommodate a relationship to chase away loneliness, bring some companionship into her life and provide an enjoyable sexual liaison. That's what she wanted. Not love. Not marriage. Not children.

Margot and Henri Deland burst into her office, abruptly bringing an end to her reverie.

"You won't believe what he did!" Margot Deland said furiously, fists clenched on her hips, cheeks flushed.

"Well, *she* started it, by God," Henri Deland shouted, staring at his wife.

Holly drew a breath. "Please sit down."

The Delands were exactly the dose of reality that she needed right now.

THE LUSH AROMAS of baking sausage, pepperoni and fresh mushrooms extended as far as the street. It was one of the things Beau liked most about PJ's Pizza Place. Another thing he appreciated was the fact that PJ's retained its individuality and wasn't part of a lookalike chain. Such franchises were making inroads in New Orleans and even in the bayou area, but so far there were no cookie-cutter pizza places in Bayou Beltane.

"I should warn you," he said to Holly, sliding into an upholstered red booth across from her. "If you're pining to sample a crawfish pizza, this is the place you can get one." He laughed at her expression. "If you're not feeling adventurous, you can settle for plain old pepperoni and cheese."

"I haven't been here before," she said, tapping her fingers on the tabletop in time to a lively Cajun tune swinging out of a pair of loudspeakers near the kitchen door. "But I can tell you right now, I'm never going to feel adventurous enough to sample a crawfish pizza." She tossed back her hair and grinned at him.

"Coward."

"Absolutely," she said, laughing. "I don't like scary movies, don't like sports where the possibility of bleeding exists, and I don't eat bugs." She tilted her head and gazed at him with sparkling eyes. "What things don't you like?"

"Let's see. I don't like franchise food, don't like formal dress, don't like foreign films." He smiled. "Your turn."

"Okay, let me think a minute. I don't like card games, don't have an ear for opera, and I'm the only person in America who does not like to stay at a bed and breakfast."

"No, there are two of us. I've stayed at a bed and breakfast twice, and both times I felt as if I were invading the owner's space. And I missed room service."

"Ah, room service. You're a man after my own heart. I love room service."

"What else do you love?" he asked, smiling, liking everything about Holly Gibson.

There had been women in Beau's life, a lot of women, and he hadn't always been discriminating. It hadn't mattered if his women weren't "suitable," as his mother would have termed it, since he wasn't interested in slipping a ring on anyone's finger. That being the case, he hadn't structured his life to accommodate a serious relationship that required time and nurturing. Every morning he was up before dawn, and he usually put in a ten- or twelve-hour day working with the horses and overseeing the finances of the family business. For the past few years, he hadn't recognized weekends, per se. Winning the Kentucky Derby was not a nine-to-five dream, not a five-day-a-week goal. The dream was as much an everyday part of his life as breathing. After a long day, he occasionally stopped in at Riverwood to have a drink with his father, and then, more often than not, he met friends for dinner and occasionally followed up with an evening of club-hopping and hard playing. There was no room, no time for a steady relationship.

And then he had met Holly. And something about her made him feel that he'd been missing something important, made him realize that he wanted more than a different woman every week. He wanted intelligent conversation and true companionship. As trivial as it sounded, he wanted private jokes and easy laughter. He wanted to *know* Holly and wanted her to know him. And he wanted sex that was meaningful instead of casual.

Since meeting Holly, he'd been paring back his work schedule, making changes. Jax and Shelby had noticed, and they had teased that he was finally ready for a relationship.

That thought made him smile. It occurred to him that a man was ready for a relationship when the right woman came along.

"What do I love?" Holly said thoughtfully, repeating his question. "I love animals, especially horses. I love summer mornings. I like to ski. When I have time, I love to read." She tilted her head, letting her dark hair fall to one side. "What do you love?"

"That's easy. Horses, horses, horses."

"What else?"

"My family," he said promptly. "And the excitement of sitting in the stands when I have a horse running. I like polo. Tennis. I like to win. I love good jazz and can listen to it for hours."

She refilled their beer glasses from the pitcher on the table and studied him with a serious expression. "What are your dreams, Beau?"

"Another easy question," he said, smiling. "I want to win the Kentucky Derby. I'm not sure it's a dream anymore. Friends tell me it's become an obsession, and maybe it has. But finally I've got a horse that could do it. Hot Shot." Leaning forward, he told her about Hot Shot's bloodlines, praised her conformation and heart. He might have continued talking if their pizza hadn't come. "Sorry," he apologized with a sheepish smile. "I can talk about Hot Shot until your eyes glaze over. I hope I didn't bore you."

"Not at all," she said, her gaze soft. "It's nice to hear you talk about something you love so much. You're grooming Hot Shot for next year's Derby?"

He nodded. "Everything we do between now and next May will be calculated to get her in the best shape possible. As you know, we'll only have one chance."

"Actually, I don't know much about Thoroughbreds or racing. My experience is of the Wyoming kind." She smiled and handed him a pizza slice. "When I was in high school, my father bought me a quarterhorse. You'll probably be horrified to learn that I rode him in the junior rodeo—barrel riding," she said with a grin. "That's a far cry from what you do."

Beau laughed. "I'm trying to picture you dressed in Western gear, racing around barrels."

"I entered the rodeo every year until I graduated. I never won the competition, but I took second place one year. So, when you say that you and Hot Shot only have one chance at the Derby, I don't really know what that means. Why only one chance?"

"The Derby is for three-year-olds." He shrugged. "Hot Shot will be three only once. Therefore...one chance."

"How about Ma Chere?"

"If something happens and Hot Shot can't run, God forbid, Ma Chere is my backup. She's paid up." He thought about it a moment. "Ma Chere isn't as powerful as Hot Shot, but who knows? We'll see how she does in the Stakes race." When Holly seemed to expect more of an explanation, he lowered his slice of pizza. "There's an old saying. Breed the best of the best and hope for the rest. But beyond that, certain horses simply stand out from the others. There's something about them that's hard to describe, but you know it when you see it. Heart, maybe. Class. Maybe it's their spirit or intelligence, or a will to win. It's difficult to explain. But Hot Shot is one of those special horses. She always has been, and everyone at the farm knows it."

"I believe in dreams, Beau. I hope Hot Shot makes it."

"I do, too," he said, looking at her. He was glad she didn't ask why he was smiling, because it would have embarrassed him to tell her that he was thinking that his description of Hot Shot applied equally to her. Holly had class, heart, spirit and intelligence. And she was special.

Neither of them noticed Chief Jake Trahan until he was standing next to their table. "Excuse me," Jake said, clearing his throat. "I spotted the Porsche outside...Beau, could I speak to you a minute?"

He shook Jake's hand, noted that he was in uniform. "Is this about the shots in the woods?" When Jake nodded and slid a look toward Holly, Beau gestured toward one of the chairs in the middle of the room. "Pull up a seat. Holly has an interest in whatever you've discovered. She was there when it happened. Have you met Jake?" he asked her.

"I believe so, yes." She smiled. "It's nice to see you again."

Jake pulled a chair toward the table and refused the beer Beau offered him. "You were right to call the department. I'd say the shooting was not an accident," he announced solemnly.

Beau pushed the pizza tray away, his expression instantly sober. "I'm surprised," he said after a minute. He truly had wanted to believe the incident was accidental. Anything else seemed unthinkable. "How did you reach that conclusion?"

"The ground was damp that morning, and the shooter left tracks. It appears someone made a nest in the underbrush and waited. He was there long enough to drink a cup of coffee. We found a crushed paper cup."

Holly's eyes widened. "Good heavens." She blinked at Beau, then looked back at Jake. "You're referring to this person as 'he.' You're certain it was a man, then?"

Jake shrugged. "Either a man or a woman who wears a size ten boot." He turned back to Beau. "The shooter was careful. He picked up the casings. Let me ask you something. Did you go back and dig the bullets out of the tree?"

"No," Beau said shortly, studying Jake's expression. Jake spoke in a matter-of-fact voice, all business, but Beau saw the concern in his eyes.

"Well, someone did. By the time I got there, the bullets were gone. Nothing to mark the tree except two gouged-out holes." He returned Beau's sober gaze. "The shooter didn't leave anything that would track backward except the paper cup, and we can't be absolutely sure the cup was his."

Beau nodded, his thoughts racing. "So, who would take a shot at us?" he mused, thinking out loud. It was no longer playful speculation. If Jake was correct, someone had planned an ambush, had hidden in the brush and waited. The shots had been deliberate.

"There are two questions as I see it," Jake said. "Who was the shooter? And who was the target?" He looked at Holly. "Do you have any enemies, Dr. Gibson?"

"Me?" She looked startled. "I can't think of any reason whatsoever why anyone would take a shot at me. I'm absolutely certain that I was not the target.'' She looked at Beau and so did Jake.

"Okay, Beau. How about you and Shelby?''

Beau regretted that no bullets or casings had been recovered that would have identified the type of weapon. Instinct and the sound of the shots suggested the weapon had been a rifle. If Jake was correct, and the incident truly had been deliberate, then the shooter knew in advance the distance involved and would have selected a weapon more accurate than a handgun.

"Would you agree the weapon was probably a rifle?''

Jake considered. "There isn't much to go on, but...'' He nodded. "Considering the setup, I'd guess it was probably a rifle. Why?''

"A rifle argues that the shots were meant as a warning of some sort. Or maybe just intended to frighten us.''

"They sure frightened me,'' Holly said promptly.

He reached across the table to take her hand, aware that Jake didn't miss the gesture. "Someone concealed and waiting could take his time setting up a shot,'' he said to Jake. "If the shooter had wanted to score a hit, he could have.'' This explanation felt right. The more he thought about it, the more convinced he became. "So, I don't think someone was trying to kill us.'' He couldn't believe he was saying this. "The shots were meant as a warning.''

Jake leaned back in the chair, his eyes on Beau's face. "You aren't answering the question. Who wants to send you or Shelby a warning, if that's how you choose to look at it?''

"Hell, Jake, in my case it could be any one of half a dozen people. You know about the lawsuit against the art gallery. Maybe old man Louis is getting a little crazy.'' He shrugged. "Maybe I've got an angry ex-employee out there that I don't know about. Maybe the owner of a rival horse farm decided to take a shot at me. Maybe one of my horses won a race that someone else thinks we shouldn't have won and he's carrying a grudge.'' Beau pushed a hand through the hair falling forward on his forehead. "Who knows?''

"How about Shelby? Who wants to 'warn' her about something? Who knew she'd be riding with you that morning?"

He hesitated. The old murder case that Shelby was investigating involved mostly family members. It was a huge stretch to imagine that his great-uncle Philip or grandfather Charles or his great-uncle William would hire someone to take a shot at blood kin. Uncle William was a priest, for heaven's sake. On the other hand, Beau didn't know all the particulars. Maybe someone was getting anxious and angry about Shelby's investigation. Beau had tended to dismiss Shelby's interest in the old case as a frivolous pursuit. Maybe he was wrong.

"You'll have to speak to Shelby. She can answer those questions better than I can," he said finally. None of his bright, articulate sisters would appreciate having anyone else speak for them. Besides which, he didn't know how much Shelby wanted to reveal about the old case.

Jake sighed, then smiled. "I figured that's what you'd say." He stood, nodded to Holly, then looked at Beau again. "Until we get this straightened out, I'd suggest that you don't place yourself in a vulnerable position. Stay out of the woods."

After Jake left, Beau became aware that Holly was staring at him. "It's okay," he said automatically, more to assure her than because he believed it.

She was still holding his hand across the table, and she gave his fingers a squeeze. "You weren't the target," she said in a low, firm voice. "It was Shelby. You need to tell her and urge her to be very careful. She's in danger."

Startled by the utter conviction in her voice, he blinked. "You sound as if you know that for certain."

A blush heated her cheeks and she released his hand. "I'm sorry, I didn't mean to sound so emphatic. You're right, of course, I don't know for certain. It's just that..."

"Holly?"

She spread her hands. "All of my life I've gotten strong hunches. While you and Jake were talking, the feeling grew that the shots had nothing to do with you. It was Shelby."

"Premonitions?"

"I prefer to think of them as hunches," she corrected him,

frowning. "I know this sounds...well, naive, but more often than not my hunches are correct." Looking as if she regretted saying anything, she drew a deep breath. "This time my hunch says you're right about the shots being a warning, and the warning was intended for Shelby." Her chin came up and she met his eyes directly, almost daring him to laugh at her.

He didn't laugh, but he didn't buy into premonitions, either, no matter what she called them. "Honey," he said, reaching for her hand again, "every time I go to a racetrack I get hunches. If there was any validity to those feelings, I'd be a lot richer." He smiled at her. "A hunch and half a dollar will get you a cup of coffee."

"Your hunches, maybe." Her chin went up another tiny notch and a stubborn glint came into her eyes. "My hunches tend to be on target."

"Good," he said, determined to lighten the conversation. "The next time I go to the track, I'll take you along. We'll make a fortune betting your hunches."

"Beau, please. Don't joke about this."

"All right," he agreed, examining her expression. It was going to disappoint him greatly if she turned out to be one of those flakes who was into occult beliefs. A scientific interest in voodoo, well, he could almost understand that. "But I have to ask...do you believe in astrology?"

"What?" Her eyebrows arched. "I can't resist my horoscope in the newspapers, but I don't *believe* in astrology. It's amusing nonsense."

"How about flying saucers and alien abductions?"

She stared at him, then laughed. "What are you trying to say?"

"Well, first you tell me that you believe in voodoo, and now I find out you have premonitions. I was just wondering how far this goes with you." He kept his voice light, letting her know that he was teasing. But he also wanted to hear her answer.

"Wait a minute. I didn't say that I believed in voodoo. I said I wanted to study it and eventually write a book examining the power of mind-altering beliefs. And I don't have premonitions," she insisted stubbornly. "I have hunches."

"You don't attend séances or commune with ghosts?" he

asked, grinning. The color in her cheeks was charming. He wondered if her face flushed when she was aroused.

"Would it make a difference if I did?" She smiled, and he could have sworn that she was staring at his mouth.

Dropping his gaze to her eminently kissable lips, he felt his stomach warm. "I don't think so," he said in a husky voice. At this point, she could claim her best friend was an invisible creature from another galaxy and he would still want her. He would still fantasize about her silky hair fanned over his pillow, would still want to run his hands over her naked body.

Once such thoughts entered his mind, they were hard to banish. He watched her walk out of PJ's after they'd finished their pizza and admired the way her stride combined grace and sexuality. A few minutes later, as they strolled along Azalea Street, listening to various combos and small bands, he held her hand and noticed other men looking at her. The glances she attracted swelled his chest with pride and sank a barb of possessive jealousy in him that he hadn't felt in a very long time. Holly Gibson had become important to him, more important than he'd been willing to admit.

"Having a good time?" he asked, handing her a strawberry ice-cream cone. He paid the vendor, then took his own chocolate cone.

"Yes," she said, smiling at a couple doing the Cajun two-step in the middle of the blocked-off street. "Do you like to dance?"

"Finish your cone and we'll give that couple a run for the glory."

"You're on," she said, looking as if she were about to say more, but she suddenly stopped speaking.

Following her glance, he saw Desiree Boudreaux standing near the Cajun musicians. She was staring across the street. Or, to be more precise, Desiree was staring at Holly. Frowning, he looked down at her, concerned by the strange trancelike expression stealing across her face.

"Holly?"

"She's agreed to see me," she whispered. She gave her head a shake, then looked up at him with a pleased smile. "This is wonderful news! I was afraid I'd have to attempt the book using only secondary research. Do you realize what this means? I'll have an opportunity to observe firsthand!''

Confusion deepened his frown and he looked back at Desiree, but she was no long standing beside the band. ''You didn't speak to her,'' he said. ''How could you know—''

It was as if Holly hadn't realized that she and Desiree had not exchanged a word until he pointed it out. A startled look raised her eyebrows and a flush rose from her throat. She waved the cone in a gesture of momentary confusion that mirrored his own feelings.

''I just...never mind.'' She gave him a smile that was clearly intended to distract. ''Hurry up and finish that ice cream, mister. I believe you promised me a dance.''

He frowned at the spot where Desiree had been standing, then looked at Holly while ice cream melted down across his fingers, and he experienced a premonition of his own.

Holly, the woman he was falling in love with, was circling around something that could be very dangerous.

CHAPTER FOUR

THE AIR WAS BEGINNING to warm, the early sun burning off wisps of ground mist as the grooms led Hot Shot and Ma Chere onto the training track and guided them into a prerace exercise routine.

Holly folded her arms on the top rail of the fence that circled the track and watched Beau confer with his head trainer, Robert Bearclaw. She let her gaze travel over Beau's crisp white shirt and tight-fitting riding pants, then she swallowed hard and made herself look at the horses instead.

They were both beautiful animals, high spirited, sleek and well groomed. Although Hot Shot and Ma Chere looked enough alike that they could have been twins, Holly could tell them apart. Exactly as Beau had said, there was something about Hot Shot that commanded attention, that made her stand apart from other horses. When Holly had watched her run the day after the Music Festival, she had done so in utter silence, too moved by Hot Shot's power and beauty to speak. Although this morning was not about Hot Shot, Holly had jumped at Beau's invitation to watch her run again.

After accepting a steaming cup of coffee from one of the grooms, she turned slightly so she could see Beau. This morning's workout had occupied most of their conversation last night when they had taken a drive after work. Because Jackson Boudreaux might show up today, the purpose of the race had changed from a routine training session for Ma Chere into an opportunity to fake out Beau's uncle Philip.

That's why Hot Shot was running this morning. Ma Chere would not show as well next to Hot Shot. To make doubly certain, Ma Chere would be carrying more weight than she would have if Jackson Boudreaux hadn't been expected to carry a report back to Philip Delacroix. The training session was, in fact, rigged to show Ma Chere in a less-than-favorable light.

Shaking her head and smiling at the machinations of the racing world, Holly sipped her coffee and watched everything with interest. It surprised her how many people were required for this morning's exercise. At least five grooms worked with or near the horses. Exercise boys stood by, waiting to hot walk the horses when they came off the track. She spotted several assistant trainers.

She didn't realize that Detective Jackson Boudreaux had arrived until he leaned on the rail next to her and spoke as casually as if continuing an on-going conversation. "I didn't know you were interested in horses."

"I've always loved horses, Mr. Boudreaux."

He was a handsome man and wore his uniform well, Holly noted. She found herself comparing him to Beau, as she'd been doing with all men recently. Jackson was probably a year or two older than Beau, but several inches shorter. His hair was a shade darker and his eyes were deep brown rather than smoky gray like Beau's. Oddly, she saw similarities between Jackson's profile and Beau's. If she hadn't known better, she might have guessed that Jackson and Beau were distantly related.

The thought made her smile. It was a perfect example of how emotions could distort perception. She was so infatuated with Beau Delacroix that now she was seeing reminders of him in every man she met. Shaking her head, she glanced toward Beau and Bear and noticed that the two men had spotted Jackson.

"Yeah, well, finding you here is a surprise," Jackson continued, his gaze following the movements of the horses. "I thought your only interest was in helping murderers get over any small twinges of guilt they might be feeling."

Holly straightened and her head whipped around. She stared at him. "Excuse me?"

"I heard how you worked with Nikki Gideon after she beat the rap for murdering my brother." He turned his head to gaze at her with flat dark eyes.

For a moment, Holly was dumbstruck. Then hot color flooded

her face and she frowned. "The defense proved that your unfortunate brother died from a snakebite. Steven was not murdered."

He studied her expression for a moment. "Some might say the only thing the defense proved is that Delacroix money can buy whatever testimony the family needs."

Holly gripped her coffee cup and shifted to fully face him. "Surely you don't believe that."

"Think about it. All the evidence proved that Nikki killed my brother. She was staring a conviction in the face. Then her lawyers, one of whom was her mother, a Delacroix, sprang a surprise witness who said Steven didn't die because little Nikki beat him with a tire iron. Oh, no. Steven died of a snakebite." Disgusted, Jackson turned away and spit on the ground. "Someone remembers to do some tests right before the case goes to the jury, and—gee, what a surprise—the tests conveniently show that Steven died of a snakebite. Like hell he did! All the evidence showed that Nikki tried to murder my brother, and shame on her, but, hey folks, the evidence is wrong. We shouldn't blame poor little Nikki for beating Steven and leaving him to drown. We should blame some bad ole snake." His lips curled. "Now, isn't it lucky for Nikki that venom showed up in those last-minute tests? Unbelievably lucky." He stared at her. "If you believe that fairy tale, Dr. Gibson, then no wonder you want to interview my grandmother. You're as gullible as they come."

Holly didn't know where to begin. Blood pounded in her temples and her hands shook around the paper coffee cup. She'd spent hours and hours and hours with Nikki and knew how devastated the teenager had been by Steven's death. She also knew that Steven Boudreaux had beaten Nikki and frightened her. And she knew beyond any shadow of a doubt that Nikki had acted in self-defense and had not attempted to kill Steven. When Nikki drove away from the lake that night, Steven had been alive.

Her instinct was to defend Nikki and to insist on the truth of the evidence. But it was clear from Jackson's stony expression that nothing she said would alter his opinion.

"I'm sorry you feel that way," she said finally, turning to look at the track. The jockeys were up and moving toward the gates.

Her comment was grossly inadequate and didn't express a tenth of what she was feeling, but it was the only neutral statement she could think of.

"I also regret that you seem to view me as some kind of bad guy," she added stiffly. "I assure you that is not the case. I'm sorry for the loss your family suffered." Several responses to his charge of gullibility hovered on her tongue, but she made herself swallow the remarks instead of stating them. She didn't want to prolong this conversation. In fact, she was looking for a way to escape Jackson's company when Beau joined them.

"Hello, Jackson," Beau said, extending his hand. After the two men shook hands, Beau leaned on the railing. "Nice morning for a workout. Not too hot yet."

Still upset, she stepped away from Jackson and moved closer to Beau. When he felt her shoulder against his, he looked at her and smiled. The smile faltered when he saw the heat in her cheeks and the anger in her eyes.

"I take it you and Jackson are getting acquainted?" he asked, studying her expression.

"Yes," she said shortly, crushing the paper cup between her hands.

Beau turned to look at Jackson. "How's the family?" he asked in a pleasantly cool voice.

Jackson studied Ma Chere when the horses passed them on the way to the gate. "Your lady friend has caused a bit of a flap. Ma and Grandma have been arguing like cats and dogs about her poking her nose into things that don't concern her."

Beau straightened and his eyes narrowed. "It's my understanding that Desiree agreed to meet with Holly."

Holly placed a hand on his sleeve. The way the two men were sizing each other up, squaring off, made her uneasy. "If your grandmother would prefer not to meet with me..." she began. But Jackson cut her off.

"That's the problem," Jackson said, staring at her. "Desiree insists on meeting with you. She told me to tell you to come tomorrow afternoon. It's Ma who doesn't want you. And why should she? You tried to help the person who murdered her son."

Holly tightened her grip on Beau's arm when she felt his muscles tense beneath her fingertips. "Please tell your grandmother that I'll be there."

"I don't like your tone, Boudreaux," Beau said sharply.

Jackson shrugged. "You asked how the family was. I told you."

Holly stepped backward, away from the waves of hostility rolling off Jackson Boudreaux. Blinking, she released Beau's arm and let her weight sag against the fence railing.

A bell sounded and Ma Chere and Hot Shot sprang out of the gate. She watched the powerful animals sweeping around the track, and some part of her mind registered their grace and fluid beauty.

But her primary focus remained firmly on Jackson Boudreaux and the impression she was picking up. This was a ruthless man capable of great cruelty. She felt this and didn't doubt it. Disturbed, she turned to look at his intent face. His mouth was pressed in a thin, hard line, and his eyes were narrowed on Ma Chere. In this unguarded moment of fixed concentration he was easy to read.

Holly stared at him and understood that despite his job and the uniform he wore, Jackson Boudreaux had absolutely no scruples. Whatever was right for him was right, period, regardless of ethics, morality or the law. This was a self-pitying man seething with frustration and resentment. A man capable of egregious acts if he saw an advantage or benefit to himself.

Shuddering, Holly turned her glance back to the track in time to see Hot Shot fly over the finish line, her mane and tail fluttering proudly like ribbons of dark silk.

"Damn," Beau muttered, staring down at a stopwatch as Ma Chere finished half a length behind Hot Shot. Although Holly knew the race was a charade staged for Jackson's benefit—and ultimately Philip Delacroix's—Beau sounded genuinely disappointed in Ma Chere's showing.

Jackson eased back from the rail and grinned, his gaze darting to the time clocked on Beau's stopwatch. "If that's the best she can do, I think I'll put my money on Camptown Racer." Needing to rub it in, he added, "If I were you, I wouldn't even bother to enter Ma Chere in the Stakes."

Beau watched the grooms handing the horses over to the exercise boys, who would walk them until they cooled off. "She's having an off day," he said in a flat voice. "I expected better."

"Sure," Jackson said, unconvinced. Laughing, he lifted a hand, then walked away from them, heading toward the parking lot.

When Jackson was out of earshot, Beau put his hands on Holly's waist and grinned. "I think he bought it. Now," he said, looking into her eyes and letting his expression grow sober, "do you want to tell me what's upsetting you?"

She loved the heat of his large hands on her waist, liked the way he held her far enough from his body that they wouldn't create a spectacle, yet close enough that she was very much aware of him.

"Beau? Tell me about Jackson Boudreaux."

He fetched them more coffee, and when they had fresh cups, they leaned on the rail. Beau watched Hot Shot walking off the race, and Holly watched the sunlight playing in Beau's dark hair.

"What do you want to know?" Beau asked.

She told him what Jackson had said to her. "I have a definite impression that Jackson deeply resents the Delacroix family. He seems to believe that Joanna or maybe even your great-uncle Philip bought and paid for evidence to rescue Nikki. Yet you said he was a direct conduit to Philip. What are the relationships here?"

Beau sighed, his gazed fixed on Hot Shot. "It's complicated, and I'm not really certain that I know all the answers. Desiree Boudreaux has been part of the family for as long as I can remember. She's always been around."

"Desiree is part of your family?" Holly looked surprised.

"In the same way as a long-term servant might be considered part of a family. When she was a young woman, she worked for my great-grandparents and later for my grandparents."

He hesitated, and suddenly Holly realized he was about to reveal a family secret. Flattered and pleased by his confidence in her, she touched his arm.

"We just recently learned that after my great-grandparents lost a child, Desiree gave them her infant son to raise. In gratitude, my great-grandfather deeded over the swampland around Desiree's home. My grandfather later offered to send Desiree's daughter to college, so the story goes. Eventually Flora got pregnant with the child who grew up to be Jackson. The two families have been entangled for generations.''

''Who is Jackson's father?''

Beau shrugged then tasted his coffee. ''Who knows? I don't mean to sound cold, but it's possible that Flora doesn't know herself. I've been told that Desiree's daughter was a beautiful and wild young woman, no better than she needed to be. Maybe that's true, maybe it isn't. But it is true that no one in Bayou Beltane knows who Jackson's father is. Including, I assume, Jackson himself. If he knows his father's name, he's certainly never mentioned it, and I've known Jackson all of my life.''

''That's sad,'' Holly said, standing away from the rail. ''It's hard on a young boy to have no father and a mother who's the object of gossip.'' Beau stood, too, and they walked toward the barn.

''Don't waste too much sympathy on Jackson,'' Beau said with a humorless smile. ''He was a bully in grade school and in and out of trouble from then on. In a way it isn't surprising that he chose police work for a profession. The uniform and the right to carry a gun are an extension of the same tyranny he exercised as a kid.'' He looked down at Holly. ''If Jackson hadn't succeeded in police work, he could have gone the other way and ended on the opposite side of the law.''

She loved it that she could read his expressions now. ''Say the rest,'' she prompted gently.

He hesitated. ''There are rumors about Jackson,'' he said finally and with obvious reluctance. ''Some talk that he plays both sides of the fence and observes the law when it suits him and violates it when it's to his advantage.''

''I'm amazed that he's still with the police department,'' Holly commented, matching her stride to his.

''Oh, Jackson is clever. Maybe *sly* is a better word.''

''What's his connection to your uncle Philip?''

''I'm not sure, except there definitely is a connection. Some say Jackson is one of Philip's henchmen, one of the goons who does Philip's dirty work.''

"Do you believe that?" Holly asked, studying his handsome face curiously.

Beau shrugged again and tossed his coffee cup into a trash receptacle. "Let's say it wouldn't surprise me if it were true." Placing his hands on her shoulders, he looked into her eyes. "Holly, tell me that you're not going to go into the swamp and visit Desiree."

Her chin lifted stubbornly even as a tiny thrill of pleasure rippled over her skin at his touch. "You bet I am," she said firmly, meeting his gaze. "This is too good an opportunity to pass up even if I wanted to. And I don't. This is what I came to Louisiana to find, Beau. I'd be a fool to walk away from it."

"Even if I asked you to?" he said softly.

"I hope you're a good enough friend that you won't do that," she answered, trying to decide if his eyes were the color of charcoal today.

He stared at her, then threw back his head and laughed. "That's a 'gotcha' if I ever heard one."

Smiling, Holly moved out from under his hands and took a step toward the parking lot, glancing at her watch. "Thanks for inviting me to watch Hot Shot and Ma Chere."

"Dinner tonight?"

"I'd love to," she said, meaning it. "But I've got a group session this evening. Can I take a rain check?"

"How about tomorrow? I'll go with you to Desiree's and then we'll catch a bite to eat."

She thought about the suggestion, not answering immediately. Desiree had not invited Beau along; she might be offended if Holly brought additional company. Besides, it annoyed her slightly that Beau seemed to feel she couldn't handle the interview by herself.

When he noticed her hesitation, he gave her an appealing grin. "I'll wait outside. I won't rush you."

"Beau," she said, frowning, "I'm in no danger. I'd sense it if I were."

"Really? You don't consider snakes and gators dangerous?"

"Oh." She hadn't been thinking along those lines. Now that she was, she remembered Steven dying of a snakebite.

Laughing at her expression, Beau lifted a hand in a wave and moved toward the cutoff leading to the barn and his office. "I'll pick you up at the clinic about two o'clock, okay?"

"Okay," she said, feeling foolish.

JACKSON FELT GOOD. He'd shown Holly Gibson that her beauty and her fancy degree didn't impress him one iota. And he'd gotten a good look at Beau's stopwatch and knew that Ma Chere's time was nothing to crow about.

Since things were going his way this morning, he decided he'd pay Philip a visit and hit the old man up for a loan. Huey was getting impatient for his money. If Jackson didn't pay something soon, things would get ugly.

And he couldn't afford to let that happen.

If the chief of police discovered that Jackson was in this deep with a loan shark notorious for ties to organized crime, he would take Jackson's badge in a New York second. And if Philip found out that he had any ties to Huey, his days as Philip's right-hand man would be over so fast it would make his head spin. Ever since Philip had announced his candidacy for reelection as state senator, he'd been playing it close to the vest, attempting to tidy up his image. Even so, he was taking a beating in the straw polls. If he found out about Jackson's association with Huey, Jackson would be out on his butt. Philip wouldn't risk even a remote connection with the loan shark.

Well, he didn't have to worry. It wasn't going to happen. If push came to shove, he would wave Philip's name around and Huey would give him another extension. Huey wasn't stupid. He wouldn't rough up a man who had the ear of a state senator. On the other hand, Huey wanted his money. He wasn't going to wait forever.

Pulling a handkerchief from his back pocket, Jackson mopped his forehead. It was getting hot and the humidity was high today. Damn. He wished Philip was showing better in the polls. If Huey decided Philip might lose, then Jackson could find himself in serious problems quicker than a cat could blink.

Easing the cruiser to the side of the road, he dialed Philip's office on the car phone. "It's me," he said when Philip picked up his private phone. "You have a few minutes?"

"Use the back entrance," Philip said, and hung up.

"Bastard," Jackson muttered, slapping his car phone into the holder. Philip couldn't say "Good morning." Or "How are you?" A familiar burning heated his rib cage and he gripped the steering wheel, staring through the windshield. His good feeling was gone.

There were times when he believed that Ma was just blowing smoke when she promised that Philip Delacroix would eventually acknowledge Jackson as his son. And times like right now when Jackson believed it would never happen. Flora could hex Philip until the next ice age and the old bastard wasn't going to budge.

On the other hand, he thought, tapping his fingers on the steering wheel, Ma had a way of getting what she wanted. And who was he to say that the gris-gris she made didn't have something to do with it? He'd seen things in his time. Maybe she really would turn Philip around and get Jackson what he deserved.

Slapping the cruiser into gear, he drove down Main and turned off at the café. He parked his car on a side street near the dress shop, waited until there was no pedestrian traffic, then walked up a block and slipped into a recessed, unmarked door at the back of Philip's building. A flight of stairs led up to a small foyer that few people knew about. Annoyed that there was no doorknob on this side of the door, Jackson pressed a button, which flashed a small light inside a bookcase within Philip's line of sight. After what seemed like several minutes—Philip always made him wait—the door clicked open and he walked directly into Philip's expensively furnished office.

Those were real Oriental rugs on the floor. Real leather chairs, not the imitation kind. He couldn't begin to imagine what the artwork was worth, but the paintings reminded him that the thirty thousand dollars he so desperately needed was only pocket change to Philip Delacroix.

"Sit down," Philip said without looking up from his desk. "What do you want?"

The question almost made him laugh. Philip knew damned well what he wanted. He wanted a piece of the Delacroix pie. He deserved a Porsche and a string of polo ponies. He deserved a big house and a bottomless wallet just like all the other Delacroix girls and boys. He wanted to tell Beau and Philip's son, Drew, all of them, that he was as much a Delacroix as they were. He wanted to wipe the superior smiles off their smug faces.

He cleared his throat and touched his uniform tie. "I'd like to borrow some money. I'm thinking about buying a house."

That got the old man's attention. Philip leaned back in his desk chair and pushed two antacid tablets into his mouth. He stared at Jackson, chewing slowly.

"How much money?" he asked, brushing his fingertips across a maroon bow tie.

Philip was the only man Jackson had ever seen who didn't look foolish wearing a bow tie. "Thirty thousand dollars."

Philip made a snorting sound and moved forward to face Jackson squarely. "If you want a house, you can work for it like everyone else."

Jackson felt the heat rise in his face, and he dug his fingers into the soft leather armrests of Philip's chair. "I need that money."

His tone inspired one of Philip's rare unpleasant smiles. "You make a decent salary. I pay you. And I suspect you supplement your income from additional sources, as well." He stared at Jackson with cold eyes. "Have you been playing the ponies again?"

It was dangerous to lie to Philip, so he evaded the question instead. "I'm thirty-three years old. It's time I bought a house." He sounded whiny. What was it about this gray-haired old man that intimidated him so much? No one else on earth intimidated Jackson Boudreaux. Just Philip Delacroix, his father. "I found a nice place over near Slidell, in that new subdivision. Hell, it isn't like I'm asking for a handout. I'm asking for a loan." He rubbed his hands on the thighs of his uniform pants and played his card. "I know Ma Chere's latest track time," he said smugly, implying the information was worth the loan he was asking.

"No, you don't," Philip snapped, his expression irritated. "What you saw this morning was a setup." He studied Jackson's surprised expression and his lips curled. "The jockey was heavy and held back. Did you imagine that you're my only source of information? Thankfully you're not, since you got taken in."

A dark flush rose on Jackson's cheeks and he made a silent vow to get even with Beau. "Philip, I really need the money," he said again, hating the edge of desperation in his voice.

"I'm not a bank. I don't make loans." He waved a hand, indicating the subject was closed. "I do have a job for you, however."

Philip was not going to give him the money. That was bad. Very bad.

Leaning back in his chair, Philip stared at him in a way that told Jackson something was coming that he wasn't going to like. "The bleeding hearts always want to stop progress."

"That's a fact," Jackson said, but he didn't have a clue what Philip was talking about. He was seething about the money. Philip would have given his son Drew thirty thousand dollars. Hell, he could hand Drew three times that amount and never miss it.

"This area is starting to stagnate because growth is limited by the swamps. Any fool can see the answer is to drain the swamps and develop the land."

Now Jackson understood. Philip was still smarting because his plan to drain and develop the swamp and wetlands had been stopped cold by the Louisiana Department of Environmental Standards. He shrugged. "You can't fight an injunction."

Philip leaned forward over his desk. "It's my land and I should be able to develop it if I damned well want to!" Philip opened a prescription bottle and put a pill on his tongue, then washed it down with a drink of water poured from a crystal carafe. "That would be happening right now if Desiree hadn't interfered."

"And Remy's wife. She's the bleeding heart environmentalist who started the trouble."

Philip waved a dismissive hand. "Kendall wouldn't have been a problem if Desiree hadn't influenced her." He fixed Jackson with a steady look. "And the problem could have been dealt with if Desiree hadn't sprung the surprise that she holds a deed for land right smack in the middle of *my* land."

Philip wasn't the only one who had been surprised. Jackson

doubted that even Ma had known Desiree owned the land her shack sat on.

"I want that land," Philip stated flatly. "Being sole owner of the land in question is the first step toward getting the injunction lifted. I want you to convince Desiree to sell me her place."

A burning sensation spread beneath his chest. His grandmother would never sell her land, not in a million years. "There's no way that will ever happen," he said after a minute.

Philip pushed an envelope across his desk. "Make it happen."

"Even if Desiree agreed to sell, and she won't, that's no guarantee you'll get the injunction lifted." The envelope was fat but not too fat. Not fat enough to solve his problems with Huey.

"We'll deal with the injunction once I own all the land involved." Philip shrugged. "People can be bribed, blackmailed...but first, I need the deed to Desiree's land. Once she's out of there, I can move on the injunction."

"How much is in the envelope?"

"Five thousand dollars."

He picked it up, surprised as usual by how little a stack of hundreds weighed. "You're asking me to sell out my grandmother," he said, tapping the envelope against his palm. "It's going to take more than five thousand dollars to ease my conscience."

Philip laughed, the first time Jackson had heard him laugh in years. Then his eyes went hard. "If you persuade Desiree to sell, we'll talk about a bonus. If you fail, then you repay the money. I'm not paying for failure, I expect success." He pulled a file across his desk and opened it in front of him. "That's all. You can go."

He ought to toss the money back in Philip's face, Jackson thought, looking down at the envelope. Five thousand dollars was a drop in the bucket. It wouldn't get him off the hook with Huey. It wasn't enough to compensate him for the aggravation he was going to face with Desiree.

But he didn't have a choice. Biting down on his back teeth, he tucked the envelope inside his uniform jacket, then walked away from Philip's desk. He waited until he'd opened the door to the private foyer before he said, "I'll tell Ma you said hello," knowing any reference to Flora upset Philip. He let the door click shut behind him and clattered down the staircase.

The five thou would quiet Huey down for a week or so and buy Jackson a little more time. But Huey was getting impatient. And that was bad.

Pushing Huey out of his mind, he shifted his thoughts to Desiree and her property in the swamp. There was opportunity here, he could smell it. And his nose told him that Philip would pay a lot more than five grand to get his hands on Desiree's deed. He would pay a fat bonus, as well.

If Jackson played this right, he could get the thirty thousand he needed and possibly a lot more. And Desiree could demand a fortune for a shack that was worth a few thousand bucks at best. A million dollars wasn't out of the question. That would only be a fraction of what Philip stood to profit if he could develop his swampland.

As Desiree's only surviving grandson, Jackson could conceivably become heir to a million dollars. He wouldn't mind that at all. Then he remembered his mother; Flora would get her hands on the million before he did.

Two million, he thought, amending his original selling price. They needed two million. Philip, the old bastard, could afford to spend two million to make tens of millions.

Frowning, he drove aimlessly, his mind racing. There was too much at stake to rush a confrontation with Desiree. He needed to think about this.

CHAPTER FIVE

THE MORE HOLLY THOUGHT about Beau accompanying her to Desiree's place in the swamp, the more irritated she became. She didn't need a baby-sitter, didn't need someone to hold her hand. The protectiveness of Southern men was legendary, and Holly knew there were times when it felt good to rely on a man, but this was not one of them. If she was not self-sufficient enough to conduct her research on her own, then she had no business even thinking about writing a book on a subject with dark undertones.

After her last appointment, she entered the private bathroom adjoining her office and changed out of a skirt and jacket and into a pair of jeans and a light blouse.

She didn't think what she was doing was remotely dangerous. It wasn't as if she believed in vodun as a choice for herself. She wasn't seeking out Desiree as a first step toward becoming a card-carrying member of a voodoo group.

Frowning, she peered into the mirror, ran a brush through her hair, then tied it at the back of her neck with a piece of blue ribbon that matched her blouse.

Hers was a scientific, analytical mind. All she wanted to do was stand back and observe. Gather firsthand information for her book. But Beau's insistence on escorting her made her feel as if she were undertaking some perilous journey, as if she were fool-ishly disregarding everything reasonable and sensible.

Or, she thought suddenly, pausing, was it possible that she was merely erecting defenses against falling in love with him? Frown-ing, she studied herself in the mirror. The mind was a strange thing, capable of disguising one problem as another. Was she really and truly irritated that Beau insisted on accompanying her to Desiree's? Or was she reacting to the fact that she seemed to think about him all of the time? Was she trying to push him away because he was getting under her skin?

"You're doing it again," she said, making a face at herself. "You should know better than to try to analyze yourself. That never works."

By the time Beau pulled up in front of the clinic and she slipped inside the cool interior of the Porsche, her mood had softened, but she was no closer to understanding her reasons for resenting his insistence on coming with her today.

"It really isn't necessary for you to take time away from your work to accompany me," she commented as she fastened her seat belt.

"I'm glad to do it." Beau glanced at her as he eased away from the curb, managing to convey admiration and a spark of concern. "Are you nervous about visiting Desiree?" he asked, misinterpreting the hint of sharpness in her tone.

"I'm not a child, Beau. I'm perfectly capable of driving to the swamp, hiring a swamp boat and going to Desiree's on my own."

"I know you are," he said easily. "I'm here because I want to be, not because I think you can't manage on your own."

"And not because I asked you to go with me."

"That, too," he agreed pleasantly. But he took his gaze from the road to give her a long look.

"I'm sure you have better things to do than spend your afternoons waiting for me to finish my initial interview with Desiree."

When they were out of town, he pulled the Porsche to the side of the road, then turned to look at her. "Whoa. What's going on here? You aren't usually this prickly."

For a moment she sat stiffly staring out the windshield, not answering. Then she lifted a hand to her forehead and sighed. "One of the first things that happens in an important relationship is that one or both people surrender their independence." She had seen this again and again in her counseling practice. And maybe that was what she was feeling in this incident.

"It starts with an urge to please," she continued, shifting on the seat to face him. And her heart sank. He was so handsome, so unconsciously sexy. And genuine concern darkened those smoky eyes. Despite suddenly feeling foolish, she blundered on.

"You want to please me, so you give up an afternoon you could spend in better ways. I want to please you, so I don't put my foot down when you insist on coming with me. Consequently, we each feel a kernel of resentment."

"I don't feel any resentment. I'm glad to be here." He placed his arm along the seat back, and let his thumb gently stroke her cheek. "Another way to look at it is that this afternoon is an opportunity to be together."

"But that's not why you're here, is it?"

"That's the biggest reason," he said, leaning to place a light kiss on her lips. "Also, I want everyone involved to know that I'm looking out for you."

Her lips tingled where he had kissed her, but she resisted an urge to lift her fingertips to her mouth. "Everyone involved? What does that mean?"

He was silent for a moment, as if carefully considering his reply. "I suspected Flora and Jackson Boudreaux would have a hard time accepting that Steven died from a snakebite, but your conversation with Jackson confirmed it."

"Beau, Steven's death has nothing to do with me."

"Anywhere else, you'd be right. But this is the bayou, Holly. Things aren't as simple here. Because Nikki was a client, you were on her side. That's how Flora Boudreaux will see it." He hesitated. "Flora isn't like her mother. Desiree has a good heart and I really believe she's harmless. But Flora is a bitter woman, seething with all sorts of resentments. What happened to her son Steven is just her latest reason to hate the world. Flora is not harmless, Holly."

The proprietors of the voodoo shops had mentioned both Desiree and Flora, and Holly was well aware of the differences between them. Desiree was widely regarded with great respect, admiration and affection, but Flora's name was whispered with a frown and a backward glance. She couldn't be certain that the shop people feared Flora, but she'd received that impression more than once.

She lifted an eyebrow. "If you're suggesting that Flora might cast a spell on me... I thought you didn't believe in hexes or spells."

"I'm not talking about voodoo," he said, dropping his arm and glancing into the rearview mirror before he pulled back onto the road. "Flora's a spiteful woman. Things happen when she holds a grudge against someone. I suspect Jackson's used his badge and uniform to cover up Flora's malicious mischief on more than one occasion."

Interested, Holly studied his profile as he drove. Sitting this close to him, looking at his strong jawline and kissable lips made her feel fluttery inside. Instinct told her that their desire for each other was growing. Soon they would have to decide if they were ready for the next step. Just thinking about going to bed with him sent a pleasant shiver down her spine.

"What kind of things happen?" she asked when she remembered what they were talking about. "Can you give me an example?"

"Let me think a minute. Okay, last year Flora got crossways with the woman who owns the dress shop. I never heard why. But shortly after, a gris-gris appeared in the shop and some signs were drawn on the sidewalk. Then someone broke a back window on the shop and stuck a garden hose through. That was on a Friday night. By the time the shop opened again on Monday, the place was flooded. Cartons of unpacked inventory were ruined. All the floors had to be replaced. It was an expensive mess."

"You're suggesting that Flora was responsible?"

"Hell, everyone in town believed Flora was responsible. But there was no way to prove it."

"Beau," Holly said gently, touching his arm. "If you're right, what Flora did was wrong and mean. But it didn't endanger anyone."

"I could tell you stories about pets that vanished or died, about people who were indeed endangered by odd occurrences, people whom Flora accused of doing her wrong. The only reason I'm not mentioning these incidents is because there's no proof that Flora was responsible even if a lot of people think she was. And, Holly, a lot of folks believe that Flora has come this close to causing someone's death." He gave her a long look. "All I'm saying is that Flora Boudreaux is not someone to underestimate."

"Interesting," Holly commented, her mind running with the

information. "Desiree is the positive side of vodun. Flora is the negative side."

Beau groaned. "Don't tell me that all I've accomplished is to make Flora more interesting to you."

"I've love to interview her, too." Questions sped through her thoughts. Did Flora really believe her spells caused misfortune to those she disliked? Or did she take matters into her own hands? Did she make her own gris-gris? Or buy them from the voodoo shops? Did she have a following?

"Holly..."

When she saw his expression, she raised a hand. "Please don't say anything. You and I are not going to agree on this subject, Beau. What you need to understand is that I'm not going to be dissuaded. I'm committed on a personal and professional basis to writing about vodun, and I've waited several months for an opportunity like this one. Meeting people like Desiree and Flora is what I hoped for when I came to Bayou Beltane."

"Nothing I say is going to change your mind," he said unhappily.

"That's right."

After a long pause, he sighed, then lifted a hand from the steering wheel in a gesture of exasperation. "You Western girls are as stubborn as mules."

Holly laughed. "Southern girls are more pliant?"

He thought a minute. "Well...it depends. My sisters sure aren't."

"That reminds me. Have you spoken to Shelby recently? Did Jake Trahan tell her about the shooter in the woods?"

Beau nodded and turned off the highway. "She's absolutely convinced that the incident has something to do with that old case she's investigating. And she's more determined than ever to go forward with it." His smile didn't reach his eyes. "Talk about stubborn."

The ground was marshy here, and they drove past a house raised on stilts. A sluggish flow of water ran in a wide ditch beside the road, and more wildlife began to appear. Holly spotted a heron high-stepping along the banks of the ditch and glimpsed a small furry creature as it darted away from the side of the road.

"That was a nutria," Beau answered when she asked him about the animal.

"Like in a nutria fur coat?" Holly shook her head and smiled, feeling a long way from Wyoming.

They left the pavement and turned onto a dirt road that skirted the lake, passing a place named Willow Island Swamp Tours. "I could swear I just saw the name Delacroix," Holly said, looking back.

"That's my uncle Remy's place," Beau said uncomfortably. He gave her a weak smile. "Frankly, I'd rather not have the whole family know where we're going and why. There's another place farther up the road. Actually, it's closer to Desiree's place, anyway."

"You're really not comfortable with this, are you?" she said softly.

His jaw set. "All I'm saying is that I'd rather not open myself to a lot of family teasing if I can help it." A few minutes later, he parked the Porsche in front of a tumbledown shack bearing a faded sign that read Dandy's Boat Rentals. Signs stuck on the front window advertised bait, cigarettes and ice-cold beer.

"I doubt I would have come here on my own," Holly murmured, skimming an eye over an upturned boat rotting in the hot sun. "I would have chosen your uncle's place."

Beau grinned before he got out of the car and walked around to open her door. "Dandy's a good old boy. You'll like him."

When Holly stepped out of the Porsche, she inhaled the pungent fishy odor of bait and tackle. A pier extended out over the water and a flat-bottomed pole boat rocked gently on the surface. Suddenly, she was very glad that Beau had come with her.

"Beau, my man! Been a coon's age since I seen you."

"Dandy, if you get any bigger you aren't going to fit in your boats."

The man Beau shook hands with was enormous—tall and weighing close to three hundred pounds. At some point his nose had been broken; he was missing several teeth and part of his right ear.

"Dandy, meet Dr. Gibson. Holly, this is Dandy Dog Verona.

If you were a wrestling fan in the eighties, you would have seen Dandy Dog taking on the biggest names in the sport."

Holly's hand disappeared in Dandy's massive paw, and he surprised her by gently raising her fingers to his lips for a courtly kiss. The moment she touched him, Holly knew that Dandy Dog was a sweet man without an ounce of malice in his huge body.

"I'm sorry I didn't see you wrestle," she said with a smile.

"You didn't miss much, pretty lady," he answered. "Truth is, I was paid to make the stars look good. You folks want a cold beer?"

Coupled with the humidity, the heat was thick and oppressive. Holly suspected it would be even worse within the swamp. "Do you have anything nonalcoholic?" she asked.

"We'll take it with us," Beau said, following Dandy Dog into the shack. He returned with an icy can of soda water for Holly and a Dr. Pepper for himself.

Dandy popped the tab on a cold beer and nodded toward the pier. "You're all set up and ready to go. There's a basket inside for Desiree. Some fried chicken and gumbo. You tell her that's from the missus. Tell her the pain went plumb away."

Holly considered him for a moment, wanting to ask a couple of questions, but Beau had started toward the pier, rolling up his shirtsleeves. He dropped into the boat, checked everything, then extended a hand to help Holly down. When she was seated beside the basket for Desiree, Beau balanced himself then dipped the pole in the water and pushed away from the pier.

"You know the way?" Holly asked uncertainly.

"Honey, I used to play in these swamps when I was a kid. I know this section like the back of my hand." Certainly he maneuvered the boat as if he'd been doing this all of his life. They floated out of the hot sun and into the dense shade of a cypress glade. "My best friend in junior and high school was Paul Gerard. He's a marine biologist now. He and I explored every inch of the swamps near Bayou Beltane."

"Did you visit Desiree?" Holly asked curiously, trying to imagine him as an adolescent. The same lock of dark hair would have fallen forward on his forehead then as now, she decided. He would have been as tanned and energetic. Every girl in school would have had a crush on him.

"We used to try to sneak up on Desiree's shack," he said with a smile. "It never worked. She'd be sitting in her rocker on the porch, lemonade and sandwiches waiting for us."

"You didn't wonder how she knew you were coming?"

"Sure we did. Spooked the hell out of us," he said with a grin, leaning on the pole. "It was years before we understood that we'd flushed out enough wildlife to announce ourselves a dozen times over." He nodded at the brown thrashers rising from the treetops. "We'll tie up at Desiree's pier in about thirty minutes, but I'll bet she already knows we've left Dandy's place."

The swamp was not silent as Holly had supposed it would be. Nor was it all water. Soggy islands appeared here and there, thickly covered with oak, holly, prickly ash and dense undergrowth. Once she heard something crashing through the brush, and Beau told her that he guessed it might be a feral hog. She was aware of splashing sounds and flocks of cardinals and jays chattering overhead. She didn't see any gators during her first trip through this strange watery world, but she saw more waterfowl than she could identify and spotted a bald eagle that she would have missed if Beau hadn't pointed it out.

His mastery of the pole boat and his knowledge of swamp flora and fauna were a side of him that she hadn't suspected. It occurred to her that perhaps this was part of his reason for wanting to accompany her today. If so, she guessed that he didn't share this side of himself with many people.

"It sounds like you had a happy childhood," she said. "But you must have worried your mother half to death."

He smiled and took a long swallow of his cold drink. "I remember one time...Paul and I climbed one of those tall cypress trees. We'd treed a racoon and we were trying to capture him. Turned out that racoons were feistier than we knew. That critter took a swipe at me, I jerked back and fell out of the tree. Landed on a stump like that one and broke my arm."

Holly gazed at the bared muscles of his arms, trying to guess which one had been broken. Then she glanced down at his thighs as he braced to lean into the pole. Suddenly the heat seemed more intense, more centered in her own body.

"After all the excitement, my mother settled me on a sofa and sat beside me. She sighed and said she'd ask me never to go into the swamps again, but that would only make a liar out of me and eventually force her to punish me. Instead, she asked for my promise to be more careful in the future."

"You miss her, don't you?" Holly asked quietly.

"Every day." He met her eyes. "When I learned that my parents would divorce, it was the biggest shock of my life. Until then, I hadn't suspected how unhappy my mother was. In retrospect, I should have seen it. I should have realized that two nice people had drifted apart, should have seen how empty my mother's life became after her children were grown."

"Children seldom see their parents' lives," Holly offered. "I know my parents fight like cats and dogs, but I can't even guess what the underlying issues might be. I used to wish they would get a divorce without having any real idea what that would have meant to them. For whatever reason, and I certainly don't understand it, divorce has never been an option."

And there it was, the obstacle neither of them could overcome. Disappointed, Holly watched Beau pole the boat around rotting stumps sticking out of the water. She wished they hadn't talked about their families, about why marriage was a choice neither of them would ever make.

Other women entered a relationship hoping it would "work out," which meant they hoped it would lead to marriage and a family. The best Holly could hope for was that she and Beau would remain friends when their relationship ended, as it inevitably would.

It was discouraging to think about, depressing to see their future so clearly.

"A penny for your thoughts," Beau said, examining her expression.

"I...was just wondering if we're about there."

"Look behind you as we come around this curve."

She did, and smothered a small gasp at the picturesque beauty of the setting. Desiree's unpainted shack sat on stilts sunk in marshy ground that was chaotic with ferns and lush growth. Cedars and live oaks soared overhead, draped with wispy streams of Spanish moss. It reminded Holly of an illustration in a children's book, an enchanted cottage in a magic forest.

In this instance, the cottage was weathered wood and the magic forest concealed snakes and gators and the other dangers that Holly wasn't sure she wanted to know about. But the sunlight filtering through a dense canopy of moss and leaves possessed a watery gold-green quality that gave the scene an ethereal hint of unreality.

"It seems so quiet here," Holly whispered. "I wonder if Desiree remembered that I was coming today."

"She remembered," Beau said, guiding the boat toward a rotting pier as voices erupted from inside the shack, shattering the illusion of silence.

"You had no right to bring her here!" The shout wasn't from Desiree. Flora? Holly peered toward a torn screen door and wondered uneasily if the "her" was herself. She suspected it was.

"Hush your mouth," a quieter voice said. Desiree. "Go out the back."

Beau put two fingers between his lips and whistled, then he applied himself to tying the boat to the pier. Holly waved when Desiree stepped onto the porch, then didn't look up again until she was out of the boat and off the pier.

Desiree looked much the same as when Holly had first met her in Beau's barn. She wore a bright red bandanna wrapped around her hair and a faded print dress beneath an apron with bulging pockets. She beckoned with a pipe, then returned the stem to her mouth, speaking around it.

"Come on up to the house," she called, walking across the porch to a pair of rocking chairs. After settling herself in one of the rockers, she watched Holly and Beau come up the spongy path, and Holly had a feeling that those old eyes missed nothing. Desiree saw Beau's hand on Holly's elbow, saw sparks invisible to the rest of the world.

"'Afternoon, Desiree," Beau said, patting her shoulder. "Dandy Dog sent this basket. Said to tell you the missus's pain is gone."

Desiree glanced at the basket and smiled. "Glad to have it. Smells like chicken. You know where to put it," she said to Beau. Then she nodded at the rocking chair beside her and spoke to Holly. "Sit yourself down and rest a spell."

Holly watched Beau carry Dandy's basket inside the shack and smiled at the irony that Beau was permitted inside but apparently she was not.

"All in good time," Desiree remarked as if she had read Holly's thoughts. She rocked, smoked and stared out at the watery sunshine dappling the water.

Removing a handkerchief from her purse, Holly mopped her throat. "Hot today," she said, wondering how to introduce the reasons for her visit.

Desiree laughed. "Child, it's always hot in the swamps. I hope you sprayed that pretty skin of yours with bug repellant. Skeetas are out in force today."

"I did."

When Beau banged out of the screen door, Holly understood they would not discuss anything of substance with Beau here.

He made a few minutes of small talk with Desiree, then smiled at Holly. "I'm going to pole up about a hundred yards and see if that old fishing hole is as good as I remember." He glanced at his watch while Holly silently thanked him for his sensitivity and understanding. "I'll return in about an hour. Is that enough time?"

Desiree smiled, flashing white teeth against skin the color of coffee with cream. "You bring me a mess of catfish up the house, hear? See if you can catch Old Whiskers."

"This time I'll get him," Beau said. To Holly, he added, "I've been trying to catch Old Whiskers for fifteen years. Biggest catfish you ever saw, and the sliest." With a wave and a smile, he strode down the old pier and dropped into the boat, then pushed off with the pole. Holly watched him glide through the sunlight and shadows.

"Beau's going to make someone a mighty fine husband," Desiree said, puffing on her pipe.

A flush of color warmed Holly's cheeks and she lowered her

head. "His parents' divorce left him disillusioned about marriage."

"It's better if he learns from his daddy's mistakes instead of hiding himself away. I expect he'll understand that when the time is right."

Holly drew a breath. "May I ask what service you provided Dandy Dog's wife?"

"Raylene came to me complaining of a pain in her chest and stomach. Every Saturday the pain came." Desiree rocked back in her chair and gazed at Holly. "What do you make of that?"

"Possibly psychosomatic," Holly speculated.

"I don't know about any psycho whatever."

"What happens on Saturday in Raylene's life?"

"Now you're getting it. Every Saturday, Dandy Dog goes up to the roadhouse between here and Slidell. Stays out until the wee hours drinking with his buddies. A woman can't get pregnant when her husband's at a roadhouse and she's at home waiting for him."

"So what did you do for Raylene?"

"I made a poultice for her pain and put a powerful spell on it." Twinkling dark eyes slid toward Holly. "That spell is much too powerful for a woman. Dandy himself had to apply the poultice to Raylene's breasts and stomach and he had to do it exactly at midnight on Saturday."

Holly laughed. "Very clever. And what was the poultice made of?"

Desiree shrugged and examined the bowl of her pipe. "A little swamp mud, some sweet-smelling herbs." Leaning back in her chair, she sucked on the pipe again, let a stream of smoke leak from her lips. "Dandy isn't a bad man. The minute Raylene catches a baby, Dandy won't be going to the roadhouses anymore."

"What would you have done if Raylene's pain had signaled a real disease?"

Desiree rocked back and forth, her gaze on the changing surface of the dapple water. "What do you do when someone comes to you and the disease is real?"

Holly placed her hands on the arms of the rocker and her eyebrows rose in surprise. "Do you believe that what you and I do is similar?"

"Those who can pay take their troubles to someone like you. Those who can't pay bring their troubles to someone like me." She shrugged. "There isn't a dollar's worth of difference, the way I see it."

"I wouldn't have sent Raylene away with a swamp-mud poultice," Holly said quietly. Frowning, she thought about it. "I would have spoken to Dandy Dog and suggested that he stop going to the roadhouse and spend more time with his wife."

Desiree smoked and nodded. "And Dandy would have followed your advice because he loves Raylene. But it wouldn't have been his idea, do you understand?"

"He would have stayed home, but he would have resented it. Is that what you're saying?"

"Could be. But he doesn't resent staying home to rub Raylene's breasts and stomach. And that might lead to other things. It might just lead to that baby Raylene is longing for."

It was vaguely discomfiting to realize that Desiree's swamp poultice and spell were probably a better solution than any Holly might have suggested. And odd to think that in Desiree's opinion at least, she and Holly shared the same profession.

"Suppose that Raylene's chest pain had been heart trouble...you didn't answer as to what you would have done in that instance."

"I'm not a doctor, chère amie. It's not my place to say this pain is disease or that pain is gas or that pain is a curse set on you by an enemy, or this or that." She stared at Holly with clear dark eyes. "The pain could be any of those things. I listen, the same as you do. And like you, I try to help where I can." She waved the pipe and gave several examples of symptoms she had cured, talking for nearly thirty minutes. "Sometimes a spell works. Sometimes it doesn't."

Fascinated, Holly leaned forward. "Would you say that your role is to serve as a folk healer? Is that part of your faith?"

Desiree returned her gaze to the murky water gently lapping at the pier. "Would you understand the meaning if I told you that I'm too old to be a horse anymore?"

A tiny shiver raced through Holly's body and unconsciously her muscles tensed. "Yes," she said, trying to keep the excitement out of her voice. "It's said the gods choose certain individuals to ride as their horse." It was a euphemistic expression for possession.

"Not the gods," Desiree corrected her. "The Loas. Papa Legba, Wedo...Dambala."

"Go on," Holly urged.

"Too old," Desiree murmured, shaking her head. "I can't serve anymore."

But it sounded as if Desiree *had* offered herself for possession in the past. She would know what it felt like, could describe it. Holly practically vibrated with excitement. Here was someone who had experienced a hysterical trance state to the point of believing a disembodied spirit had entered her body and taken control of her mind.

"I'd like to hear about the times when the loas rode you," she said evenly.

"I'm just a conjurer now," Desiree said with a sigh. "Doing the good work in a different way."

When Holly spotted Beau poling around a curve, a twinge of disappointment tightened her chest. The time had passed so swiftly and she'd only scratched the surface. Frustration ruffled her brow. "There are so many things I want to ask you," she said. "Your knowledge shouldn't be lost."

Desiree looked at her fully. "You have the knowledge yourself," she said quietly. "It's understanding you seek, and that I can't give you. You must find understanding yourself. That is the way."

"I'm sorry, I don't know what you're saying," Holly said with another frown.

"Often the power passes from mother to daughter, but not always. When it does, understanding comes easier through observation. I think this is not so in your case. You didn't have an opportunity to observe, so now you seek to learn and to understand from others. That is good. I can guide you, but your answers won't come from an old woman like me. They come from here." She closed her fist on her chest and stared at Holly.

"Oh, wait. I believe we have a misunderstanding here." She returned Desiree's stare, mesmerized by the force of the old woman's gaze. "I'm not seeking induction into the vodun faith. I want to learn what you do and how you do it to preserve the knowledge and to write a book about what I learn. A lot of nonsense has been written about voodoo, but I intend to treat it seriously. I'd like to write an account from the point of view of a devout practitioner."

Desiree watched Beau tie up at the pier, then lift a string of catfish for her to see. "You want to know why you sometimes sense what will happen before it occurs. You want to know why your dreams are so real. You want to know if you can rely on your impressions about people. You want to know how to use your power."

Holly's eyes widened and her mouth dropped open.

"Hey, it's not *that* impressive a catch," Beau said, laughing as he carried the string of catfish up onto the porch. "I didn't even catch a glimpse of Old Whiskers. Where do you want me to put these?" he asked Desiree.

"There's an ice cooler inside," she said, leaning back and puffing on her pipe.

"How do you know that I sometimes see things before they happen?" Holly whispered.

Desiree smiled and rocked back and forth. "The next time you visit Beau's office, turn down the sweatband on his hat and pin two needles there, crossing each other. Lie with him on a Tuesday, but well before midnight. Not after."

Holly's mouth dropped open and hot color flooded her cheeks. "Desiree—"

The old woman stood and stretched her back against the flat of her hand. "Come back tomorrow." She met Beau as he was walking out of her screen door. "And you," she said, looking deeply into his eyes. "You take care of this child, hear me?"

"If you mean Holly, she's prickly about letting anyone take care of her," he answered, smiling. "But I'll do what I can."

Desiree placed a hand on Beau's sleeve and held his gaze for a long moment before she stepped inside the shack and let the screen door bang behind her.

Watching them, Holly frowned. She had the oddest idea that they were speaking in a shorthand form that they understood but she didn't. If asked to guess the meaning of what had just transpired, she would have said that Desiree had issued a warning and Beau had pretended to make light of it.

Troubled, she followed him back to the boat.

CHAPTER SIX

As BEAU POLED AWAY from Desiree's pier, he looked back but didn't spot Flora.

He'd seen her when he returned to the shack from the fishing hole. She'd been standing pressed against the side of the shack, eavesdropping on Desiree and Holly. It was a good guess that Desiree knew Flora was listening, but he doubted that Holly had known.

Even without Desiree's veiled warning, he sensed that trouble was brewing.

"Did the interview go as you expected?" he asked cautiously. There was no point in mentioning Flora. He didn't want to pique Holly's curiosity more than he suspected he'd done already.

Holly mopped a light dew of perspiration from her forehead and throat, appearing to consider before answering. "I'm not sure what I expected. I guess I'd hoped we would discuss more of the belief system associated with vodun, but we didn't do that. However, we made a beginning and I'm pleased about that. Desiree gave me a lot to think about, and she agreed to see me again tomorrow." A challenging tilt of her chin almost dared him to object.

Beau frowned and leaned his weight onto the pole, moving the flat-bottomed boat through the sluggish water. He didn't like any of this. It didn't make sense to him that Desiree, whose loyalty was almost a legend, was willing to cause problems between herself and her daughter for the sake of spending time with Holly, a stranger to her. And he sure didn't like it that Flora appeared to be developing a resentment toward Holly. That worried him a great deal. Finally, it bothered him that Holly was pursuing this subject at all.

"What am I going to do with you?" he asked quietly, gazing down at her.

Dappled sunlight slid through her glossy auburn hair. Loose tendrils floated around heat-flushed cheeks. There was something incredibly arousing about the damp crescents on her shirt beneath her breasts, and looking at her, he felt himself stir and a wave of desire quickened his heartbeat. He wanted Holly Gibson as he'd never wanted another woman in his life. Going slow and letting their relationship mature into something more than a physical itch was one of the hardest things he'd attempted in recent years.

"What would you like to do with me?" she asked, her voice teasing and as sultry as the heat enveloping them. Her gaze held his, and the muscles in his thighs twitched as he recognized an answering look of desire narrowing her eyes. When she broke their locked stare, she let her gaze drop to his opened collar then flicker to his wide-legged stance.

There was no aphrodisiac as powerful as knowing the object of one's desire was equally aroused. He drew a low breath between his teeth and tightened his grip on the pole. He wasn't sure what had brought matters to a head so unexpectedly. Perhaps it was the sweltering August heat, or the musty exotic scents of the swamp and the mystery of watery silence closing around them. Perhaps it was the age-old eroticism of a man standing over a seated woman, muscles bulging with effort, emphasizing mastery over the elements.

He stared at her and felt the blood throbbing in his body. "What would I like to do with you?" he repeated hoarsely. "I'd like to undress you slowly and then run my tongue over every inch of your body. I'd like to explore you with my fingertips and my lips until I know you as intimately as I know myself. I'd like to kiss you until we're both breathless and gasping for air. I want to tease you until your body gleams with sweat and you beg me to take you."

"Oh, God." The words sounded like a moan. Her eyes closed and her head fell backward. Her breast rose and fell in quick breaths.

The tension between them was as tangible as the fragrant cedars overhanging the watery channel. Alone in the timelessness of the swamp, they might have been the last two people in the world. That was how the moment felt to Holly, primal and elemental, ripe with the steamy urgency of man and woman.

"I know we said we would wait," Beau murmured hoarsely, unable to look away from her. He wanted to lick the perspiration from between her breasts, wanted to peel the damp clothing from her lovely body and caress her until she was as wild with wanting him as he was with wanting her. "But..."

"I know," she whispered, looking up at him with half-lidded eyes that were dark with desire. "Perhaps we've waited long enough...."

If they had been anywhere near a private patch of dry, solid ground, Beau would have poled straight to it and taken her while they were both enchanted by the magic heat of the swamp. His second instinct was to say something like, "Tonight." But that would have destroyed the spontaneity of what they were feeling right now. Now was the moment and he didn't want it to slip away from them. Unfortunately, there didn't appear to be any choice.

"Soon," he said in a thick voice, staring at her. "Soon."

"Yes."

The promise in her husky whisper made his heart soar. He hadn't been certain until now where their relationship was leading. He'd hoped, but he hadn't known. Now that he knew she wanted him as urgently as he wanted her, he should have relaxed. Instead, he felt the tension of anticipation and the frustration of knowing they had to wait.

She was the first to smile and then laugh. "Does the swamp have this effect on everyone?"

He grinned at her, then leaned on the pole, moving them forward. "Remind me to bring you here more often."

"There's something exotic and mysterious about it." Lifting her head, she smiled at a pair of egrets watching them from the banks. "It's a different world from anything I've ever known."

"Someday you'll have to show me Wyoming."

She laughed. "It's nothing like this."

"I want to know your world, too," he said softly. The truth of his statement surprised him. Usually he took the background of his dates for granted, knowing they came from an insular community similar to his own. Until Holly, he hadn't cared enough about any woman to want to know what had formed her or to want to see the environment in which she had grown to maturity. Knowing Holly was changing him in subtle ways that he was only gradually beginning to recognize.

"Over here!"

Dandy Dog's call caught his attention and he laughed aloud. If Dandy hadn't shouted, Beau would have drifted past the pier. He and Holly smiled at each other, regret that the swamp journey had ended evident in both their expressions.

Trying to hold on to the magic, they didn't speak often during the drive back to town, but Beau was aware of her gaze and the nearness of her body next to this. After he pulled up in front of her small rented house, he took her hand in his.

"Dinner tonight?"

She turned his hand between hers and ran her fingertips lightly over his palm, the gesture oddly erotic. "You're a good man, Beau Delacroix," she said softly. "Strong, compassionate, loyal."

"Are you a palm reader, too?" he asked, smiling at her. "Or is that one of your hunches?"

"Intelligent, dedicated, ambitious. Very appealing to women," she added, lifting a teasing eyebrow.

"There's only one woman I hope I'm appealing to," he said, wanting to kiss her.

Her gaze flicked to his lips, then she glanced out the car window at a neighbor who was mowing his lawn. She gave Beau a rueful smile. "I'd love to invite you inside right now. But what I need most is a shower. Then I want to make some notes about the interview with Desiree while my impressions are fresh. Is eight o'clock too late for dinner?"

"It's perfect. Are you sure you won't change your mind between now and then?" They both knew that dinner was merely the prelude to something more important.

"Thinking about the next step wouldn't hurt either of us," she said lightly. Then she gazed into his eyes and her voice again took on that husky timbre. "But no. I'm not going to change my mind, Beau."

He hoped the disappointment caused by having to wait until tonight was not as obvious as it felt. "I'll cook for you." He twined his fingers through hers and thought about kissing her, but he knew she wouldn't be comfortable knowing the neighbor watched them. "My place. Eight o'clock. I live in one of the cottages between the barn and the big house."

For a long moment she held his gaze, and it was all he could do not to pull her into his arms and plunder her lovely mouth.

"It sounds wonderful," she said, then she laughed self-consciously. "I'll see you then."

He waited until she ran up the porch steps and waved before she stepped inside the house, then he pulled from the curb, whistling between his teeth. He was still whistling and planning for the night ahead when he slid out of the Porsche back at the farm.

But his good mood didn't last long. In his absence all hell had broken loose.

Bear intercepted him before he reached his office. "I don't know if our people have suddenly turned careless as hell, or if we've been a victim of malicious mischief."

While Beau listened with a deepening frown, Bear listed a series of events that left him reeling. A person or persons had opened the stall doors and all the horses had poured into the paddocks. There, too, gates had been left open and several prized Thoroughbreds had gotten loose and galloped into the woods.

Bear raked a hand through his hair. "We've rounded up all the animals except Toulouse and Many More."

"Hot Shot?" Beau asked in a terse voice.

Bear nodded. "Back in her stall. Matt Taggart is with her. There's nothing serious," he added hastily when he saw Beau's expression. "Just a few small lacerations. Matt's checking all the animals." He scowled toward the woods. "I've got a dozen men searching for Toulouse and Many More. Meanwhile—" he drew a breath "—Mr. Fujimoto arrived about one-thirty. We didn't know how to reach you, so he waited here until a few minutes ago. He left a number for his hotel in New Orleans."

Beau swore. "Fujimoto wasn't scheduled to arrived until next week."

"He said he received a phone call from your secretary informing him to come a week earlier. Today."

"What? You know I don't have a secretary."

"I know it, but Mr. Fujimoto didn't." Bear shrugged. "We didn't make a very good impression, Beau. Loose animals all over hell and gone, chaos like you wouldn't believe. Then Fujimoto ran into the IRS auditor. And he was present when some lawyer fella showed up saying he had an appointment with you to take a deposition in a lawsuit."

Beau tugged his collar away from his throat. "How did you explain my absence?"

"I said you had an urgent matter to attend to in New Orleans."

Both men walked toward the barn. "Thanks for covering for me. Believe me, if I'd known any of this would happen, I would have been here. But Fujimoto wasn't due until next week and I didn't have any appointment for a deposition." He bit down on his back teeth. "See what you can do to discover how the horses got loose." He paused, thinking about it. "I would have sworn such a thing simply wasn't possible. This was no accident, Bear. We both know it."

"I probably shouldn't mention this..." Bear hesitated.

"Spit it out."

"One of the grooms—old McIntyre—said he thought he spotted Jackson Boudreaux shortly before the horses broke loose. He wasn't sure. And one of the grooms said he saw a stranger coming out of the barn at about the same time." Bear shrugged again. "I don't know how much weight I'd put on either of those stories. The groom probably saw the lawyer who was here for the deposition, and old McIntyre only said that he saw someone who looked like Boudreaux. At a distance he might have mistaken the IRS auditor for him. The auditor is about the same size and coloring as Boudreaux."

"Which leaves us nowhere," Beau said, feeling a wave of frustration tighten his muscles. "Damn it."

The first thing he did was go directly to Hot Shot's stall. The horse was still excited and restless, tossing her head and pawing at the bedding. "Nothing serious, right?" he asked Matt, who was wiping his hands on a towel and studying Hot Shot.

"A few cuts, that's all." Matt looked tired. "The hunter-jumpers got out, too. Jax is fit to be tied. One of the jumpers got a serious leg cut. He'll be off the circuit for the rest of the season." He picked up a case of medical supplies. "I've still got three horses to check. I won't leave until they find Toulouse and Many More."

"Thanks, Matt," Beau said, running his hands over Hot Shot, speaking to her in a soothing voice. Fifteen minutes later, he checked on Ma Chere and the rest of his racehorses. Then he looked in on the hunter-jumpers. He heard Jax's angry voice before he saw her reaming out one of the grooms.

"Come on, Jax," he said, putting his arm around her. "What happened wasn't this man's fault."

She whirled on him with flashing gray eyes so like his own. "So whose fault was it, Beau? And where the hell have you been? Did you know that Mr. Fujimoto waited for you all afternoon?"

"I heard," he said grimly. "Come on, let's go to the office."

She stared at him a minute then sighed and fell into step beside him. Of all his sisters, Beau felt the closest to Jax. Pulling her arm through his, he gazed down at her. People said they looked alike, having the same smoky eyes and dark hair, but he saw his mother when he looked at Jax. "I haven't seen much of you since you and Matt got married," he said. "And now with the baby coming..." He spoke with affection, but the truth was, he missed the time they had spent together before she and Matt fell in love.

At the mention of Matt's name, her eyes softened and an unconscious smile curved her lips. "I miss you, too," she said. "But Matt is the best thing that ever happened to me. He and the kids have changed my life."

"I think you've changed some lives, too. Amy and Jeff worship you."

She dug her elbow into his ribs. "Matt's crazy about me, too!"

They laughed together, going up the staircase to the office, but the smiles faded quickly. Jax threw herself on the old sofa and crossed her boots on a scarred coffee table. "What a day!" She closed her eyes for a minute then looked at him. "Want to start by telling me where you disappeared to?'' After she'd heard about his afternoon in the swamp, she blinked and her expression sobered. ''It *has* been a while since we've talked. I didn't realize you were that serious about Holly.''

''You know me. I'm not going to get serious about any woman until after I win the Kentucky Derby.'' He moved a pile of messages to another corner of his desk. ''Holly and I aren't looking for anything serious, as you put it.''

''Really?'' She gave him a knowing look. ''You might be able to fool yourself, Beau Delacroix, but you can't fool me. Holly Gibson is making a dent in that bachelor armor of yours.''

''She's very special, but...'' He looked at her and frowned, realizing he'd said too much. ''Don't we have other things to discuss besides my love life?''

Jax grinned. ''Okay, I'll let you off the hook. But only if you promise that I'll be the first to know when you pop the question.''

''That's not going to happen. Look, did you talk to Mr. Fujimoto?''

''Are you kidding?'' She spread her hands. ''It was chaos around here. I brought Fujimoto up to your office, spent about ten minutes telling him that we weren't prepared for his visit, then ran back outside. He was polite, but very confused.'' Her expression sobered. ''Beau? Who would have called Mr. Fujimoto and rescheduled his visit?''

''I don't have a clue. Everyone knew he was coming to inspect our breeding stock. Last week Bear had the grooms clean the breeding shed from top to bottom. We knew Fujimoto would want to see it.'' He shook his head. ''Fujimoto's visit wasn't a secret. I think everyone here knew how important he could be to us.''

''Well, I think we can forget about Mr. Fujimoto making any offers. It must have looked to him as if we're running a very sloppy operation. And meeting the IRS auditor had to have raised some alarms. If it didn't, then learning that you're being sued certainly would have. I'm assuming the attorney was here about the suit against the gallery?''

Beau picked up one of the messages on his desk, then let it fall from his fingers. ''No, this is yet another lawsuit. The attorney represents a man named Max Sloan. Mr. Sloan claims he came to the farm to look at a horse he wanted to buy, got into an altercation with me, and I assaulted him.''

Jax stared. ''You're kidding. Did this Sloan character file a police report?''

''Jax, the incident never happened. I've never met anyone named Max Sloan. He was never here, and I never assaulted him or anyone else.'' Frustration and anger were evident in his voice. ''It's strictly a nuisance suit. Dad's firm has discovered that Sloan has pulled this kind of stunt before. You'd be surprised how many people simply pay him to drop the suit and go away.'' He clenched his fists on top of the desk. ''We're not going to do that.''

''Okay,'' Jax said after a minute. Holding up one hand, she began ticking down her fingers. ''So Mr. Fujimoto thinks we're careless enough to let our stock run wild. He thinks we're cheating on our federal taxes. And he probably thinks you're some kind of violent maniac who assaults people like himself who want to buy some prime breeding stock.'' She made a face. ''Yeah, we can kiss that connection goodbye. Mr. Fujimoto is undoubtedly thinking he made a very long trip for nothing.''

Beau nodded, tapping a pencil on the desk. ''The longer we talk, the more it feels like someone here at the farms is feeding information to someone outside.'' To his great-uncle Philip, maybe? He hated thinking one of his employees might be on Philip's payroll, but that would explain a lot. ''Several days ago, I made a notation in my appointment book that I'd be out this afternoon.'' A wave of his hand indicated his cluttered desk. ''Anyone could have come up here and noticed that Mr. Fujimoto was scheduled for next week. And there was a phone number beside his name.''

But whoever changed Mr. Fujimoto's arrival date couldn't have known that Beau would be out this afternoon, not if Mr. Fujimoto had been contacted last week. Beau's absence would simply have been an added bonus, one to take advantage of by setting the animals loose and informing Max Sloan's attorney to come this afternoon.

''Beau?'' Jax asked, studying him. ''What's this all about? Why are we having so many hassles lately?''

"Damned if I know."

They sat in silence for a full minute, then Jax stood and crossed the room to the coffeepot. She poured two cups and set one on his desk. "I guess you've heard that Uncle Philip is taking a beating in the preelection polls?"

Often, like now, Jax seemed to read his mind. He nodded. "With Philip's poor showing in the polls, the Delta Stakes might loom larger. He might feel he *needs* to win," Beau said, thinking out loud. "I can see Philip engineering a stunt like setting the horses loose in the hopes that Ma Chere might get hurt and be unable to run in the Stakes. As for the audit and the frivolous lawsuits...if Philip's behind these problems, they might be intended as a slap at Dad or even at grandfather Charles. Philip might not be aware that most of the fallout's on me."

Jax lifted an eyebrow.

"All right," Beau conceded with a sigh. "He'd know that. But he'd also know how upset Dad and Grandfather would be when they heard about it."

"Can you think of anyone else who might want to cause you trouble? Who might be able to bribe or intimidate one of our people into feeding him information?"

Jackson Boudreaux sprang into his mind, but he couldn't justify why, other than a long-standing rivalry that stretched back as far as high school. Even then, the ill will had come from Jackson rather than Beau. For some reason, Jackson had considered himself in competition with Beau. It had always seemed ridiculous and a little sad in Beau's opinion, since their circumstances were vastly different.

"Not really," he answered after a minute. He and Jackson Boudreaux would never like each other, would never be friendly. But he had no reason to believe that Jackson had suddenly decided to act on old hostilities that stretched back years. As for McIntyre's claim that he'd spotted Jackson at the farm, he had most likely made a mistake. But even if McIntyre had seen Jackson here, that wouldn't be all that unusual. Jackson was interested in racing and he liked to watch the horses work out. Usually he requested permission first, but not always. And even if Jackson had dropped by, it didn't necessarily follow that he was responsible for opening the stalls. McIntyre wasn't claiming that he'd seen Jackson in the stables.

"Well," Jax said after she finished her coffee, "I want to check on my horses, and I know you want to look in on Hot Shot and Ma Chere again and see if the boys have found Toulouse or Many More yet."

"And I need to track down the IRS auditor, then phone Mr. Fujimoto and see if he'll agree to meet with me this evening." If Max Sloan's attorney wanted to talk to him, he could call back. Beau wasn't going to chase him down.

"Matt and I are having dinner with Dad tonight. I'll fill him in."

Dinner. He'd have to call Holly and ask for a rain check. Frustration darkened his eyes to a stormy gray. Damn. He knew her well enough now to anticipate that she would be gracious and understanding. But he was feeling less charitable. If he ever found out who had caused this mess, they were going to pay for wrecking the wonderful evening he'd planned with Holly.

Swearing beneath his breath, he reached for the phone and dialed her number.

WEARING THE LIGHTWEIGHT robe she'd put on after her shower, Holly fixed a grilled cheese sandwich for dinner and carried her plate into a second bedroom that she'd fixed up as an at-home office. She turned on her computer, intending to make some notes about her visit with Desiree, but found herself daydreaming about Beau instead.

His disappointment about canceling tonight had been flattering and had matched the letdown she, too, experienced. After those intense moments in the swamp, she had felt the time was right for them, had realized it was foolish to delay what they both knew would happen between them.

"The right moment will come again," she said, staring out the window above her computer. It was a hot, moonless night. Crickets strummed a monotonous melody against the still air. The only sound in the house was the gentle whir of the ceiling fan in the living room and the hum of her computer. The lack of distractions made a perfect situation for analyzing her time with Desiree and composing her thoughts.

But Beau kept intruding.

When she had taken his hand in the car, she hadn't been reading his palm. She knew nothing about palmistry and didn't believe in such things, anyway. She'd simply held his hand and opened herself to the impressions she received. Her hunches.

Since her impressions often seemed to be correct, she had long ago made a rule that she would not "read" the people close to her. Would not open herself to hunches about their personalities or nature, would not let herself receive feelings about their thoughts or what was really going on in their lives. When she'd done that in the past, all too often she had opened herself to upsetting information.

This had been the case with Beau, too. She'd mentioned aloud the positive impressions she had received, but she hadn't told him about the disturbing images that bothered her now. Frowning, she bit into her sandwich and thought about the impressions she had picked up when she'd held his hand and let herself connect.

She had seen dark and misdirected forces swirling around him. In truth, it hadn't surprised her when he phoned to cancel their plans for the evening. She had anticipated that chaos awaited him back at the Delacroix Farms. And she knew the problems he was experiencing were neither coincidence nor accident. From there it got murky.

When Holly realized the direction of her thoughts, she smiled and shook her head. She didn't *know* anything, she reminded herself. It was all merely hunches. Just silly impressions that her intellect rejected when she thought about them.

This line of thinking led her to Desiree's statement. *You want to know if you can rely on your impressions of people.*

Frowning, Holly set down her sandwich and stared at her computer screen without really seeing it. Desiree's comments had indicated that she believed Holly's interest in vodun was not scientific but personal. And Desiree had, in fact, been uncomfortably accurate on a couple of points. Holly *did* wonder if she could rely on her impressions. She *did* wonder if her dreams carried meanings beyond the explanations of her profession. And it did indeed startle her when she had a hunch that something would happen and then it did.

Standing, she carried her plate back to the kitchen, rinsed it and placed it in the dishwasher. Then she studied her reflection in the window above the sink.

She didn't know what Desiree was talking about when she said that Holly had power. That didn't make sense to her. What kind of power? For what purpose? Just thinking about it made her feel deeply uneasy.

There was something else. A hunch told her that Desiree didn't care about aiding a scientific study of vodun. The hunch said that Desiree was interested in the mysterious power that she felt Holly possessed. This imaginary "power" was the reason Desiree had agreed to see her and why she would continue to see her. Desiree was interested in whatever she imagined she saw in Holly.

Holly studied her reflection in the dark window, striving to see in her eyes and face what it was that Desiree saw. After a moment, she turned her back to the window and the sink and drew a deep breath.

A flood of thoughts swamped her mind.

Suddenly she questioned the wisdom of pursuing a book about vodun. She wished Beau had not challenged her by telling her to drop it. Now pride was a factor. She wished she had a clearer vision of her motives. Wished she understood where she and Beau were going. Wished her hunches would either vanish or be more explicit.

Dropping her head, she closed her eyes and rubbed her temples. "Oh, Beau," she whispered. "I wish you hadn't had to cancel tonight. I wish we were together right now."

CHAPTER SEVEN

WHEN BEAU ARRIVED at Riverwood to have breakfast with his father on Saturday, he found Justin outside on the sun-drenched terrace. Pausing just inside a set of french doors, he gazed at his father with affection.

Holding a cup of coffee, frowning and pacing beside the wrought-iron railing, Justin spoke into his cell phone. He gave Beau a wave, finished his conversation, then the two embraced and sat down at the umbrella table. Justin poured coffee for them both. "Good morning, your honor," Beau said, smiling at his father.

"Sorry I was tied up when you arrived. I don't regret taking a seat on the bench, but occasionally I do regret the politics involved."

Lifting the silver lid of a serving salver, Beau served himself to scrambled eggs, then found the sausage and grits. His father had mellowed over the years, but certain things had not changed. Breakfast had to be eggs, sausage and grits. "You're looking very dapper today."

His father smoothed the gray at his temples, then touched his tie. "Later this morning I'm meeting with Armand Louis's attorney in regard to the lawsuit over the damned painting." Scowling, he scraped butter across a piece of toast. "I hope you made it very clear to the new manager of the gallery that we do *not* purchase any piece, no matter how much a bargain it appears to be, unless the piece is accompanied by a bona fide provenance."

"Oh, yes," Beau said grimly. "But in fairness to the manager I fired, the provenance looked authentic at first glance. There was no reason to suspect a forgery."

"He should have given it a thorough second glance," Justin

said sourly. They ate in silence for several minutes, then Justin pressed his napkin to his lips and leaned back in his chair. "Did you track down Mr. Fujimoto?"

Beau suddenly lost his appetite. "I persuaded him to speak to me, then spent about four hours with him at his hotel." He shook his head. "Fujimoto was polite, said he understood, and then very cordially declined to return to the farm." A line appeared between his eyebrows. "We've met twice since then, but Mr. Fujimoto hasn't changed his opinion. The group he represents will not be buying any breeding stock from Delacroix Farms. Damn it." He flung down his napkin.

Justin nodded and sighed. "And the audit?"

"We'll finish next week. When I spoke to the auditor yesterday, he indicated that we'll most likely come out of this with the IRS owing us a refund of almost a thousand dollars." He didn't care about the money, he just wanted the audit finished and the auditor out of his office. He longed for life to return to what he thought of as normal chaos.

One of the most upsetting aspects of the recent problems was Beau's concern that he had disappointed his father. He couldn't help wondering if Justin looked at the spate of lawsuits and the accumulation of recent difficulties as evidence that Beau was an incompetent business manager.

Leaning forward, he refilled their coffee cups with a deepening frown. Although Justin did not address the issue, Beau sensed that his father was never going to believe that Beau had made the right career choice until one of his horses won the Kentucky Derby. Or perhaps he needed to win the Derby to prove to himself, not to his father, that choosing business and the farm over law had been the right choice for him.

Over second and third cups of coffee, they discussed the lawsuits and the horses getting loose, then talked about politics and local events and other members of the family.

Beau smiled politely after hearing about his sisters' latest matchmaking efforts for his father. The stories were amusing, but he listened with mixed emotions. After ten years, he no longer harbored any illusion that his parents would reconcile. But neither could he imagine another woman in Justin's life. As selfish as it sounded, he wasn't certain how he would feel if his father or mother ever married someone else.

"You know, don't you, that your sisters are shopping for new ensembles to wear to your wedding?" A twinkle appeared in his father's eyes. "They've stopped thinking about finding a good match for you."

"What?"

"That may be a bit of an overstatement, but Jax and Shelby believe that your bachelor days are numbered. When do you plan to bring Dr. Gibson to the house for dinner? I've been hearing about this young woman from your sisters. When will I meet her?"

Beau shrugged awkwardly and tugged his collar away from his throat. Today was going to be a scorcher. "The next time the subject comes up," he said, stating his standard response, "please inform my nosy sisters that I don't plan to even think about marriage until after I win the Derby."

"That may never happen," Justin said quietly. "It's starting to sound like an excuse."

"I really believe that Hot Shot can win," Beau said irritably, feeling the sun hot on his face. "You've seen her run. Delacroix Farms has never had a horse like Hot Shot."

His father was silent for a full minute. "At your age, I was married and had started a family."

"I have plenty of time. I'm in no hurry." The sadness in his father's eyes disturbed him. It hadn't occurred to him that his father held an opinion one way or another concerning his bachelor state. Also, he realized that his own response had been automatic. He'd been waving off any possibility of marriage for so many years that he no longer questioned if that's how he still felt. Maybe it was time to take stock and decide if he still believed that winning the Derby was more important than a family of his own. Since this thought was disturbing, his mind darted away from it. First the Derby, he thought stubbornly. And then *maybe* marriage.

"Don't make the mistake of believing all marriages have to end as your mother's and mine did."

The comment astonished him. Was he that transparent?

"I believe your sisters understand that one marriage does not represent all marriages, Beau, but I'm not certain that you do. I'm to blame for the failure of my marriage to your mother, not the institution itself. Many good marriages exist. There's no reason to believe that you won't learn from my mistakes and create a solid marriage of your own."

This kind of discussion made him extremely uncomfortable. He didn't want to know the intimate details of his parents' divorce, didn't want to feel as if he needed to choose sides. And he most definitely did not want to be pushed into marriage.

When he said so, his father responded by commenting, "I'm not pushing you toward anything. I'm merely saying that I'd hate to see you end up alone and lonely. I'd rather see you happily married and raising a family that will bring you as much joy as you and your sisters have given me."

Beau definitely did not want to think of his father in terms of being alone and lonely. Pushing back his sleeve, he made a show of consulting his watch. "I'm sorry to cut this discussion short, but I have a full day ahead. The farrier's coming this morning, then I'm meeting with Matt about the gash on Toulouse's flank. Bear wants to breeze Hot Shot and Ma Chere. I have to find some additional records the auditor wants, and I told Bear that I'd call the Devoux brothers and ask if they can help out for a week or two."

His father lifted an eyebrow. "Are you shorthanded?"

Relieved to be talking business again, Beau nodded and stood. "In addition to the other nonsense going on at the farms, someone has been leaving voodoo markings where the grooms will find them." A look of exasperation pinched his mouth. "Three of our walkers quit, saying they wouldn't work with horses that are hexed."

"Sounds like you have your hands full," his father said, standing to squeeze his shoulder.

"That I do," Beau agreed. "But it's nothing I can't handle."

Except Holly Gibson, he thought as he drove away from Riverwood. And the reason he couldn't handle Holly was because he hadn't seen her in almost a week. Either she had been busy with work-related obligations or he had. But tonight, come hell or high water, he was going to keep his date with her. If he was very lucky, they would pick up where they had left off and it would be a wonderful evening.

THE FIRST TWO TIMES that Holly had poled the swamp boat to Desiree's shack by herself, she'd been worried that she would get lost or upset the boat. She had even been concerned that she might be attacked by an alligator or a snake or God knew what else.

Now those fears impressed her as foolish and amusing. As long as she kept Dandy Dog's boat in the widest channel and didn't drift into any of the branching forks, she wouldn't get lost. Dandy himself had given her a demonstration showing how hard it was to actually overturn one of his wide-bottomed boats. And although she had observed more varieties of wildlife and waterfowl than she'd ever seen in her life, she had yet to spot an alligator or a dangerous snake.

Smiling at her earlier concerns and feeling very self-sufficient, Holly tied the boat at Desiree's pier and climbed a weathered ladder. Before she went up to the house on stilts, she took a moment to look around the glade and appreciate its beauty. The swamp channels were never clear, but today, with the sun almost directly above, the water looked like amber flowing through emerald underbrush. The scent of moss and damp earth and cedar permeated the air, and clouds of insects danced in bars of dappled sunshine. She could almost persuade herself that time didn't exist here, that the quiet heat and lush peacefulness would continue unchanged until the end of time.

Then she heard angry voices coming from the house, shattering any illusion of peacefulness and quiet.

By now she recognized Flora's voice, although they had yet to formally meet. When someone shouted, "I will *not* leave! I'll be damned if I'll let that conniving bitch drive me out of my house! I live here, too!" she knew it was Flora.

After clearing her throat, she called, "Hello? Desiree?"

Instantly the voices inside the shack dropped to whispers. Holly couldn't make out any words as she came up the front steps and rapped against the screen door, but she felt waves of dark emotion washing toward her.

The hostility emanated from Flora, she thought with the beginnings of a frown. The impressions she received from Desiree were intense but always calm, always positive and centered, always warm and healing. If Holly had been asked to describe Desiree in terms of color, she would have promptly said that she had an aura of pure blue-white. In stark contrast, Flora left curls of ugly purple in her wake. Holly had sensed malevolence on previous visits, had glimpsed traces of the unpleasant purple.

Today, it seemed, they would finally meet.

"Come in," Desiree called. She said something else in a hissing whisper that Holly couldn't overhear.

Tentatively, she pushed open the screen door and stepped inside the shack. By now she was familiar with the strings of drying herbs suspended from the ceiling and hanging along some of the walls. She had observed Desiree grinding seeds and roots in the mortar with a stone pestle, and the jars of herbs and powders weren't as mysterious as they had seemed on her first visit inside the house. A side table covered by burning candles and pictures of Catholic saints continued to fascinate but wasn't a surprise.

She placed a basket on a table covered by a faded oilcloth that once had been vibrant with color. "I brought you some bread pudding and whisky sauce from the café in town," she said, smiling at Desiree and nodding politely to the scowling woman standing next to her.

"This is my daughter, Flora," Desiree said. Her dark eyes flashed a warning that Flora ignored.

"You got no business coming here," Flora said, baring her teeth and leaning forward. A dull purple shadow outlined her form. "We don't want you here!"

"Hush your mouth," Desiree snapped. "Where are your manners?"

Holly had grown up in an angry household and she confronted angry clients every day at work. She didn't back away from Flora's furious eyes. "I'm sorry you feel that way," she said in a level tone. "I'm here at your mother's invitation. If she would prefer that I come back at another time…"

"You got her bamboozled, but you don't fool me. I know what you're doing!" Spittle flew from Flora's lips, and her handsome face had turned a dark plum color. "You're spying for those Delacroix. Looking for evidence to use against my murdered son."

Surprise lifted Holly's eyebrows. "The trial is over. And it wasn't directed against your son. It was—"

"We don't want you here!" Flora shouted. She flung out a shaking arm and pointed at the door. "Get out and don't you ever come back! I'm warning you."

Desiree stiffened her shoulders and her eyes narrowed. "That's enough, Flora! You can go now."

Flora whirled toward her mother and purple flared around her, speckled with black. She started to protest, then stepped backward, her lips curled away from her teeth in a hiss. "Someday I'll be stronger than you are, old woman. Someday." She glared at Holly, spit on the floor, then turned in a swirl of pale cotton and dashed out the back door, banging the screen behind her.

Holly placed a hand on her chest, feeling the thud of her heart beneath her palm and waiting for the dark waves of hostility to recede. Flora lived up to Beau's description, she thought. There was no doubt in her mind that Flora Boudreaux was as potentially dangerous as Beau had insisted she was.

"Don't pay Flora any attention," Desiree said, lifting the cover of the basket Holly had brought to inspect the bread pudding. "Jackson and I tell her over and over that she can't appeal Nikki's acquittal, but she won't listen. She keeps talking about another trial." Sadly, Desiree shook her head. "Sit down and I'll fix you some tea to settle your nerves."

"I'd like that," Holly murmured, pulling out a chair. The impressions rolling off Flora had rattled her. "Desiree," she said after a moment, "if my visits are creating a problem..."

Desiree waved a hand of dismissal. "Flora's just angry and jealous, that's all."

"Of me? But why on earth would Flora be jealous of me?"

Ignoring the steamy August heat, Desiree placed a battered kettle on top of a wood stove and set out two beautiful china cups. "She's mad because she thinks you're on Nikki's side against her. And she's jealous because she suspects your mojo is stronger than hers. She's right about that."

"I counseled Nikki during the trial, that's all. I'm genuinely sorry for the loss your family has suffered. As for the mojo part, I'm sorry, but I'm afraid I don't understand."

"The power," Desiree said, measuring a mixture of crushed tea leaves and powders into a ball strainer. Lifting her head, she looked out the window and frowned. "Flora wants it so bad," she said, speaking softly, almost talking to herself. "She claims the loas ride her, but I think she's only pretending. All of her life, I've been telling her the power grows by giving it away. Like you do. Like I do. But her? No, she wants to keep the power for herself and use it for profit." She shook her head. "That child was born mad at the world and wanting to swallow it whole. She can't be happy with what she has, she always wants more."

Holly experienced a sudden throb of excitement. "Are you saying that Flora attends voodoo ceremonies?" That was the implication.

Desiree blinked, then smiled and poured boiling water over the tea strainer. "It's too soon to talk about that. Though you're coming along right smartly," she added, glancing at Holly's tape recorder and notepad. "Tell me what color you see around Flora," she demanded abruptly.

"Purple," Holly answered, keeping any hint of judgment out of her tone.

A sigh lifted Desiree's chest. She filled the teacups and carried them to the table. "What color do you see around Beau Delacroix?"

Holly smiled. "Blue, mostly." She laughed. "Sometimes flares of red or orange."

Desiree laughed. "Green, too, sometimes. That boy is a whole rainbow. But he's a good man." She tasted the tea, offered a grunt of satisfaction, then studied Holly's face. "What's that fancy word you call the colors?"

"Auras."

"Not everyone can see auras like you and me."

Holly hesitated, then admitted, "I don't always see them, either."

"You will if you trust the power and let it flow through you."

As always, Holly experienced a mixture of fascination and resistance when the conversation focused on her. Looking down at her notebook, she drew a deep breath. "When I was a child, my father became very angry when I mentioned seeing colors around people." She bit her lip as a trickle of perspiration ran down her neck. It had to be over a hundred degrees in the shack. "I wanted my mother to intercede on my behalf but she never did."

"Either your mother didn't have the power or she quashed it early on," Desiree said with a shrug. "Sometimes it happens that way." She turned her face toward the screen door. "And sometimes it happens that the mother has the power but the daughter doesn't inherit it."

"Could we talk about where the power comes from?" Holly requested, adjusting her tape recorder.

Desiree smiled. "Me, I say the power comes from Dambala. You, you probably say the power comes from God. Someone else might say the power comes from trees and plants and all living things. Another person might claim the power comes from little bitty folks flying around in saucers from Mars. The source doesn't matter as long as you use the power wisely and remember to say thank-you."

Holly smiled, enjoying Desiree's company more than she had expected to. The old woman had surprised her by exhibiting a sly sense of humor on occasion, and an appealing earthy wisdom. When talking to her, Holly often forgot the great difference in their ages. At those times, Desiree became the teacher and she the admiring student.

"This tea is very good." She did indeed feel calmer. "What's in it?"

The corners of Desiree's mouth twitched and she smoothed down her apron. "All this week we've talked about herbs. What do you think is in the tea?"

Holding a sip on her tongue, Holly considered before she swallowed. "Chamomile, for certain. And...a touch of mustard," she said with surprise.

"And..." Desiree prompted, looking pleased.

"And...walnut? Yes, a touch of walnut."

"Excellent. Now we'll take a walk and pay our respects to the plants that have soothed us." She gazed at Holly for a long moment. "And we'll take some of that bread pudding to the tree where the strong spirits live."

"An offering?" Holly asked, her eyes glowing. Offerings of food were common in the vodun faith. She'd even observed bowls and platters left beside the tombs in the cemeteries. What she didn't yet know was what kind of ceremony attended the offering, if any did. "May I bring along my recorder?"

Desiree glanced at the tape slowly revolving within the machine. "I think your notebook will be enough."

Bending, Holly concealed her excitement by pretending to examine her heavy boots. Until today Desiree had not objected to the tape recorder. That she did so now suggested they were progressing toward a deeper level.

Holly was about to witness an offering made to the tree spirits. Truly, they were making remarkable progress.

She followed Desiree out the back door but put a hand on the old woman's arm before they set out into the marshy undergrowth. "Thank you for trusting me with this opportunity and this information," she said softly.

Desiree looked pleased, but she brushed aside the comment. "This is how you learn. Maybe I'll give you some homework today," she said with a chuckle, pushing through an explosion of ferns. "When's the last time you thanked your house spirit for watching over your house?"

A startled look raised Holly's eyebrows, then she smiled. "I don't believe I ever have."

"That isn't wise." Desiree threw a stern look over her shoulder. "If your house spirit treats you well, you should express your gratitude. Otherwise, you're taking a risk. It wouldn't hurt to leave a small offering of appreciation."

"Perhaps I will," Holly said, hurrying to keep pace.

Then she smiled, glad that Desiree didn't see. She wondered what Beau would say when he saw the offering to her house spirit.

"THAT'S WHAT?" Beau repeated, leaning over a bowl of fruit, cooked shrimp and a chunk of bread flanked by two pale burning candles. A cross suspended from a silver chain was propped against the bowl.

Smiling, Holly handed him a glass of chardonnay. "It's an offering to my house spirit."

He straightened with a frown and stared down at her. "Tell me that you don't really believe some spirit is going to bip down here and eat that food."

"Not just any spirit, my house spirit," she said, teasing him with sparkling eyes. Lifting the lid from one of the pots bubbling on her stove, she closed her eyes and inhaled the aroma of shrimp gumbo. "It smells wonderful, but I have to tell you I'm a little nervous about this dinner. This is only the second time I've attempted gumbo. Back in my neck of the woods, we grill steaks for guests."

"Steaks would have been fine," Beau said absently, sitting on one of her kitchen stools. "How do you know that your house spirit isn't allergic to seafood?"

She chose to ignore the attempt at light humor. "*You're* not allergic to shrimp, are you?" The possibility hadn't entered her mind until this minute.

"I'm not allergic to anything. But how about your house spirit?" He tasted the wine, watching her over the rim of his glass.

She tilted her head and thought a minute. "I'm new at this. I don't even know if that's where the offering should be placed," she said, waving a hand at the countertop. "It just seemed logical since the kitchen is usually the heart of a home."

Beau placed his glass of wine on the countertop and reached for her as she came around the counter. He caught her by the waist and drew her between his outspread legs, holding her loosely against his body. "You mentioned on the phone that you were going out to see Desiree every afternoon, but you didn't tell me that you'd joined the club." He kissed her lightly on the chin. "What's next? Casting spells on the neighbors? Dancing around a bonfire?"

Though she felt her blood pounding at the touch of him, Holly's good mood evaporated. Using the pretext of checking the dishes she was preparing, she moved out of his arms and back to the other side of the countertop. It was simply impossible to have a coherent conversation with Beau when his arms were around her.

"All right, it's a silly thing to do," she said, glancing at her offering to the house spirit. "But that's how people learn, Beau, by doing. If I hadn't set up that offering, I might have overlooked some questions I now need to ask. How is the food choice determined? Is the arrangement of the items significant? Are different-colored candles preferred by different spirits? How long should I burn the candles?" Picking up a spoon, she gave the gumbo a stir. "This may seem like a joke to you, but I've already learned a lot. And more importantly, I've learned how much I don't know."

"Holly, I wish you could hear yourself." A frown appeared between his smoky eyes. "You're wondering what color candle your house spirit would prefer. You don't think that's a little bizarre?"

She gazed at him across the countertop, wondering how it was possible to feel annoyed and aroused at the same time. Tonight Beau wore a polo shirt that fit almost like a second skin, outlining his trim, muscled chest. Instead of the riding pants she was accustomed to, he wore a pair of well-fitting jeans and expensive sandals. He looked like a very sexy model for casual weekend attire.

Occasionally, like now, she looked at him and felt her breath stop. She had dated good-looking men before, but there was something about Beau Delacroix that made the others fade from her mind. It wasn't only that Beau was so much better looking, it was also the way he moved and carried himself, his easy, almost unconscious sexuality. And there was his considerable charm, his almost courtly manners, the way he looked at her with genuine concern.

"I'm not sure we're ever going to be able to discuss this subject without disagreeing," she said after a minute. "Why can't you accept that this is important to me?"

Instead of giving her a flip answer off the top of his head, he took a moment to consider the question. "I do understand that writing a scholarly treatment is important to you," he said finally. "I understand goals and dreams and determination."

"Then...?"

"Let me ask you this. Have you met Flora yet?"

She frowned. "Yes, I have. Earlier today, in fact."

"And what was your impression?"

"You're a clever devil, Beau Delacroix," she said with a smile she couldn't suppress. He was maneuvering her into agreeing with his assessment of Flora Boudreaux.

He returned her smile but the warmth didn't quite reach his eyes. "So tell me. Are you and Flora bosom buddies now?"

"Hardly." She pushed the wine bottle toward him and watched as he refilled their glasses. "I suspect Flora resents the time Desiree is spending with me. I wouldn't go as far as to say that I think she believes I'm usurping her place, but something like that."

Beau swore softly. "That's exactly what I'm worried about. Holly, Flora is going to make a dangerous enemy."

The comment made her laugh. "I've never had an enemy in my life." She pushed back a wave of hair. "What will Flora do? Put a hex on me?"

"I don't get this," Beau said slowly, his gaze on her mouth. "One minute you're setting up a minishrine to your house spirit, and the next you're laughing and waving off the possibility of a hex. Which is it, Holly? Are you going deeper into this or making fun of it?"

Her expression sobered. "I'm not making fun of it, that's for certain," she snapped. "But that doesn't mean I fear being the object of a spell. I keep telling you, my interest is scholarly."

"If we're talking about Flora Boudreaux, then maybe you *should* fear any spells she might send your way."

"Now who's taking this too seriously?" She stared at him. "I'm puzzled, too. One minute you're telling me vodun is superstitious nonsense, but now you're saying beware of voodoo spells. You can't have it both ways, Beau."

They studied each other in tense silence. "Flora is no more a voodoo queen than I am," Beau said finally. "But she'd like people to believe she is because it gives her a sense of power. That's how I see it, anyway. To protect that sense of power, it has to appear that her spells are effective. So if Flora places a bad luck spell on someone, she has to make certain that person experiences bad luck. That's what I think she does. And that makes her dangerous, Holly.''

"That's conjecture on your part.''

"Agreed. But I've lived in Bayou Beltane a lot longer than you have. There are people here who fear Flora and with good reason. Some believe her spells and signs can conjure evil spirits. Others believe the only wickedness involved is Flora herself. But just about everyone agrees that Flora is bad news. Not a person to cross. So, yes, there's no doubt in my mind that if Flora Boudreaux places a spell on you, you can bet that trouble is sure to follow. It won't come from any supernatural source,'' he said, waving a hand toward Holly's offering to the house spirit. "But there *will* be trouble.''

"I'll keep that in mind,'' Holly said coolly. She busied herself with the pots and pans on her stove. "I think we're almost ready here. I wonder if you'd mind filling the water glasses on the table.''

Beau stood and walked around the countertop. He took the ladle out of her hands and laid it aside, then drew her into his arms. "I apologize. I didn't mean for this conversation to get out of hand. I wanted tonight to be wonderful and lead to...well, I wanted it to be wonderful.''

"So did I,'' she murmured, pressing her forehead against his chest and closing her eyes. "I'm sorry, too. I should have known better than to get into this subject. We should have restricted our conversation to the horses and the farm.'' If he was half the man she believed he was, he wouldn't accept this. She hated putting him to the test, but she needed to know how much of a problem they were facing.

Beau shook his head and eased her back so he could look into her eyes. "If anyone knows better than that, it's you. You know a relationship won't work if the only thing we talk about is what's important to me. I want to know what you're doing, too.'' He kissed her lightly on the lips, then looked at her again. "We'll find a middle road, Holly.''

"Will we?'' she whispered, gazing into his beautiful gray eyes. "I hope so.''

"What I want you to understand is that I care about you. I'd hate to see you get in over your head, that's all. I certainly don't want you to get hurt.''

"I'm not going to—'' But she broke off her protest. She didn't want to throw them right back into another disagreement. Lifting on tiptoe, she returned his light kiss, then stepped away. "Let's have dinner and you can tell me what you've been doing all week.'' Smiling, she raised a hand. "Not because I think you're uninterested in my pursuits, but because we've finished with that topic.''

But they weren't, not really. The earlier conversation had placed a damper on Holly's mood and, she suspected, on Beau's too. Midway through dinner she accepted that the evening was not going to end as she had hoped it would.

Disappointment washed over her after she cleared away their dessert dishes. "Would you like another cup of coffee before you leave?''

He picked up on the "before you leave'' and his jaw tightened. "I'm sorry, Holly. We got off on the wrong foot tonight, and it's my fault.''

"I remember getting in a few licks, too,'' she said, gazing at him across the candle in the center of the table. "It wasn't anyone's fault, Beau. Vodun has been a touchy subject from the beginning.'' She thought about the new lingerie she was wearing and the clean sheets she had put on the bed and suppressed a sigh.

Leaning forward, Beau reached across the table and took her hand. Immediately, Holly felt a tiny thrill shoot up her arm. But she had never doubted the chemistry between them. From the first, they had been electric together.

"I don't want to let another week go by when we don't see each other,'' Beau said. "Talking on the phone every night is good and I've enjoyed it, but it isn't the same as seeing each other in person.''

"I agree.'' She rubbed her thumb over the back of his hand, feeling the strength in those long fingers.

After bringing her hand to his lips and kissing her palm, he said in a husky voice, "You haven't forgotten the Stakes race on

Tuesday, have you? I'd really like you to be there to cheer for Ma Chere.''

"I have Tuesday afternoon scheduled out on my appointment calendar. I wouldn't miss that race." Or you, she added silently.

"Wonderful. Afterward we'll celebrate with dinner and see where the evening leads us."

Desiree had said their first time together should occur before midnight on a Tuesday. Smiling, Holly nodded. "I'd like that. A lot."

"Good. We won't talk about your book or your research, and we won't talk about the problems at the farm. Tuesday will be just for us."

She walked with him to the door, her arm around his waist. And she sent him a silent word of thanks. Many men wouldn't have been as sensitive. She suspected that Beau had arrived tonight with the same hopes and expectations as she'd had. But he hadn't pushed the issue. Clearly he wanted their first time together to be as perfect as she did.

At the door, they turned to each other and stood for a moment, holding hands and smiling. Then Beau kissed her. His kiss was ardent enough to tell her that he was disappointed by the evening's outcome, but tender enough that she didn't feel he was pressing her to change her mind. The kiss was as wonderful as he was.

"Thank you for dinner. Your gumbo doesn't have to take a back seat to anyone's.''

"Wait until you taste my steaks," Holly said, smiling into his eyes.

"If that's another dinner invitation, I intend to hold you to it." He touched her cheek, then pushed open the screen door. "I'll phone you tomorrow about the same time as—"

He stopped so abruptly that Holly bumped into his back. "What is it?"

Swearing, he snapped on the porch light as Holly stepped up beside him.

When she saw what was on her front porch, she gasped and her fingernails dug into his arm.

CHAPTER EIGHT

"I'M SORRY," Holly apologized, gingerly stepping out onto the porch. "I didn't mean to overreact, I was just startled."

"Hell, who wouldn't be?" Beau muttered, rubbing his arm.

Dropping to her knees, Holly held herself very still and examined a crude set of symbols drawn with colored salt. "This is a poor representation of Baron Samdi's veve," she explained, speaking slowly. "But it's been bastardized. This isn't a classic presentation. And whoever drew it added some original touches." She pointed, indicating a small bleached skull positioned on top of a roughly drawn salt cross. "Although death and skulls are associated with Baron Samdi, no actual skull is placed on the classic veve. This looks like it might be the skull of a chicken." Although she was trying to maintain a scholarly detachment, a small shudder of revulsion ran through her. "What do you think? A chicken or some other kind of bird?"

When she looked up, Beau was staring down at her. He started to say something, then reconsidered and closed his lips. "I'll get a broom and dustpan," he said finally, reaching for the screen door.

"Wait." Holly stood, then entered the house before him. "I want to get my camera—take some photos of this." When she returned to the porch, Beau was right behind her with the broom. She tested the flash on her camera, then moved around the veve, taking photos from several angles. "Black and purple sand," she murmured, speaking more to herself than to Beau. "The colors are correct for Baron Samdi. And it's Saturday, Baron Samdi's special day." She advanced the film and took another shot. "Am I imagining it, or do you smell rum?"

"I smell it, too," Beau said, glaring down at the sand drawing. "Despite the cross, that's a nasty-looking thing."

"The nastiness is a bit of originality on the part of whoever drew it. The chicken skull. The phallic suggestions. Ordinarily, Baron Samdi's veve isn't quite as ugly or offensive."

Beau set the broom against the side of the house and pushed his hands into his pockets. "I hate myself for asking this, but who in the hell is Baron Samdi?"

Kneeling, Holly took a close-up shot of the salt drawing. "Sometimes he's referred to by other names. In the vodun pantheon, Baron Samdi is the leader of the spirits of the dead, the Gede."

"Holly, how can you be so calm about this?"

Actually, her hands were shaking slightly and she wasn't entirely calm. At the moment, however, she chose to focus tightly on the opportunity to observe and photograph an actual veve. Later she would compare her photographs to drawings of veves from Haiti and other areas, looking for regional differences and variations of interpretation. Already she knew this veve had strayed far from the standard representation.

The question was why? Did the addition of the chicken skull and the phallic suggestions indicate ignorance on the part of the person who had drawn it? Or had markings in the New Orleans area developed a character of their own that differed from representations of the same loas in Haiti, for instance? To answer these questions, it would be helpful to observe several drawings dedicated to the same loa.

"Have you seen this particular sign before?" she asked Beau, snapping another photograph. "I think you mentioned more signs at the farm. Have any of them featured an actual animal skull as part of the presentation?"

"Holly." Gently, Beau pulled her to her feet and gazed into her eyes. "I'm trying to understand your fascination. But the bottom line here is that someone crept up on your porch while we were having dinner a few yards away. That same someone spent several minutes drawing symbols that border on the obscene and then arranging a chicken's skull and then sprinkling the whole ugly thing with rum." He stared down at her. "This isn't the work of a welcoming committee, honey. This is a warning. Maybe a hex. Who the hell knows? But I know this. You were wrong about not having any enemies.''

The concern in his eyes broke through the detachment she'd been striving to maintain. For an instant a jolt of blind, unreasoning fear shot through her body. Then her intelligence swam to the surface again.

''It's unnerving to find this on my porch,'' she agreed, turning her head to glance at the veve. ''More disturbing still to realize that someone wants to frighten me or wish me ill luck.'' Lifting a hand, she pushed a wave of hair off her forehead. ''But, Beau, I don't for a minute believe that some lines of dyed salt and a chicken's skull can cast a spell or a hex.''

''Who do you think that 'someone' might be?'' he asked, still looking deeply into her eyes.

She sighed and stepped away from him, reaching for the broom. ''You want me to say Flora Boudreaux.'' In less than two minutes she'd swept the salt, skull and a couple of small bones into the dustpan. Opening the screen door, she carried the dustpan into the house and into the kitchen, bending to empty the contents into the garbage pail beneath her sink.

Beau followed and removed the bag lining her garbage pail. He folded the top and took the bag to the trash container in the garage. When he returned, he opened one of Holly's cabinets and removed a bottle of Scotch. While Holly washed her hands, he poured two drinks and handed her one.

''Forget the scholarly pursuits for a minute,'' he said, leaning against the countertop. He took a drink from his glass and considered a minute before he spoke. ''The signs appearing at Delacroix Farms have a random feel about them. Aside from the markings in the stables aisle the day Hot Shot colicked, the signs we're finding are scattered from the paddocks to the path leading to the parking lot. There doesn't seem to be a specific target. To tell the truth, the signs have a mischievous feel about them. Like a kid throwing a handful of stones, hoping one of the stones might hit a target.''

''Are the signs drawn in salt like this one was?'' The Scotch burned down her throat and settled in her stomach. The warmth felt good. Even though the evening was warm, her skin felt chilled and her palms were slightly clammy.

"Some are drawn in the dirt as if the person doing it had used a stick. Some are raised, made out of mud, I think."

"How about the chicken skull and the loose bones? Are you finding anything like that?"

"Not so far. But, Holly, the appearance of the veves is not the point. The point is that the thing we found on your porch is specifically targeted at you. There's nothing random about it. That symbol was intended to frighten *you*. Whoever left it is an enemy who hopes something bad or unpleasant will happen to you."

Turning away from him, Holly walked to the kitchen sink and looked out the window. The nearest streetlight was at the corner, half a block away. Shrubbery hemmed the porch. It would not have been difficult for someone to come onto her porch unobserved.

"It gives me the creeps to think about someone being on the porch while we were having dinner and we didn't know it." A light shiver ran down her arms and she took another sip of the Scotch. "All right," she said, turning to face Beau's steady regard. "The sign is intended to frighten me and/or bring me bad luck. And the person who did it is most likely Flora Boudreaux."

"Excellent," Beau said with a humorless smile. "We're making progress."

"I'm angry that Flora would come to my house and do this. But she's wrong if she thinks a pile of salt and some chicken bones are going to scare me away from pursuing my research with Desiree." Her chin came up and her eyes flashed. "I hope you're not thinking that, either, Beau."

Sighing, he glanced at the burned-out candles flanking her offering to her house spirit. "I admit I had a flicker of hope for about a minute. Look, would you like me to stay with you tonight?"

For an instant the suggestion was appealing, and realizing it annoyed her. Intellect told her that she was correct; a pile of salt and bones couldn't harm her. Yet these items somehow managed to speak to her on a primitive level, as well. That was the most irritating of all. There was no reason on earth why she should feel even a pinprick of apprehension. She knew better.

"Thank you, but no," she said, managing to smile. "I'm fine. Really."

"It wouldn't be a bad idea to phone Jake Trahan and let him know about this."

"Call the police?" Her smile widened.

"We probably shouldn't have swept up the mess until Jake took a look at it."

"Beau, based on my impressions when I interviewed the proprietors of the voodoo boutiques, I'd guess this kind of thing occurs rather frequently. The shops don't carry bags of colored salt for nothing. People buy them and presumably use them to draw veves."

He frowned. "If Bayou Beltane is experiencing an outbreak of voodoo activity, I sure haven't heard about it."

"Sure you have," she said, correcting him gently. "It's right under your nose. Didn't you tell me that a couple of your employees quit rather than work with hexed animals?" She paused and tilted her head. "Did you think the markings you've discovered at the farm were enough of a concern to call Jake Trahan and ask him to drive out and take a look at them?"

A dark flush rose in his cheeks. "This is different."

"No, it isn't." Setting aside her drink, she walked to the stool where he was sitting and placed her hands on his shoulders. "I'd feel foolish involving Jake or anyone else. I feel about this the same way you do about the markings you've found out at the farm. It's petty mischief, that's all."

He slid his hands to her hips and frowned. "I'll do whatever you want, Holly. But I'd like you to think about mentioning this to Jake, because it isn't the same as what's happening at the farm. In this instance, there's a specific target—you. You don't have to make a big thing out of it with Jake if you don't want to. But it seems like a good idea to put this on record. If nothing else, Jake and his men could do more drive-bys and make sure no one is on your porch."

Leaning down, Holly kissed him on the mouth, letting her lips linger. His protectiveness charmed her. "Can we agree to this? If anything else happens, I'll talk to Jake.'' He didn't look happy, but he finally nodded.

At the doorway they kissed again, a long, lingering kiss that made Holly's blood rush, and they said good-night again. "I hate to leave you," Beau murmured against her hair.

Earlier in the day when Holly had been planning and thinking about this evening, she had imagined him saying something similar, but for different reasons. Regret filled her gaze as she brushed her fingertips across his lips. "Call me tomorrow."

"Count on it," he said gruffly, skimming his hand from her cheek to her throat.

She stepped onto the porch and watched him walk to his car, loving the fluid grace in the swing of his hips and his long stride. Then, when she realized how vulnerable she felt, standing in a pool of light cast by the porch lantern, she reached inside the door and snapped off the light. Beau touched the horn lightly then pulled away from the curb and headed slowly down the street.

Folding her arms across her chest, Holly leaned against the front of the house listening to the quiet sounds of a summer night. She had never been a skittish type of woman. She wasn't the type to frighten easily or jump at every unexpected noise. As a woman living alone, she locked her doors at night and took reasonable precautions, but she had never feared solitude or living by herself. She simply wasn't the type to imagine things or see shadows where none existed.

So why was her heart knocking against her chest? Why did her fingers begin to tremble when she gazed at the spot where the ugly veve had been?

Annoyed with herself, she went inside, closed and locked her front door, then cleaned up her kitchen and flipped on the dishwasher. As she worked, she tried to analyze her reaction to the salt drawing.

In hindsight, her insistence on treating the veve as a professional opportunity seemed a little defensive. A posture that insulated her from having to consider the event on a personal level. That made sense. What didn't track was her emotional response. Without Beau to convince, with nothing between her and the truth, she had to admit that finding a veve on her doorstep was more upsetting than she had been willing to concede. And that surprised her.

Giving in to a silly impulse, she walked through every room in her small rented house, clicking on the light, looking around carefully, then turning the light off again. She didn't really expect to find anything amiss and she didn't.

Smiling at her foolishness, she prepared for bed, then slipped between crisp, cool sheets and sighed. The evening had not gone at all as she had expected and hoped it would. Tonight should have marked the beginning of a new and wonderful phase in her relationship with Beau. But instead of ending up together in her bed, they had parted uneasily, both aware of a wedge between them.

Holly folded her arms behind her head and stared up at shadowy patterns playing across her bedroom ceiling. The wedge was her fault. She could dissolve it as easily as snapping her fingers. All she had to do was abandon her dream of writing and publishing a scientific analysis of fringe faiths. If she let go of her ambition to write the book, then there would be no point in continuing the research with Desiree. Flora would be happy. So would Beau.

Holly had a hunch that she might be relieved and happy, too. *Might* be.

The thought surprised and irritated her. Damn it, she had as much right to pursue her ambition as Beau had to pursue his dream of winning the Kentucky Derby. A scholarly publication would be a credible addition to her résumé. The proposed book was one of the reasons she had come to Louisiana.

It was not logical to halt her research and give up the book to smooth the rough edges of a relationship that could only be temporary at best. If she ever gave up the book, it had to be because that's what she wanted to do, not because it would make things easier between her and Beau. If she abandoned her dream for Beau's sake, resentment was sure to follow.

Groaning softly, she rolled over and pressed her face into the pillow. The dangerous thing was that she would even consider compromising her ambitions for Beau's sake. And there was something else even more important. She had a worrisome suspicion that a temporary relationship wouldn't be enough because...she was falling in love with him.

That was a mistake. Beau had been honest about having no desire to marry, and he believed she felt the same way. Which she did. She really did.

"Come on, shrink. Heal thyself," she whispered, squeezing her eyes shut. "This is turning into a mess with a huge potential for getting hurt." But she knew better than to attempt self-analysis.

Finally, near dawn, she fell into a restless sleep. And dreamed again of walking into a blazing building.

JACKSON HATED THE SHACK in the swamp. When he was growing up, calling a family "stilt people" was the same as calling them trash. Now, high-ticket homes were going up in marshy subdivisions that required the houses to be lifted on stilt foundations. This amazed him. He couldn't believe people actually paid six-figure prices to buy a stilt house. It didn't matter how lovely the homes were, they were stilt houses.

After tying his boat to the ramshackle pier, he frowned at the shack where his mother and grandmother lived. Old Desiree liked living in the swamp, and it was going to be hard to pry her out of here. She'd always said living in the swamp was the same as living in a pharmacy. She was ancient and she didn't care about having things, didn't care if some people thought she was stilt trash. His mother, now that was a different story.

Flora understood things. And she was smart. Jackson believed her when she claimed that she lived in the swamp because it gave her a certain mystique and lent credibility to her powers. That was true. A lot of people feared Flora Boudreaux, and that made him proud. He would have liked it better if his mother lived in a mansion like Belle Terre—Philip's place—but he understood her reasoning. When push came to shove, it was better to have power than a fancy house and all the trappings. The best of all worlds would be to have both. Thanks to Philip's greed and ambition, having money *and* power was now possible.

"You're right on time, *chéri*," Desiree said, smiling at him before she turned back to the chicken sizzling on top of the wood stove. "Help yourself to a beer out of the ice chest. We'll be ready to eat in about fifteen minutes."

"Open a beer for me, too," his mother said. She sat at the table, fanning herself and frowning out the screen door. "When I get rich, I'm going to move someplace where it's cool in the summer."

Jackson grinned. Flora wouldn't object to selling the place for a fortune. Already he saw her as an ally. "With what you've got socked away, you could buy a place with air conditioning right now." She cried poor, but she earned plenty with her spells and charms and hexes.

"That's the trouble with you," Flora said, swinging her frown toward him. "You think I'm made out of money." After taking a long drink, she rolled the chilled beer bottle across her forehead.

Jackson sat across from her at the table and glanced toward the strings of drying herbs and the sealed bottles that contained God knew what. He recognized the labels that read Aniseed or Aloe or Mistletoe. He didn't have a clue what might be inside jars labeled Adam and Eve or Kava Kava. Since he didn't like to look at jars of stuff with names like Bloodroot or Devil's Cup, he turned his gaze to Flora.

Even when his mother scowled, she was a handsome woman. It didn't surprise him that Philip had pursued her in her youth. She must have been a shake and bake, a real beauty. The thought made him shift uncomfortably in his seat.

Flora shoved at a loose tendril of hair and glared at him. "Anytime you talk about money, begging for a loan always follows. The answer is no. I'm not lending you any more money."

She saw through him like he was made of glass. She always had. Leaning forward, he cleared his throat and began an appeal. "I need thirty thousand dollars, Ma, and I need it bad." He flicked a meaningful glance at Desiree. "This time I know how I'll pay it back."

Flora stopped fanning long enough to study his newly acquired black eye and cracked lip. "Did Huey's boys do that?" Her upper lip curled in disgust and she waved the fan at her throat. "You oughta know better than to borrow money from a loan shark like Huey. What was it? Some tip on a sure thing?" Her disgust deepened. "I've told you and told you to stay away from the racetrack. But you won't listen. By now you should know that those sure things have a way of coming in dead last. Well, you got yourself in this mess and you can just get yourself out."

Gingerly, he touched the scab on his lip and wondered if anything in Desiree's jars might help the injury heal faster. Asking for help might soften her up. Might be a way to lead into Philip's offer. On the other hand, working with her remedies might remind her of how much she liked living here.

"This is the last time I'll ask for a loan, Ma, I swear it."

"I've heard that before, too." The bodice of her loose dress was sticking to her chest and she pulled it away from her skin and waved the fan. "Must be a hundred degrees in here, and not much cooler outside."

"Next time, Huey's boys aren't going to let me off with just a black eye and a fat lip." Real estate deals didn't close overnight. Even if he persuaded Desiree to sell out, the sale wouldn't occur swiftly enough to keep Huey from breaking a few of his bones. Or worse.

Giving Huey's boys the five thousand from Philip had saved him temporarily, but it also created another problem. His son-of-a-bitch father wanted the five thousand back if he didn't persuade Desiree to sell, and now of course he didn't have it. He had to find a way to open the subject of Philip's offer.

Following his instincts, he told Flora how he had humbled himself and asked Philip for a loan and how Philip had refused him. Instantly her attention sharpened as he had known it would. She stared at him with narrowed eyes and he saw the fire and fury in her gaze. Philip's name always stirred her up.

"If his precious Drew had asked for a piddling thirty thousand, he would have written a check so fast it would make your eyes blur to watch," she snapped.

At once he saw that stirring her up wasn't the direction to take and he shifted gears. "You always said you were going to make Philip acknowledge me as his son and you said we'd get some of that Delacroix money." He leaned back as Desiree set a heaping platter of fried chicken and mashed potatoes in front of him. He looked at Flora. "I don't see much progress in acknowledging me, but..." He paused, stringing it out until he had both women's full attention. "I have to give you credit, Ma. Philip is willing to hand over a whole lot of Delacroix money."

"What are you talking about?" Flora demanded. "Did he finally rewrite his will and provide for us?"

"It's better than that. We don't have to wait for Philip to die. We can get a chunk of his money within weeks." He thought about Beau Delacroix's green Porsche and women like Dr. Holly Gibson. There were a lot of things he wanted right now. "Philip is willing to pay a fortune for this old shack and the land it sits on!" He gave them a triumphant smile as if he had come up with the idea and put the deal together. "He wants to buy this property."

Desiree lowered her fork and stared at him. "No. I will never sell my home."

Jackson leaned over the table. "Grandma, Philip wants this place bad. I think we can get at least a million dollars, maybe even two. With that kind of money, you can live wherever you want, buy a whole swamp somewhere else. We'll all be rich!"

Standing, Desiree gazed down at him, anger and sadness in her eyes. "Never."

Frowning, Jackson turned to his mother. "Talk some sense to her. Tell her to think of us if she won't think of herself!"

Flora leaned back in her chair and stared. "How could I raise such a fool?" she said with a look of incredulous disgust. "First, I'll bet everything I own that you plucked that million-dollar figure out of thin air. The day Philip Delacroix writes a million-dollar check to a Boudreaux is the day I'm crowned queen of England."

He'd expected her to be on his side. Thinking she didn't understand, he told her about Philip's plan to find a way to lift the injunction prohibiting development of this area.

"Use your head," she said sharply. "Until the injunction is lifted, if it ever is, this land isn't worth a plugged nickel! That will be Philip's argument and he's right. So he'll only offer us a couple of thousand dollars. A million dollars?" She gave him a nasty grin. "You're dreaming."

Jackson fell backward in his chair and blinked. She was dead right. Why hadn't he seen it? That's why Philip wanted to buy Desiree's land before he attempted to lift the injunction. After the injunction was lifted, this land would be worth a million, but not a minute before.

Desiree stood at the stove, poking a fork at the skillet. "This is my home, I've lived here most of my life. I know every root and every herb in this swamp." Her voice tightened. "You tell Philip Delacroix that even if he did offer a million, I'll never sell."

Flora nodded. "Tell that old bastard we're not as stupid as he thinks we are! You tell him to get the injunction lifted and *then* make us an offer." She ignored Desiree's tight lips and narrowed eyes. "Meanwhile, Mama is right. We'd be fools to leave here for a few thousand dollars, and do what? Go where? To town?" She made a snorting sound. "Where are we going to find the herbs we need in town? Where are we going to hold our ceremonies? You go back to Philip and throw his offer in his face!"

Their angry expressions told him they wouldn't budge. And now he was in deeper trouble than before. He still owed Huey twenty-five thousand, and Philip would demand his five thousand back. He couldn't pay either one.

Throwing down his napkin, he walked to the door and stared out the screen. "I know what you've been doing over at the Delacroix Farms," he said, needing to show Flora that he wasn't as stupid as she thought he was. "Philip asked you to leave a few signs and stir things up over there, didn't he?"

"What I do is none of your business," Flora said, casting a quick glance at Desiree.

"It is if you're willing to help Philip, but not me. You could give me a loan."

"The trouble with you is you don't think things through." Flora dropped a bone on her plate and leaned back. "First, Philip isn't going to scratch my back unless I scratch his. And I'm not talking about his insulting offer to buy this place, I'm talking about the real money. But before he changes his will, he's going to want a whole lot of scratching on my part. So...Beau's Ma Chere isn't going to win the Delta Stakes. That horse is already spooked and you can take it from me, it's going to get spooked worse. You need some money? Bet on Philip's Camptown Racer.''

"I thought you said I should stay away from the track."

"Huh. Like I believed you ever would." She rolled her eyes above a humorless smile. "I'm thinking Beau deserves a little payback for tricking you about Ma Chere and making you look bad in front of your father. If you see a way to benefit—" she shrugged "—so much the better."

Learning that Ma Chere had no chance on Tuesday was good news. Philip's Camptown Racer would win the Stakes easily, since Ma Chere had been the only other real contender. Unfortunately, Camptown Racer was a favorite and the odds were low. A winning ticket wouldn't pay much. To make any real money on this deal, Jackson would have to bet at least ten grand on the nose. He didn't have that kind of money and was tapped out on places where he might borrow a few thousand.

When he turned around, he discovered his mother and grandmother were arguing again.

"You leave Beau Delacroix alone," Desiree was saying. "He hasn't done anything to you."

Flora exploded. "I'm sick and tired of you always defending the goddamned Delacroix! What did they ever do for you that you think they're all such saints?"

"I didn't say the Delacroix were saints. Philip certainly isn't." A thin smile played around Desiree's lips. "But the Delacroix have been good to me and mine." Her smile faded and her eyes sharpened. "All I'm saying is you leave Beau and his young lady alone."

"His young lady!" Flora's lips curled and she jumped up from the table, her hands clenched into fists by her sides. "That bitch is this tight with the little slut who murdered my son!" She held up two crossed fingers. "*Your* grandson, in case you've forgotten!"

"Steven died from a snakebite. Whether you like it or not, that's what happened and that's the truth. I know it." Returning to the table, Desiree lifted a forkful of potatoes to her mouth.

This was what happened every time he came for Sunday dinner. A family fight. "Can we get back to the subject of the land?"

Both women looked at him as if they had forgotten that he was present.

"Are we agreed that we'll sell if Philip gets the injunction lifted?"

"The injunction will never be lifted," Desiree said calmly.

Jackson gazed into her eyes and his heart sank. She had that strange otherworldly look that stole over her expression when she was gazing into the future. When this happened, she was never wrong. Philip could spend a fortune in bribes and try blackmail and threats, but the injunction would hold. This swamp would never be developed.

Jackson scowled at his dinner plate and felt his dreams deflate. It wasn't fair. A note of desperation entered his voice when he addressed his mother. "I have to have five thousand dollars and I need it immediately."

"I swear. You're jumping from subject to subject so fast, I can't follow you."

"You can afford it," he said flatly. "You could at least give me five thousand. Ten would be better."

"I'll loan you five thousand," Desiree said suddenly, surprising the hell out of him. "If you and Flora swear to leave Beau and his young lady alone. I don't want either of you messing with those young folks."

He exchanged a quick glance with Flora and knew she wouldn't honor this condition any more than he would. "Could you make it ten thousand?"

"No. And I want you to swear you'll leave Beau and Holly alone."

Five thousand would have to do. "We swear," he said sullenly.

When Desiree turned to her daughter, Flora ground her teeth together and nodded. "Outside with you," Desiree ordered, rising from the table. His grandmother didn't want them to see where she hid her money.

He and Flora went out onto the porch, letting the screen door slam behind them, and sat in a pair of weathered rocking chairs.

"Some day," Flora muttered, rocking back and forth, her eyes on the water sluggishly flowing past the shack, "Ma and me are going to go one on one, and then we'll see what's what."

For the first time in three days, Jackson smiled with genuine amusement. "If I were you, I wouldn't challenge Grandma no way, no how."

He'd heard whispers that in her time Desiree had been a great voodoo queen. Some said she'd been as impressive as the legendary Marie Laveau. But Desiree had never capitalized on her fame and powers. She wouldn't throw tricks against anyone, wouldn't use her power to harm or frighten. He hated to think of the income she'd lost by being so stubborn.

Flora hissed at him between her teeth. "Dambala himself rides me as his horse!" She pounded a fist against her chest. "Not her anymore. Me! That's *my* snake in the crate out behind the shed, not hers. And it's *me* who sends out the call for a ceremony!"

He didn't want to argue with her, but he also didn't want to see a showdown between her and Desiree. Flora had power. He didn't doubt that, even if she helped things along on occasion. But Desiree didn't have to help things along. His grandma *knew* things. She talked to her ancestors and she honest-to-God communed with nature. If Flora called down the spirits against him, he'd worry about it. But if Desiree did the same thing, he'd run for his life. That was the difference.

"Now, Ma, how many people would show up for those ceremonies if Grandma wasn't present?"

His effort to head off a showdown backfired. Flora jumped out of the rocking chair and shook her finger under his nose, spittle flying from her lips. "I've got a following and don't you forget it! Those people come to see me and I direct the loas! If you have any doubts, then come to the next ceremony. I'll send Simbi into you and watch you throw yourself and that fancy uniform into the swamp! Watch you roll in the mud and mash mangos all over your pretty face! I'll let Simbi ride you hard, boy, and when it's over, *then* you tell me how I don't have any power!"

"Ma," he said, following her back inside the shack. "I never said you didn't have power." He was talking to air. Flora stormed into her room and slammed the door. "Well, damn." Frustrated, he pushed a hand through his hair and cursed the lack of air-conditioning.

"Here's your money." Desiree tucked an envelope into his

uniform pocket and studied his eyes with a steady gaze that made him look away. "You promised not to mess with Beau or Holly Gibson."

"I said I wouldn't."

"You said you wouldn't go to the track anymore. And you said you wouldn't borrow more money from those sharks, either."

"I won't bother Beau and his shake and bake, all right?" He swore and jammed his hat on his head. "I'm not going to stand here and take any more of this. I'm going."

"Jackson? I'm never going to sell this place, so don't talk about that again."

He waited until he was out of sight of the shack before he pulled the pole into the boat and let it drift long enough to count the money Desiree had pushed into his pocket. It was all there.

For a minute he considered giving the five thousand to Huey and reducing the amount he still owed to twenty thousand. Or...he could put it all on Camptown Racer to win. Both options exerted equal appeal, with Camptown Racer coming out a little ahead in his inclinations.

And then he thought about Philip. He didn't need any special powers to know that Philip was more dangerous than Huey ever dreamed of being. The money had to go to Philip.

Brooding, he slid the pole back into the muddy water and leaned on it. Damn Beau Delacroix. Old Desiree wouldn't give her own grandson a red cent when it was just him asking for it. But she'd hand over five grand to protect Beau. He thought about that distinction, getting madder by the minute.

None of this was fair. He had just watched a million dollars evaporate before his eyes. He had a hot tip on the outcome of the Delta Stakes but lacked the funds to capitalize on it. Huey was after him. Philip would demand his money back the minute Jackson reported that Desiree would never sell.

Somehow Beau Delacroix was to blame for all of these problems. Logically, Jackson knew that wasn't true, but emotionally it was. And Beau would have to pay for that.

CHAPTER NINE

THE DELTA STAKES DIDN'T run until two o'clock, but Beau was at the Bassier City's track's shedrow by six in the morning. Excitement mounted and would continue to accelerate as the clock neared post time. Already, the tension along the shedrow resonated with palpable force. Beau's skin tightened and even his scalp felt taut and tingly. These were familiar feelings that he welcomed, part of the thrill and mystique of racing, an adrenaline high that made his blood race and his heart pound. He loved it. There was nowhere else he would rather be than standing here in the early morning sun, inhaling the sweat of men and the good clean scents of horses and saddles, sipping hot coffee laced with hope and anxiety and expectation.

Despite the large number of people working or milling about the receiving barn, this area was not open to the public. This was the working end of the track, and the activity was intense. Grooms bathed the horses, brushed and curried them. Stalls were being mucked out and new bedding laid down. Trainers endlessly debated the proper mixture of oats, bran and molasses, or secret lucky combinations mixed with hay and special treats. Assistants oiled or polished tack. Vets did last-minute checks. Trainers, assistants and owners conferred about problems real or imagined. Track officials hurried here and there. Blood samples would be taken minutes before each race and again from the winner after the race.

As the morning progressed, the jockeys began to arrive for their weigh-in, posturing for status, inspecting their silks, looking in at their rides, examining saddles and tack, conferring about weights and the condition of the track. Beau respected the jockeys, especially Ace Crowder, who would ride Ma Chere today. But he privately considered them prima donnas and a giant pain, as well. Ace Crowder threw his weight around like a man three times his size, but most jockeys did.

Since the Stakes race was an important showcase and the purse substantial, Beau expected his uncle Philip to put in an appearance, but to his surprise, Philip still hadn't appeared by an hour to post time. He thought he glimpsed Drew, Philip's son, but he wasn't certain. He had started forward to check, when Bear called him to take a look at Ma Chere.

Tapping an empty coffee cup against his thigh, Bear stood at the door of her stall, a frown fixed on Ma Chere, who moved restlessly from wall to wall. "She's tossing her head and swishing her tail—bad signs," he said, focusing intently on the horse. "She can't seem to settle down."

"Did Matt check her thoroughly?" Beau asked, concerned. Usually Ma Chere exhibited a calm temperament. She wasn't prone to anxiety or restless movement.

Bear nodded. "She's fit as a fiddle according to Matt. There's nothing physically wrong."

"What did she eat today?" Beau listened carefully but didn't hear anything unusual in Bear's reply. Neither he nor Bear subscribed to the theory of giving a racer special feed on post day. Ma Chere had received her customary breakfast. "How about yesterday? Did she travel well? Have a good night?" Ma Chere moved inside the stall as if she had an itch that she couldn't scratch. Her behavior didn't make sense.

"Yes to everything," Bear said, still frowning, watching as Ma Chere tossed her head and pawed at the bedding material. "This is her first time in actual competition. Maybe she's just picking up the excitement."

"That's usually the mark of an eager competitor." Beau thought about it. If Matt had checked the animal out, then there was no physical problem. He trusted Matt's judgment completely. Still, Ma Chere wasn't behaving in her usual calm manner. Beau considered Bear's stern expression. "I have a feeling there's something that you aren't telling me."

"It's nothing important," Bear said after a minute. His mouth tightened and he made a sound of dismissal at the back of his throat.

"We're grasping at straws here, so tell me, anyway."

"Hell, Beau. We found one of those ugly gris-gris things in the travel trailer after we unloaded her late yesterday afternoon." He spit in disgust. "You don't believe in that crap, and I don't, either. But..."

Beau nodded, trying to keep the anger out of his voice. "Are we going to have any trouble with our people about this? Did it spook any of the grooms? The walkers?"

"I don't think so. Pooch found it, and I asked him to keep the discovery to himself. So far, it looks like he has." Bear hesitated. "Look, I don't want you to think I'm placing any validity on a handful of old bones, a hank of hair and some evil-smelling black stuff."

"I don't think that."

"She's upset because her routine has been disrupted, that's all. She'll settle out when Ace goes up and she's in the gate. Ma Chere is a competitor. She's just wound up because she has a little stage fright. Isn't that right, girl? You're gonna do just fine."

Beau nodded, but without real conviction, and glanced at his wristwatch. The hours had flown past and the time surprised him. "Well, I'll leave you to it," he said reluctantly, hating to depart the shedrow. However, at this point, he was just in the way. From the corner of his eye, he noticed Camptown Racer's trainer leading the horse out of her stall. His scalp prickled as it always did at this point, and he grinned to relax his face muscles.

Stepping inside the stall, he stroked Ma Chere's velvety nose and moved backward as the horse pranced sideways, nudging him with her shoulder. She rolled her eyes at him and stamped the floor. "You can do it. You go out there and show those other horses how to run a race. Bring home the blue."

As if a floodgate had opened, he was suddenly surrounded by people, all edging him out of the way to attend to Ma Chere. After glancing again at his watch, he shook hands with Bear and with Ace, then he walked swiftly toward the stands.

The Delacroix box was already crowded, but he didn't spot Holly. Jax and Matt were present, of course, and it touched him to see that his sisters Marie and Charly had come to offer support along with the men in their lives, Lucas and Marshall. Shelby gave him a note from their father expressing regret that he couldn't be present and wishing Beau and Ma Chere luck. On the bar was a stack of good-luck messages from friends and well-wishers.

"Would you like a glass of champagne before you leave us?" Jax asked, smiling at him with sparkling eyes. They all knew his habit of watching alone when one of his horses ran.

"Not yet," he said, leaning to scan the crowd below the box. "Have you seen Holly? I've never known her to be late before."

Shelby overheard the question and frowned. "Actually, I thought I spotted her about fifteen minutes ago." She consulted a slim gold wristwatch. "I thought for sure she'd be here before now."

"Oh, no." Beau slapped his forehead. "I'm an idiot. I told her to ask directions to the Delacroix box."

Jax groaned. "They must have sent her to Philip's box."

"Bye, everyone," he called with a hasty wave. "See you after the race." Pursued by shouts of cheer and good-luck wishes, he dashed down the row of private boxes, following the curve of the stands.

Once he rounded the curve, he saw Holly at once, standing just outside Philip's box. She held her purse in front of her with both hands, and she scanned the faces of the people passing by. When she spotted him hurrying toward her, her face lit in a radiant smile that made his heart skip a beat.

She was easily the most beautiful woman in the stands. Today she wore her glossy auburn hair loose, and it curled softly on the shoulders of a cream-colored linen suit. As she turned to face him, he noticed a green silk blouse that brought out the emerald flecks in her eyes. It occurred to him that whether or not he won the Stakes race, he was a lucky man, indeed.

"I'm sorry," he apologized, placing his hands on her shoulders and looking down into her lovely face. Wanting to kiss her. "I completely spaced out that there are two Delacroix boxes."

"I didn't doubt that you'd find me eventually," she said, smiling at him.

Looking past her, he noticed Drew sitting inside Philip's box. Annoyance flickered in his eyes. "He could have invited you inside."

"Why would he?" Holly asked with amusement. "I don't know the gentleman in question and he doesn't know me."

When Drew heard voices at the door of the box, he looked up and recognized Beau. Standing, he hesitated a minute, then walked to the door of the box and extended his hand. "It's been a while," he said coolly.

"Have you met Dr. Holly Gibson?" Beau inquired after shaking hands. His tone was polite but equally as chilly as Drew's. "Holly, this is my cousin Drew Delacroix."

"How do you do," Drew said.

"I'm pleased to meet you."

"Well," Beau said uncomfortably. He had nothing to say to Drew. "The race we're all interested in is about to begin."

Drew placed a hand on his arm. "As long as you're here..." he said, anger frosting his gaze. "Would you happen to know anything about the gris-gris that have been appearing around Dad's firm lately?"

The accusing tone in Drew's voice blindsided him. "I beg your pardon? I don't know what you're talking about, but I sure as hell resent what you're implying."

Drew glared at him. "There's been a lot of animosity between your side of the family and mine, but I won't tolerate these childish attempts to frighten my father."

Beau couldn't believe what he was hearing. Anger flooded his cheeks and his voice roughened. "I'm not responsible for any bad-luck charms left at your door, but I *am* sick and tired of the cheap tricks you and Philip have been pulling. Like siccing the IRS on us and instigating a potload of nuisance lawsuits. Or arranging for voodoo signs all over the farm and hiring snipers to hide in the woods and fire warning shots!" His lip curled. "But unlike your side of the family, no one on this side is that malicious. If someone is leaving gris-gris at your office door, you can bet they didn't come from us. And since your father has plenty of enemies, you might ask him who would have a reason to put a hex on him or the firm. I'm sure there's a long list."

Drew stepped closer and his eyes turned to ice. "I'm warning you, Beau..."

"No, I'm warning you. I've had just about enough of—"

Holly squeezed his arm and stepped smoothly between them. She smiled at Drew, then at Beau. "They're leading the horses onto the track."

Beau and Drew both turned to peer out of the box. "Damn," Beau muttered. Without bothering to say goodbye, he took Holly's arm and rushed her away from Philip's box, down a flight of stairs, then turned her toward a tier of tables positioned against a railing. "Table five is ours."

When he reached the table, he seated Holly, then remained standing, swearing under his breath and staring at the horses parading past the stands. Ma Chere was still nervous, prancing sideways, tossing her head. Even from this distance, Beau could see that Ace Crowder was frowning.

"I didn't get a racing form," Holly said, studying the horses passing in review. "What number is Ma Chere?"

"Number five. Ace is wearing the green-and-white silks." Pulling out his chair, he sat down and reached for the binoculars on the table. First he checked out Ma Chere, then he examined the rest of the field, confirming that Philip's Camptown Racer was Ma Chere's only real competition. It didn't surprise him when he glanced at the tote board in the center of the grassy area inside the track and noticed Camptown Racer and Ma Chere were both favored to win. The odds were so low that no one would make much money betting on either horse. While he watched, the payoff figures dropped another fifty cents as last-minute betters bought tickets. If Ma Chere came in in the blue, a two-dollar win ticket would only pay two dollars and twenty cents. It was the same for Camptown Racer.

"What does it mean that the odds are so low?" Holly asked.

He grinned. "It means the crowd recognizes class when they see it. Looks like everyone here is betting on Ma Chere and Camptown Racer." After another long inspection, he handed the binoculars to Holly.

She thanked him and raised the glasses to her eyes. "This is probably a stupid question, but why aren't we watching the race from your box?''

"Sheer superstition," he answered sheepishly. "The first time one of my horses took the blue, I was sitting at table five."

She lowered her binoculars, looked at him and laughed.

"Besides, if I lose, I like to have a minute alone before I face the people in the box and have to listen to words of commiseration." He shrugged, watching the horses walking toward the gate. "So. Any hunches as to which horse is going to win?"

She lifted the binoculars, hiding her expression. "No hunches today. Sorry."

His heart sank. Holly Gibson was not a good liar.

Frowning, he fixed his attention on the track and bit down on his back teeth when he noticed that Ace was having difficulty getting Ma Chere to enter the gate. She balked, balked again, then Ace walked her away from the gate and into a wide circle. Beau knew the jockey would be talking to her, soothing her with the sound of his voice, coaxing her, trying to calm her.

"There's Jackson Boudreaux," Holly said suddenly. "Standing down by the rail nearest the track."

"Honey, if you're watching people instead of the horses, would you give back the binoculars?" He cursed his lack of foresight. Next time he'd arrange to have two sets of binoculars at his table. "Thanks," he said tersely when she handed back the glasses.

Ace had Ma Chere in the gate now. But he could see that she was still fidgety. Sometimes that level of skittishness signaled eagerness and was a good sign. Sometimes it foretold disaster. Lowering the binoculars, he gazed at Holly for a moment, wondering what her hunch told her and kicking himself for harboring a set of superstitions that only flared when he came to the track.

When he heard the announcer say, "And they're off!" he spun in his seat in time to see the field of horses break from the gate. To his horror, Ma Chere stumbled, and he thought for one stunning second that she would go down. Relief flooded his body when she recovered, pulled up and leapt forward as smooth as silk. By the first turn, Ace had regained a little ground and crowded out the horse on the right. He brought Ma Chere up fast on the outside, pounded past two horses, leaving them behind, and began to gain on the horses hugging the rail. By the second turn, everyone in the stands was on their feet, shouting and cheering, and Ma Chere had moved up.

"Oh, God, she's beautiful," Holly said in a choked voice.

His own throat was too full to answer. Ma Chere's mane flowed and her tail fluttered behind her. Her chest muscles slid and worked like powerful, fluid pistons. He imagined he could hear the thunder of flying hooves tearing up the turf, could feel the animal heat rising in the midst of heavy bodies pounding and straining forward.

Coming into the turn, the field had narrowed to four horses with Ma Chere moving up fast. And then, it was Ma Chere and Camptown Racer, flying neck and neck down the home stretch. The noise in the stands had reached such levels that Beau didn't hear himself chanting, "Come on, come on, come on, baby. You can do it. Come on."

Time seemed to freeze into slow motion, and he could see the powerful front legs of both horses thrusting forward, could inspect the fire in their eyes and the spittle flying from their mouths. The powerful beauty of the animals brought moisture to his eyes and he swallowed hard.

They flew across the finish line.

"Ladies and gentlemen, we have a photo finish. Please hold all tickets until the judges confirm the winner."

Beau lowered the binoculars and collapsed into his chair, his heart thudding in his chest. Holly stared at him across the table.

"Win or lose, that was the most thrilling thing I've ever seen," she said in a voice hoarse from shouting. "I've seen races before, but nothing like this. She's a wonderful horse, Beau. A born competitor!"

He knew it. And he knew that Ma Chere would only get better. She'd tasted her first public competition and had proved herself a fierce contender. She had class and heart.

"Ladies and gentlemen…" A deep hush fell over the crowd. "The winner of the Delta Stakes by one one-hundredth of a second is…Camptown Racer!" An equal number of cheers and groans erupted from the crowd. The tote board lit up showing

Camptown Racer in first place, Ma Chere in second, and Loonie Tunes in third.

Holly reached to cover his hand. "Beau, I'm sorry."

Turning away from the sympathy in her eyes, he watched Philip's head trainer lead Camptown Racer toward the winner's circle. At the other end of the stands, Drew would be hurrying down to the track and the waiting photographers.

Standing abruptly, he clasped Holly's fingers and guided her to her feet. "Come on. Let's get out of here."

She blinked. "Don't you have to accept the trophy for second place?"

"Bear will pick it up."

Surprise and bewilderment filled her eyes. "The people in your box…"

"They'll understand."

Delacroix Farms also had a horse running in the sixth race, but he didn't want to stay here another minute. He had been so certain that Ma Chere would win, so damned certain. And she would have if…if what? Frustrated, he pushed his hands deep in his pockets and scowled at the field. There was something, he didn't know what, but something had spooked Ma Chere. This was the first time she'd been so restless, the first time she had ever stumbled on the break.

"If she hadn't stumbled…" That was the missing fraction of a second that she'd needed to beat Camptown Racer. The way he saw it, if Ma Chere hadn't stumbled, she would easily have won.

"I know," Holly said softly, studying his face with anxious eyes. "Beau, are you all right?"

"Hell no, I'm not all right," he growled, resisting an urge to kick the table leg. "I wanted to win." When he saw her expression, he laughed. "I'm a lousy loser, darlin'. Now you know the truth. We didn't watch the race from the box because the rest of the family won't let me stay there when I have a horse running. If I win, I'm obnoxious. If I lose, I'm miserable."

She lifted an eyebrow, trying to decide if he was making a joke. "If you'd rather be alone right now, I could—"

To stop the words, he kissed her, dimly aware of a spate of cheers that erupted around them. "Does that feel like I want to be alone?'' he asked gruffly when he'd released her. God, he wanted this woman. Right here, right now. Exercising all his will-power, he stepped away from her before he embarrassed them both.

Pink-cheeked and smiling, she glanced at the people watching them and cheering. After smoothing her jacket and skirt, she drew a breath. ''I think you're right. Let's get out of here.''

They drove straight back to New Orleans, speaking little during the long drive from Bassier City. But instead of returning to Bayou Beltane, Beau took her to a deserted spot that overlooked Lake Pontchartrain. After sliding out of the Porsche, she drew a deep breath of pine-scented air and gazed at the sunset reflections glistening on the water. ''This is lovely. How did you ever find this place?'' After leaving New Orleans behind, they had turned down a series of dirt roads before the lake appeared before them.

''I suspect there are a few other hometown boys who know about this place, but I like to think of it as mine,'' he called to her from the trunk of the car. Walking forward, he placed a picnic basket on the ground, then unfurled a large red-and-white check-ered cloth. ''M'lady?'' Taking her hand, he led her forward, and Holly sat on the cloth and tucked her legs beneath her.

Smiling, she peeked into the basket and discovered a bottle of champagne, which was still cold, red grapes, a wheel of Brie and sesame crackers, a pot of Russian caviar and toast points. ''If we eat all this, we won't be hungry for dinner.'' It was already past the dinner hour.

''Does it matter?'' he asked, sitting across from her and reach-ing for the champagne bottle. ''As long as I'm with you, I don't care if we're here or in a restaurant or where we are.''

The picnic was so obviously a celebration repast that it tugged at her heart. ''Beau, I'm so sorry that Ma Chere didn't win.''

''So am I. There should be a couple of glasses in the basket.''

She found two crystal flutes and held them as he poured the champagne. After he put down the bottle, she touched her glass to his. ''Here's to Ma Chere's next race. I have a hunch she'll win that one.''

He gazed at her in silence before he spoke. ''You knew Ma Chere wouldn't win today, didn't you.''

"I didn't *know* it," Holly answered uncomfortably. "This is wonderful champagne," she said, hoping to change the subject. "What brand is it? Dom Pérignon?"

"But you had a hunch."

"Everyone at the track had a hunch," she said lightly. "Some were right and some were wrong."

"You were right."

"Beau, why are you doing this?" She gazed into his steady eyes, trying to read his expression. "I thought we'd agreed not to talk about this kind of thing." Instantly she realized she had made a mistake by tying her hunches into her research and her sessions with Desiree. Thankfully, Beau didn't seem to notice. But she did, and making that connection startled her.

Consciously, she had rejected Desiree's assertion that her interest in a faith exhibiting paranormal elements was not entirely scholarly but was fed by a personal need, as well. It appeared that her subconscious didn't agree. On some level, she had placed her hunches in the same category as the mysteries that Desiree performed. Something about that thought sent a light shudder down her spine.

Dropping her head and letting her hair fall forward to hide her expression, she set out the items in the picnic basket, spread Brie across several crackers and handed a couple to Beau.

"I could do this all day," he said, smiling. "Eat from the hand of a beautiful woman."

"Flatterer," she said, laughing. "But your ploy isn't working. You get to put cheese on the next batch of crackers."

"You really are one of the most beautiful women I've known," he said in a soft voice. "I like to just look at you."

A blush of pleasure warmed her cheeks. "I never know how to respond to compliments, so let's change the subject. What was all that business with your cousin Drew?"

"That reminds me. I think I owe you a word of thanks for preventing a fistfight." Leaning back on his arms, he gazed up at the sky. "Hell, I don't know what it was about. He exploded—I exploded. Maybe he's angry that his sister came over to work for our side of the family. Does Joanna ever mention Drew?"

"She didn't the last time I saw her," Holly said with a frown.

"All we talked about was her pregnancy and how happy she is." Shifting her gaze from his face, she looked out at the water. Pregnancy was another subject that she didn't want to explore. The taboo areas were piling up. "You certainly have a tangled set of family relationships."

He laughed. "That I do."

"Still, I envy you for having a large family. When I was a child, I used to fantasize that I had brothers and sisters. I didn't know where all those imaginary siblings were hiding, but in my fantasy they were coming home soon." She smiled and extended her champagne glass for a refill. "I think all only children are fascinated by large families."

"And those of us from large families think it would be wonderful to be an only child and have all the toys and all the attention."

"The grass is always greener..."

"What would you do if for some reason you decided not to write your voodoo book? Do you have a dream to replace that one?"

"Whoa," she said, her smile fading. "That's a pretty abrupt change of subject."

"Have you thought about it?" he asked, leaning forward to spread caviar on the toast points.

She lowered her champagne glass to her lap. "Beau, don't ask me to give up my dreams or ambitions. Our relationship won't survive that."

"I'm not your father, Holly," he said, looking up to meet her eyes. "I'm not issuing orders, not telling you to do anything. If you think I am, you're making a wrong assumption. I'm merely asking a straightforward question. Sometimes, despite all our efforts, dreams don't come true. We fall short of our ambitions and goals. If that should happen to you, how would you handle it?"

Try as she might, she couldn't always shut off the analytical side of her brain. It occurred to her to wonder if he was really asking this question of her...or of himself?

"I'm sorry if I seemed overly touchy," she said cautiously. Then she considered his question, trying to do so without looking for a subtext. "It's important to me to publish," she said finally.

"For many reasons, some of which I don't fully understand myself. So I'm not going to abandon that dream." A frown puckered her brow as she thought out loud. "I think what we're really discussing here is the subject matter. If for some unforeseen reason I couldn't continue writing a book on the mind-altering effects of fringe religions, I suppose I'd select another topic."

Tilting his head, he studied her face as if trying to read her thoughts. "All right," he said slowly. "Another question."

"Go ahead." She loved the long, elegant lines of his body stretched out on the cloth. He had propped his head in one hand, his legs were crossed at the ankle. There wasn't an awkward angle anywhere; he was all grace and classic masculine beauty.

"Let's say you complete your firsthand research into vodun...what happens then? Are there other mind-altering religions you want to research before writing your book?"

At once she saw where he was leading and she caught her lower lip between her teeth, thinking about her answer. "When I began this project," she said hesitantly, "I saw it as covering several religions. For example, I thought the Moonies were worth researching."

"The Moonies have a strong base in Seattle, don't they?"

She nodded, frowning. He was really asking how long she intended to stay in the Delta area. How long would they be together?

"Lately," she said, her voice sinking to a whisper, "I've been thinking there's so much material on vodun that I could devote the entire book to this one subject." Did she see a flicker of relief in his gray eyes? Because this veiled sparring made her uncomfortable, she turned the tables. "How about you? If for some unforeseen reason Hot Shot couldn't run in the Kentucky Derby, do *you* have a backup dream?"

"Ma Chere is a definite backup possibility," he said promptly, sitting up. Stretching out his hand, he slowly ran a finger down the length of her leg from knee to ankle.

Holly caught a quick breath that was almost a gasp. "I phrased that the wrong way. If you never win the Derby, Beau...how would you handle that?"

The question affected him profoundly enough that he stood and walked away from her, standing at the edge of the lake, staring out at the water. Holly rubbed her hand along her leg where he had touched her, looking at his broad back.

"Beau?" she called softly.

"Sorry," he said, walking back to where she sat on the checkered cloth. "I was thinking about what you asked." He sat down in front of her cross-legged. "Maybe it's been a mistake, but it seems I've tied a lot of things to winning the Derby. For one thing, when I win, I'll feel that I've vindicated my professional choices to my father."

Her eyebrows lifted in surprise. "Maybe you should think about that a little. My impression is that your father not only approves of your choices but is proud of you. I base my opinion on things Joanna has said, and Shelby, and even things that you've said."

Beau remained silent for so long that she grew uncomfortable beneath his steady regard, even though she doubted that he was really seeing her. He had the look of a man deep in thought. Suddenly, he threw back his head and laughed, surprising her again.

"You know something?" he asked, taking her hands in his, caressing his thumbs across her palms. "You put your finger on something that I haven't taken a critical look at in years."

"Seriously, Beau. I suspect your father would be very surprised if he knew you want to win the Derby to prove something to him."

"That's the crazy thing. I agree with you. But I didn't realize it until right now." Leaning forward, he kissed her on the lips, letting his mouth linger before he spoke again. "My father would have liked it if I'd followed in his footsteps, but in retrospect, I can think of a dozen examples that prove your opinion that he came to terms with my choices years ago. It's time I did, too." His voice deepened to a husky register and his gaze slowly traced the full curve of her lips. "You know, I think I could get used to having my own personal shrink. Before this is over, you'll have me all straightened out and thinking clearly."

Before this is over... But she wouldn't let herself think about that. Not today, when they were forging new beginnings. Not today, when they both knew how they wanted this day to end.

"Since we seem to be on a roll here," she said lightly, her lips still tingling from his kiss, "what else have you tied to winning the Derby?"

She heard herself murmur the question but she hardly knew what she had asked. Her mind was focused on his smoldering eyes, on the nearness of his body. When he wet his lips with the tip of his tongue, she closed her eyes and let the breath slowly run out of her chest. Wanting him had become an ache deep inside that made her tingle one minute and yearn the next.

Instead of answering, Beau drew her to her feet. For a long moment he looked deeply into her eyes, then he crushed her in his arms, whispering her name. She knew exactly where his hands were because she could feel the heat of his fingertips scorching through her linen jacket as if he touched her skin instead of her clothing. When he pressed her tightly against his chest, his heart crashed against her own and their ragged breathing mingled in the electric instant before his mouth claimed hers.

This kiss was like none they had shared before. This kiss was a declaration, an act of possession. There were no inhibitions this time. No hesitation or pulling back. Desire leapt through Holly's body like a sizzle of lightning, leaving her gasping and weak in the knees. No one, absolutely no one, had ever kissed her like this. She felt his passion as if it were her own, and it was. His mouth pressed a hot brand on her lips, marking her as his alone, and right now that was exactly how she felt. His, to do with as he wanted.

She felt his body melting into hers, seeking the final union; felt the urgency of frantic kisses and flying hands, touching here, exploring there, coaxing, teasing. And she couldn't breathe, couldn't think. Her world narrowed to touch, to the sound of his breath and hers, and to the low groans of pleasure and need that each of them whispered; narrowed to the frenzied heat erupting between them from lips to knees. Holly's world burned away, leaving only this moment, this magic man and their need for each other.

Holding her, his lips trailing fire down her arched throat, Beau eased to the ground.

She had one semilucid moment where she hoped this lovely place by the lake was as private as Beau had indicated it was, then she sank into his kisses, reaching for the buttons on his shirt and let their passion for each other sweep her away.

CHAPTER TEN

"ON TUESDAY BEFORE midnight," Holly said softly, recalling Desiree's advice. Then she laughed and stretched her naked body in the shadowy twilight before she snuggled back against Beau, nestling her head on his shoulder. "I can't believe I'm doing this," she murmured drowsily. "Lying here naked. What if someone had come while we were..." Heat turned her cheeks pink. "Or even now?" It embarrassed her to think about it, but not enough that she moved away from him to get dressed. She loved the feel of his shoulder beneath her cheek, loved the long, strong length of his body curved against hers.

"Honey," Beau said, trailing his fingertips across her bare shoulder, "if anyone drove into this glade right now, they would take one very long look at you and one quick look at me, and then they would say, that is a very lucky man."

She smiled and kissed his chest, pulling her fingertips through the springy dark hair there. "Have you ever done this before?"

"Done what? Had sex before?" he asked, laughing. "Maybe once or twice."

That she knew. He was an amazing lover. Considerate, skilled, sensitive and controlled. A man who took pleasure in giving as well as receiving.

"No, you goof." She nipped him lightly with her teeth and smiled when he yelped, then laughed and held her closer. "I meant, have you ever made love outside?"

"I hope this doesn't destroy your image of me as a bon vivant, a sophisticated and worldly fellow, but the answer is no." His fingers moved to caress her hair. "Until today, I've never wanted a woman so desperately that I couldn't wait for a bed and some guaranteed privacy."

Holly lifted herself up on an elbow and smiled at him. "Desperately? I think I like that."

"Oh, cruelty, thy name is woman." He closed his eyes and groaned. "I'm trying very hard not to stare at your beautiful breasts lest you think that I'm an insensitive pig." Opening one eye, he returned her smile. "Or should I interpret your shift of position as an invitation?"

"You may interpret it as a definite invitation," she said, laughing, "but for later, not now. Right now, I'm starting to get very nervous about us lying here naked in the open air, starting to worry about someone coming here." Leaning over him, she kissed him slowly and thoroughly, drawing back to gaze into his eyes before she moved away and reached for her bra and panties.

"You really are a gorgeous woman," Beau said in husky voice as he sat up to watch her.

"Who is feeling very self-conscious at the moment. There is simply no graceful way to put on underwear." Aware that he was watching every movement, she hooked her garter belt around her waist, then sighed as she examined her stockings. "At least three runs. You wouldn't happen to have some clear nail polish, would you?"

"Sorry, darlin'. I left my clear nail polish in my other purse. Why do you need it, anyway?"

She grinned at him. "In your other purse, huh? Nail polish stops the runs from going farther. You'd think a guy with four sisters would know that."

"Holly?" The change in his tone made her look at him. The softness in his eyes and the flicker of renewed desire made her heart roll over in her chest. "This was one of the most fantastic experiences I've ever had. A fantasy come true. I'll never forget this evening and you. You were wonderful."

"So were you," she whispered, charmed by his candor. "As a psychologist, I suppose I should know the answer to this. But why is it that men have fewer inhibitions than women? You're sitting there naked while I'm getting dressed, and it doesn't seem to bother you at all."

Laughing, he stood and stretched and Holly froze in the act of putting on her blouse. He was so beautiful, his skin so taut and golden. A light sprinkle of dark hair ran down his chest like an arrow pointing to the stirring between his thighs. She closed her eyes for a second, responding to an answering heat in her stomach, before she let herself look at him again. As she would have expected with a horseman, his thighs were heavily muscled, tapering to well-shaped calves. When he bent for his briefs, she glimpsed tight, smooth buttocks.

"Oh, Beau," she said. "This was the most romantic evening of my life. Thank you for making our first time together so wonderful. I'll never forget it, either."

Even though he started dressing after she did, he finished before her and poured the last of the champagne into their glasses. "To my favorite girls," he toasted, touching the rim of his glass to hers. "Holly Gibson, Hot Shot and Ma Chere."

"I'm flattered to be included in such distinguished company," she said solemnly. Then they grinned at each other and drank the warm champagne.

"Suddenly, I'm starving," Beau said, picking up the checkered cloth and folding it into the picnic basket. "Does a later dinner sound good to you?"

"It does if you can think of a place where I won't embarrass you by wearing ruined stockings and an incredibly wrinkled linen suit."

Stepping forward, he lifted her chin and kissed her. "As a matter of fact, I can. I know a place that won't let a woman in the door unless she's wearing ruined stockings and a wrinkled suit."

"Where's that?" Holly asked, enjoying his company. Loving him. Oh, yes, she thought helplessly. She loved this man. And she was going to get hurt by him. But right now that didn't matter. The hurt was in the future. Today they were charmed by each other, entranced. And she wasn't going to spoil a minute of this wonderful day by thinking about a future they couldn't have.

"My place," he said, grinning. "I just happen to have a couple of T-bones, a couple of giant potatoes and the makings for a great salad. And that's not all."

"There's more?" Holly asked, pretending to swoon. "Oh, be still my beating heart."

"There is more, O smart-ass doctor of mine. Are you ready? You are looking at a grill master. I believe I'm not being too immodest when I say that no one in the state of Louisiana is my equal when it comes to grilling steaks. I'm the acknowledged king of the grill. Ask anyone."

"The king of the grill? Oh, no, that's not immodest, not at all."

Grabbing her around the waist, he crushed her against his body and looked down at her with a mock frown. "Do I detect a tiny hint of skepticism?"

"Not at all, your highness."

Holly hadn't giggled since high school, but she did now. She was simply giddy with loving him, with having been loved by him. Happiness sparkled in her eyes and everything seemed beautiful. Especially the man who gazed down at her with happiness shining in his eyes, too.

"I don't know what's wrong with me," she said, smiling up at him. "Everything seems funny." Laughter bubbled in her throat, spilling out in happy release. "I wish today didn't have to end."

The last two hours had been magical. For a wonderful while they had been the only two people in the world, in utter harmony with nature and themselves. Such moments came so seldom and were so precious.

"Get in the car, woman, and stop tempting me with those bedroom eyes." He gave her a light pat on the bottom and opened the car door for her. "Our afternoon isn't over. We're just entering a new phase."

"The king-of-the-grill phase," she asked, sliding into the passenger seat.

"Correct." He lifted his eyebrows and leered at her legs. "I need to eat something to keep my strength up for a repeat performance. My dear Dr. Gibson, did you know there are runs in your stockings? You look like a woman who's been making love by a romantic lake as the sun set."

"What a rude comment, Mr. Delacroix. I'm not that kind of girl."

Laughing, holding hands, they drove away from the lake, intoxicated by each other.

THE THING ABOUT HIS MA'S mumbo jumbo was that you didn't know for sure if it had actually been successful or if a coincidence had occurred or just what the hell. Brooding, Jackson sat in his car on the shoulder of the road, watching a stream of traffic curving off the causeway ramp. He wasn't on duty, but he didn't have anything else to do, so he'd parked in his usual place to watch the traffic returning from New Orleans.

Everyone in three parishes knew that either Ma Chere or Camptown Racer would win the Delta Stakes. So Flora had a fifty-fifty chance of being right no matter which horse she picked. But she'd picked Ma Chere to lose, and Ma Chere *had* stumbled on the break and lost the race. Mumbo jumbo or coincidence? Hell, he didn't know.

But he knew for sure that the tip hadn't made him any money. He'd put two hundred bucks on the nose, wagering that Camptown Racer would win, and he'd netted a smooth twenty dollars. Disgusted, he leaned his head out the window and spit on the ground.

Twenty bucks. It had cost him more than that to drive to the track and pay the gate fee to enter the stands. Toss in the cost of a racing form, a couple of beers and a hot dog, and he'd lost money on the deal.

But the day wasn't a total waste. He'd had the pleasure of knowing that Beau Delacroix had received a bit of the comeuppance he so richly deserved.

Speak of the devil. Narrowing his eyes, he watched Beau's green Porsche sweep down the ramp and flash past. Too bad Jackson wasn't on duty. The Porsche was moving at least ten clicks over the speed limit. He would have enjoyed writing Beau a ticket to top off the bastard's day.

What instantly soured an already depressed mood was noticing that Beau didn't look like a man who had just suffered a hugely disappointing defeat. He was laughing and looking at Holly Gibson, who was leaning toward him like she was about to plant a kiss on his cheek.

Jackson waited a minute, drumming his fingertips on the steering wheel, then he pulled off the shoulder and followed the Porsche to see where Beau was taking his shake and bake. Not to her place. The Porsche headed out of town on the road to Delacroix Farms. So that's how it was.

Thumbing an antacid tablet out of the tube, he popped it into his mouth and chewed. Here he was with nothing to do on a balmy summer evening and no beautiful woman sitting in the passenger seat, hanging on his every word. And there Beau was, laughing and having a gay old time, taking a gorgeous babe out to his place. *He* wasn't keeping an eye out for Huey and his boys. *He* wasn't worrying himself sick about where he was going to put his hands on twenty-five grand. The clock wasn't ticking on ole Beau. Ole Beau was leading his charmed life and about to be rewarded for owning a fancy Porsche and a stable full of Thoroughbreds.

There was no justice.

Until he turned off on a dirt logging road that was little better than a pair of ruts through the woods, Jackson didn't know where he was going. He was just driving around, killing time. But when he reached the area where the fire road passed behind the row of cottages between the farm and Riverwood, he stopped the car, sat there a minute, then got out and closed the door quietly.

He walked through about a hundred yards of forest and tangled undergrowth, then stopped just out of sight of an expanse of cleared area and the back of the Delacroix cottages. The green Porsche identified which of the cottages was Beau's.

He decided to pretend this was a stakeout and just watch for a while. Nothing happened for several minutes, then the porch light came on and Beau stepped out the back door onto a wide porch and fired up the barbecue grill. Lights came on inside the house and he saw movement inside what he assumed was the kitchen. How domestic. They were making dinner together. And not just hamburgers, either. It looked like big, thick steaks that Beau was setting on the side of the grill.

Jackson decided he could use a thick steak about now, but he didn't leave. He leaned against a tree, whittled on a piece of wood and watched the cottage.

As in any stakeout, long minutes passed when nothing happened. Finally Holly came outside, carrying plates and silverware, which she laid out on a redwood picnic table. She was wearing an oversized bathrobe and her hair was wet and slicked back, her feet bare. She went inside and Beau emerged, dressed like she was, in a bathrobe. His hair was wet, too.

Beau forked the steaks over the coals then called inside, and Holly came out again, a bowl and a plate with two steaming potatoes on it. She paused to inspect the steaks, and whatever they said to each other made both of them laugh so hard that she almost dropped the potatoes.

Jealousy flamed in Jackson's heart.

Beau Delacroix had been born standing at the front of the line, and Jackson at the back. Now, how was that fair? That's what he wanted to know. Just how in the hell was it fair that the Delacroix had everything and the Boudreaux had nothing?

Fuming, he watched Beau and Holly toast each other with glasses of red wine, then eat their nice juicy steaks outside on the picnic table. Beau lit a candle and they continued talking and occasionally kissing. Half an hour after dinner, Beau slipped his hand inside Holly's bathrobe and Jackson caught a distant glimpse of a full, rounded breast. His body rigid, he watched Beau stand, then carry her inside the house.

Enough was enough. He didn't want to stay here and imagine what they were doing inside. Screw them. He had better things to do.

This time he wasn't careful about slamming the car door. So what if they heard a noise? Did he care? Scowling, he backed down the old logging road until he found a wide spot to turn around. Spinning dirt and small rocks behind him, he gunned the motor and sped down the ruts, then burned rubber turning onto the pavement.

Fact one: Beau had not suffered more than a two-minute disappointment over Ma Chere losing the Delta Stakes. Fact two: Beau had to pay. Fact three: Jackson thought he knew just how to make Beau pay.

Hot Shot.

Driving aimlessly, his car radio set on a station that alternated

Cajun tunes with country-western, he pondered how to get the most of getting back at Beau. If he planned this right, he ought to be able to screw Beau's plans for next year's Derby *and* solve his own pressing money problems.

Biting his thumbnail, he slowly cruised past Holly Gibson's house. He wouldn't mind seeing a little bad luck go her way, too. And it would, he thought. Knowing how much Flora hated Beau's shake and bake, he could almost guaran-damn-tee that Miss Doctor's Degree had some heavy bad coming her way. A satisfied smile twitched his lips.

Now all he had to do was figure out how he could make twenty-five grand by crushing Beau's dreams.

HOLLY NESTLED INTO THE curve of his body and made a purring sound deep in her throat. "I don't think I have the energy to get dressed," she murmured drowsily.

"Flatterer." A pleased smile widened Beau's lips as he brushed aside the hair on her neck and nuzzled the tender skin at her nape. "This has been a fantastic day." It was hard to remember that today was the same day that Ma Chere had lost to Camptown Racer. The Stakes race seemed as if it had happened eons ago, before the world rocked on its axis and this wonderful woman became his.

"What time is it?"

Raising himself up on an elbow, Beau checked the luminous dial on the clock beside his bed. "Almost four o'clock." When she groaned, he chuckled. "Stay the night here, what's left of it."

"I can't."

"Why not?" he asked, kissing the back of her neck again.

"An old-fashioned streak of decorum. I don't want to risk having my neighbors see me coming home to change clothes before work, wearing ruined stockings, a suit that looks like I slept in it, no makeup and hair that looks like a flock of birds nested there." Turning in his arms, she nibbled his chin and smiled. "They'll know I've been doing exactly what I've been doing. Besides, if I stay here, I suspect that neither of us will get a wink of sleep, and we both have long days tomorrow."

That was true. With the Delta Stakes now behind them, all the farm's energy would shift abruptly from Ma Chere to focus intently on Hot Shot. His pride and joy was entered in the Bayou Derby, the region's most important race of the season. A lot was riding on that race. The purse was the largest of the year, but Beau didn't care about the money. The Bayou Derby was a qualifying race.

He'd told Holly that if Hot Shot didn't work out, he could transfer his hopes to Ma Chere. But if he looked at that option honestly and with cold objectivity, he knew Ma Chere couldn't hold a candle to Hot Shot. Ma Chere was a fine horse, and he'd make money with her over the years, but the truth was, she wasn't in the same class as Hot Shot. A horse like Hot Shot came along once in a decade. Maybe once in a lifetime. Just like a chance at the Kentucky Derby.

He tried to explain this to Holly. "Our timing isn't the greatest," he finished, stroking her arm. "The next couple of weeks are going to be frantically busy for me. I won't be able to see you as much as I want to."

She was quiet for a moment, then she kissed his lips. "I've got a lot on my plate, too. I'm trying to cram a full day's schedule into about six hours to accommodate daily visits to Desiree. And I'm way behind in transcribing my research notes." She bit her lip, studied his expression in the dim light, then gave her head a tiny shake as if changing her mind about something she wanted to say.

It delighted him that he was beginning to know her so well. "Tell me whatever it is you just decided not to tell me."

She leaned over him, her gaze searching. "It has to do with a subject we promised not to get into."

Desiree and the damned voodoo nonsense. She was correct; he didn't want to hear it. At least not now. Gently, he placed a finger over her lips. "I want to know everything that's going on in your life. But about certain things...well, not now. Okay? I don't want anything to spoil this perfect day."

"Okay," she conceded after a minute. Easing down on the bed, she snuggled her head on his shoulder, making it impossible for him to read her expression. "You know, a cooling-off period isn't a bad idea. Maybe we need a little time apart to think about…things." She hesitated the way women sometimes did before saying something important. "What happened today doesn't feel casual," she added, letting the sentence trail without indicating how she felt about what she was saying.

"No, it doesn't," he agreed after a moment.

What had happened between them today felt so right, so complete. It felt as if he'd found something he'd always been looking for, something he couldn't have defined but knew he lacked.

The realization of how important Holly was to him came as a shock. He had never anticipated feeling that way about any woman. Hadn't intended to even consider a serious or important relationship until after he won the Derby. But Holly had appeared, and their deepening relationship had catapulted him into new emotions and new ways of looking at things.

Leaning his head back on the mounded pillows, he frowned at the ceiling and warned himself to put on the brakes. His feelings toward Holly were new, but his situation hadn't changed one iota. His parents were still divorced and he still resonated with the lesson he'd learned from that: marriage didn't last. Invest your hopes and your emotions in another person and pain was the inevitable result.

He needed to keep his parents in mind because he was falling in love with Holly Gibson. And he'd seen how love had clouded the judgment of friends who had been as staunchly opposed to marriage as he was. He had watched it happen. First came a relationship that leapt from casual to serious. Then came declarations of love. Then an engagement ring. And finally that long walk down the aisle. But that's not where the path ended. Sooner or later, the road branched toward a divorce attorney's office. And that's when men like him turned into men like his father, men with sad, haunted eyes and a lonely life. Men who seemed bewildered by what had happened to them.

That was not what he wanted in his future.

"Well," Holly murmured, stirring in his arms. "I'm sorry to roust you out, too, but I need a ride home." After placing a kiss on his chest, she sat up and swung her long legs over the side of the bed.

Relief relaxed his body. They were not going to discuss what had happened today in terms of their relationship. He had a lot of sorting out to do before he'd be ready for that particular conversation. Maybe Holly felt the same way.

Standing, she stretched her lovely naked body, then peered through the darkness. "I think I have clothing scattered all over the room."

"Shall I turn on a light?"

"Whatever modesty or inhibitions I might have had disappeared during the last few hours," she said with a trace of amused embarrassment. "I doubt that I'll ever feel self-conscious with you again. But thanks for being so considerate."

"Good," he said, pleased. Snapping on the bedside light, he watched her dress, surprised by the pleasure it gave him. She was a graceful woman even when she knew he was watching, putting on her clothing with languorous movements that seemed almost erotic to him. He found himself wanting her again and suddenly wondered if he would always feel that way, if it would ever be possible to fully satisfy his need for her.

"I'm probably misquoting this, but didn't someone say that life is in the details?"

She looked up and smiled. "I think the quote is, 'God is in the details,' but I wouldn't swear to it."

He liked knowing that she put her stockings on first, then her panties and next her bra. The way she adjusted one lacy strap charmed him. When he noticed how she buttoned the emerald silk blouse, he laughed. "You're the only person I've ever known who buttons from the bottom up instead of from the top down." These were details he would always remember about her, the tiny details that lovers took delight in observing and learning.

"And you're the only person I've ever known who can dress in thirty seconds flat and still look as if you just stepped off the pages of *Gentleman's Quarterly.*" She slid her skirt to her waist and tugged up the zipper. "Still, I'd say it's time you got a move on." A smile lit her face. "I'd like to sneak into my house without running into the paperboy or the milkman. If we hurry, I've still got a chance."

Within five minutes they were driving toward town, watching

the sky brighten along the rim of the eastern horizon. The radio played softly, lulling them. Beau glanced over and saw her rest her head against the seat back and close her eyes. A smile curved the corners of her lips.

"Happy?" he asked, smiling himself.

"As happy as I've been in a long time." She shifted and opened her eyes. "You?"

He took her hand and held it. "I'm usually not a man who finds himself at a loss for words, but all I can say is that this has been the most wonderful night that I can remember. *Happy* is too inadequate a word to cover what I'm feeling right now."

No, he thought, suppressing a sigh of concern, this didn't feel casual at all.

HOLLY INTENDED TO FALL into bed and snatch a couple of hours of sleep after Beau drove away, but a quick shower woke her up and she knew she wouldn't sleep until she had thought about everything that had happened since she left here at noon yesterday.

Abandoning the idea of going to bed, she brewed a pot of coffee, then carried a steaming cup out onto the porch, stepping around the spot where the veve had been. She curled up in the porch chair near the azalea bush that crowded the railing. After tucking her terry robe around her legs, she tasted her coffee and gazed at a glow of pink and light blue spreading toward the last faint glimmer of evening stars.

It had been an incredible day brimming with firsts.

She had attended horse races before, but never when she had a personal interest in one of the contenders, and the difference had been thrilling. And then, unbelievably, the lovemaking beside the lake that followed the race. A blush heated her cheeks at the memory. As little as twenty-four hours ago, Holly would have sworn on all she held sacred that she would never, under any circumstances, make love on the ground. Such an outrageous thing would never happen. Yet it had, and the experience had been sensational. Something she would remember for the rest of her life. Just as she would remember her first visit to Beau's cottage and the first meal he cooked for her. The first night that they made love almost until dawn, reaching for each other again and again as if to reassure themselves that what they felt and shared was real and not a dream.

Frowning, she took a sip of coffee and studied the brightening sky. Exactly what had she felt? Joy. Yes, she'd experienced the joy of physical pleasure and total satisfaction. But there had also been an undercurrent of alarm as she began to understand that she was powerless to stop herself from loving Beau. Things had gone too far. That knowledge frightened her, because loving him was the first step on a journey that couldn't end well or painlessly.

Beau agreed that what was happening between them didn't feel casual, but he hadn't followed up by suggesting that he had changed his mind about serious relationships and marriage.

"Good heavens," she murmured aloud, lifting a hand to cover her eyes. What was she thinking about?

She hadn't changed her opinion, either. If she was ever tempted to consider marriage, all she had to do to shake herself out of fantasyland was to pick up the telephone and dial her parents. Her father would answer the phone in the living room and her mother would pick up the extension in the kitchen. And then they would argue for the next five minutes until Holly said she had to hang up, at which point they would protest that she hadn't said much and start blaming each other for trying to monopolize the conversation instead of letting her talk. Listening to them bicker depressed her.

No, she definitely hadn't changed her mind about avoiding marriage.

But where did love go if it didn't move toward a permanent commitment? She knew how to handle relationships that did remain casual, but somehow Beau had slipped past her defenses and invaded a heart that she had believed was well armored. What did she do now?

Desiree Boudreaux was the wisest woman she knew. Perhaps Desiree could advise her on how to avoid the pain that surely loomed in her future.

CHAPTER ELEVEN

"YOU LOOK TIRED," Desiree commented with a knowing smile. "What was yesterday? Tuesday?"

Holly hadn't mentioned Beau, but Desiree's twinkling eyes told her that the old woman knew their relationship had moved forward. After trying and failing to stifle a yawn, she gave Desiree a sheepish shrug of apology. "I shouldn't have come today. I should have gone straight home from the clinic and taken a nap. I'm not as sharp as I'd like to be for our sessions."

"When we finish feeding Dambala, we'll return to the house and I'll make some tea that will increase your vitality."

They were outside in the afternoon heat, standing behind a shed that Holly had never been invited to inspect. Vines covered the shed's only window and overhung a sagging roof. Today, however, she didn't wonder what was inside. Her attention was focused on the wooden crate set in the undergrowth behind the weathered boards.

Inside the crate was a sleepy-looking python that Desiree claimed was seven feet long when his coils were extended. The snake hadn't appeared so docile a few minutes ago before Desiree fed it the mouse. The python's head had been moving in a rhythmic back-and-forth, agitated motion, its tongue darting. She would have sworn its yellow eyes followed her with a stare that was almost hypnotic. In fact, she had gazed into the snake's eyes and felt dizzy and lightheaded, as if she were beginning to fall into a strange, beguiling darkness where whispering voices beckoned to her.

The impression only lasted a minute, probably less, but it had alarmed her and left her feeing deeply unsettled. Now, however, with the snake ignoring her, sleepily beginning the digestive process, she wondered if she had imagined the peculiar incident. As tired as she was, it wouldn't surprise her to learn that her imagination was playing tricks.

Desiree lifted the lid of the crate far enough to permit the entrance of her hand and she stroked the python's head. "Flora says Dambala belongs to her," Desiree said quietly, almost as if speaking to herself. "She's wrong. Dambala rides many, but chooses only one." Sadness infused her tone. "I wanted it to be Flora." The heat and the silence of the swamp settled on them like a moist blanket before Desiree sighed and spoke again, straightening her shoulders. "It's not my place to question Dambala's will. I give praise that he has sent me you."

Without thinking about it, Holly slipped her hand into the crate beside Desiree's and petted the snake. His skin was warm and dry, surprisingly pleasant to touch. It seemed to Holly that the python pressed back against her palm, sending a light tingle up her arm.

"Is he ever allowed out of the crate?" she asked curiously.

"Oh, yes. At the ceremonies."

Then she would see what role the snake played, because Desiree had invited her to attend a voodoo ceremony next week in the swamp. That had been the exciting news she had wanted to share with Beau. On reflection, it was probably best that he had stopped her from telling him about the invitation. She had a hunch he wouldn't approve.

"We'll go to the house now," Desiree said gently, looking at her as if repeating something Holly had failed to hear.

Holly blinked and was surprised to notice that Desiree had withdrawn her hand from the cage, but Holly had not. And she experienced a puzzling reluctance to do so. Although it seemed ridiculous on the face of it, she had an impression that the python had taken a liking to her. He seemed to be rubbing against her palm, as if he was returning her stroking.

"Dambala likes you," Desiree commented with a thoughtful expression. And suddenly Holly understood that showing her the snake and judging her reaction—and the snake's—had been the purpose of this visit to the shed.

"You have a strange way of appearing to read my mind," she commented with an uneasy smile.

"And you like Dambala," Desiree whispered. She studied Holly, then turned and strode toward the house.

Holly gazed at the python for another minute before she followed Desiree. Snakes had always made her uncomfortable, but this one didn't. And she would have assumed that watching Desiree feed the python a live mouse would have disgusted her. But it hadn't. Puzzled, she knelt beside the crate and examined the snake. It was a beautiful animal, gray and black and golden. A king in its own right. For a second, she considered lifting the lid of the crate and petting it again, then smiled at the notion and made herself push to her feet.

"Until we meet again," she murmured, half convinced that the snake watched her and listened.

Desiree waited on the porch, and Holly sat in the rocking chair beside the old woman. "Thank you for the tea," she said, lifting the steaming cup Desiree had given her to her lips. It always surprised her how refreshing Desiree's hot tea could be even on a scorching day. Whatever was in the brew, it seemed to chase the sleepiness from her mind.

"Did you put a love spell on Beau?" Desiree inquired with a smile.

"No," Holly said, laughing. "But thanks to you, I'd know how to do it if I wanted to." They rocked for a few minutes, watching sunlight glisten on the water in the swamp channel. "Neither Beau nor I want to get married," Holly said after a period of comfortable silence. "The problem is, I love him." It wasn't necessary to explain how confusing this conflict was; she sensed that Desiree knew.

After knocking the cold ashes out of her pipe, Desiree repacked and lit it. She exhaled a puff of fragrant smoke with a sigh. "Not too many pleasures left to an old woman." As she didn't seem to expect a reply, Holly remained silent. "Don't worry about you and Beau Delacroix. Everything will work out just fine. You'll see. Trust the power and listen to your voices."

Frowning, Holly gazed down at the teacup she held in her lap. "When I try to imagine the future for Beau and me, something panicky closes my throat.'' She closed her eyes and a vision of smoke and flames played against her eyelids. Startled, she blinked hard and gave her head a shake. This was the first time she had recalled the fire dream during the day and in such lurid detail. ''It's a premonition, isn't it?'' she asked in a shaky whisper. The dream was profoundly upsetting.

''Describe what you see,'' Desiree said, understanding Holly's reference.

Holly almost laughed when she realized that she had assumed Desiree could see her dream as clearly as she just had. Fatigue played strange tricks on the mind. ''I can't describe it,'' she said after a minute. ''It's too upsetting.''

''It doesn't matter, *chérie*,'' Desiree said, rocking and puffing on her pipe. ''You and Beau will be together.''

Holly noticed that she hadn't said married, just ''together.'' After a moment's reflection, she decided that maybe this was the answer she had been seeking. She'd consider the possibility when she wasn't so tired.

She finished her tea and placed the cup on the floor of the porch. ''There's something I want to tell you about. It happened last Saturday night.'' Glad to turn the conversation away from herself and Beau, she told Desiree about the veve she'd discovered in front of her door. ''Is that a common representation of Baron Samdi for this area? Or was the symbol adulterated?''

Desiree stopped rocking and stared at her with narrowed eyes. ''Did you turn the trick?'' she asked sharply.

''No,'' Holly answered, surprised by how upset Desiree appeared to be.

Without another word, Desiree hurried into the house and returned with something in her hand. ''Put this under your tongue. Don't speak until I tell you it's all right to talk.''

It was an old silver dime. A light chill ran through Holly's body as she realized that Desiree was going to test her to discover if a hex had been successfully cast. For a moment she considered protesting, not wanting to put a much-handled dime in her mouth. Then she remembered that this would indeed be firsthand research. Curious about the results, she placed the dime beneath her tongue and waited, feeling a little foolish.

When Desiree instructed her to spit the dime into her waiting palm, she did so, and frowned in surprise. The dime had changed from shiny silver to dark gray.

"This is not good," Desiree murmured, peering at the dime. "Could be worse, though. It could be entirely black. If that happened, there wouldn't be much hope. But gray...this we can work with."

It had to be a trick, of course. Holly retraced the sequence with the dime, thinking about it. Her first thought was that Desiree had switched a shiny silver dime with a darkened one before placing it under her tongue. But Desiree had not put the dime in Holly's mouth. Holly had examined the dime, then placed it herself.

All right, then the discoloration had to be the result of a natural process. Perhaps saliva interacted in some way with silver. But even as she thought this, she knew it was ridiculous. She'd check it out, but instinct and intellect told her that she would discover saliva and silver did not interact in such a way as to tarnish a coin.

When she realized that she was tense and drawing back from the darkened coin, Holly made herself relax. The gray dime was a trick of the trade. It must be. Every profession had its little secrets. And voodoo was no exception. It made sense that people would need more than an old woman's word when it came to spells and hexes. The dime acted as concrete evidence that a person was hexed. If Holly could be this unnerved by the change of the dime's color, it seemed reasonable to suppose that a person lacking her analytical mind would be utterly convinced.

Another interesting point occurred to her. Desiree had used the silver dime as a physician would use a thermometer. And the darkened dime was as effective a visual aid as the mercury in the thermometer. However the trick was accomplished, it was undeniably impressive.

"You believe Flora left the sign and hexed you."

Holly hesitated. "I have a hunch that your daughter resents the time you're spending with me, and that she doesn't agree with your decision to share your knowledge with an outsider." When Desiree continued to stare at her, she sighed. "Yes, I think it was probably Flora who created the veve. She dislikes me for a number of reasons."

Desiree lowered her head, and for an instant she looked her age. "I'm grateful that you didn't turn the trick back on the trickster. I'm in your debt," she said in a low voice.

Holly waved aside the old-fashioned phrase. "You don't owe me anything. You can't be held responsible for the actions of a grown daughter. Besides, it gave me an opportunity to study a veve. And," she added lightly, hoping to reassure the old woman, "I don't know how to turn a trick. There was never any danger that I'd spin the hex back on Flora, if she is indeed the person who drew the veve."

Desiree lifted her gaze. "Yes, you do know how," she said softly, not willing to be fooled. "You and me, we've talked about this. And you have your hunches...." She studied Holly's face, and Holly experienced another of those peculiar instances of feeling an electric connection. "Well," Desiree said eventually, breaking eye contact. "Did you do anything to stop the trick?"

"No," Holly said. It hadn't occurred to her.

Desiree closed her fist over the dime. "This you do first thing. Sprinkle salt around your house on the inside, and in front of the porch steps. Put black pepper in your purse and in your shoes. Do this for three days, four would be better. I'll give you a mustard seed, and you plant it under your porch." She glanced at Holly's heat-dampened hair. "If you want to teach Flora a lesson, hide matches in your hair." Anger infused her sharp nod. "Then she'll know her trick has been stopped but good!"

Before they parted for the day, Holly accepted the mustard seed that Desiree pressed into her hand, but she did so merely as a gesture of politeness, not intending to actually plant it beneath her porch.

So it surprised her when she returned home and found herself unwilling to dispose of the tiny seed. Standing over her kitchen sink, she examined the mustard seed and thought about the darkened dime.

"What harm would it do?" she said aloud. And then laughed at herself as she went into the garage to fetch a garden trowel. But it was uneasy laughter. And she didn't laugh at all while she planted the mustard seed and then sprinkled grains of salt throughout her house. She just did it. "In for a penny, in for a pound," she muttered when her rational mind questioned her actions.

After dinner, she typed the day's session with Desiree into her computer, recording her impressions of the python and Desiree's instructions for warding off Flora's hex. Then she worked on some files she had brought home from the clinic before she changed into her nightgown and washed her face. After she brushed out her hair, she considered her reflection in the mirror.

"You are practising voodoo," she said to the surprised image gazing back at her. Then she laughed and raised an eyebrow. When she began her research with Desiree, she hadn't imagined that she would one day be making an offering to a house spirit or planting a mustard seed to head off a bad-luck spell. "Might as well take it the rest of the way," she said, grinning at herself in the mirror before she tore a dozen matches out of a matchbook and tucked them under her hair next to the scalp. "Take that, Flora old girl. Two can play at this game."

Feeling foolish and a little silly about the salt sprinkled around her house and the matches hidden in her hair, she read in bed until Beau called about eleven o'clock.

"Did I wake you?" he asked. His voice sounded tired.

"No, but if you'd called thirty minutes later you would have. I've been dozing over the book I'm trying to read. I think I've read this paragraph three times." Covering a yawn, she smiled at nothing in particular, loving his voice in her ear as much as she loved recalling why they were both tired today. "How did your day go?"

"Good, actually. The auditor called and signed off our case. We got a clean bill of health. In fact, the IRS owes us eight hundred dollars. Not only that, but my father managed to quash one of the nuisance suits, and it looks as if he may be able to negotiate the suit with Armand Louis. Things are looking up on that front. And finally, we breezed Hot Shot and she came in with a spectacular time, her best ever."

"That's good news, all of it. Congratulations!"

He laughed. "We're not out of the woods yet, but we're moving in that direction. How about you? Did things go smoothly at the clinic?"

"I'm not sure things ever go smoothly at the clinic," she said, leaning back on a pile of mounded pillows and picturing him in her mind. Now that she had been to his cottage, she knew where his phones were and could imagine him standing in his small kitchen, his shoulder against the wall, the phone cradled beneath his ear. "I had one appointment after another. The usual things. Marriage problems. One case of depression. Two juveniles."

It seemed to her that he hesitated before asking the next question, and when he did, his voice sounded a little too casual. "Did you go out to the swamp today?" After she said yes, he paused again, even longer. "How is Desiree?" he asked finally.

"Fine." She hesitated, too. "It was a good session."

Suddenly, putting the matches in her hair seemed utterly ridiculous and she combed her fingers over her scalp to pull them out. Uncertain that she'd found them all, she sat on the side of the bed and leaned forward, shaking her head. Two matches floated toward the carpet.

"Holly? What are you doing? It sounds like...I don't know what it sounds like."

"Nothing. I just sat up for a moment."

"I missed you today. I must have thought of you a hundred times."

After giving her head another shake, she lay back on the pillows. "What? Only a hundred times? I'm disappointed."

His laugh poured into her ear, rich and intimate, and made her smile. "Honey, you wanted to tell me something last night and I cut you off. Unless you're in a hurry to read that same paragraph again, this would be a good time to tell me what you started to say."

She had changed her mind. She didn't want to report that Desiree had invited her to observe a voodoo ceremony because she knew he wouldn't approve. But secrets were like wedges that slowly pried apart the best of relationships. Therefore, with great reluctance, she told him about the upcoming ceremony. A shocked silence opened on the line. "Beau?" she said after a minute. "Are you still there?"

"Frankly, I don't know what to say."

"You could say congratulations. Very few outsiders have witnessed an authentic voodoo ceremony."

"Congratulations," he repeated in a flat voice.

Holly smothered an irritated sigh. She'd known this would cause a problem between them. "All right, go ahead. Tell me all the reasons why I shouldn't do this." Despite an effort to keep her voice neutral, she heard the anger in her tone and knew he heard it, too. "But keep in mind that I *am* going to do it. I *am* going to attend that ceremony."

"I'm not telling you what you can or can't do. You're an adult, capable of making your own decisions."

"Yes," she said crisply, "I am. I'm glad you recognize that. But you don't approve."

"You don't need my approval," he said, and now she heard irritation in his voice, too. "As you pointed out, you're going to attend the ceremony regardless of what I think about it."

"This is exactly the opportunity I'd hoped to find when I came here. But I didn't really believe I'd get a chance like this. You bet I'm going to act on it. I can't think of any reason why I wouldn't!"

"Fine, then do it. Don't give a thought to taking a boat into the swamp at night. Don't let it concern you that you're attending a meeting where violent hysteria is a prominent feature. Don't let it worry you that the only person you'll know there is a ninety-year-old woman who wouldn't be much protection if others just happen to resent the intrusion of an outsider."

Holly sat upright and swung her feet over the side of the bed. Her spine stiffened. "I'm not asking for your approval or your support, but it would be nice to have both. Especially as you know how important this project is to me. Every one of the things you mentioned has occurred to me, and, yes, I'm uneasy about some of those things. Does that make you happy? But I'm not going to allow some maybes or might-happens to cause me to miss an event that could be the centerpiece of my book!" She drew a breath. "Look. We're both tired. It's been a long day and tomorrow won't be any shorter. I think we both need a good night's sleep."

''If that's how you feel…good night.''

Holly hung up the telephone and fell back against the pillows, angrily crossing her arms over her chest. She supported his dream; why couldn't he support hers?

He made her feel like a naive child blindly walking into danger despite warnings from more knowledgeable adults. And that was nonsense. She was a scholar, a detached observer. Why couldn't Beau grasp that?

After fuming and fretting for a few minutes, she snapped off the light and slid down on the bed. She would have fallen asleep almost immediately, except something pressed against her cheek. When she investigated, she found another match.

The discovery gave her pause. All right, she wasn't quite as detached as she'd like to think. On the other hand, she didn't believe for one minute that hiding matches in her hair had anything to do with anything. It was just a bit of impulsive silliness.

That thought also troubled her. She usually wasn't prone to impulsive silliness. So why had she placed matches in her hair? Was that a rational thing to do? Did intelligent people hide matches in their hair for no reason? Or was it just possible that she had lost her objectivity and was sinking deeper and deeper into voodoo lore on a personal basis?

She was too tired to think about this now. It wasn't important, anyway.

ON SUNDAY, BEAU USUALLY had brunch at Riverwood with his father; the family had an open invitation to the lavish buffet set up on the stone terrace. Today, all his sisters were present along with the men in their lives, and Grandfather Charles arrived about the same time as Beau, which pleased his father. Justin enjoyed any occasion that brought the family together. But there was a downside as well. When the family gathered, they were all aware that one person was missing. Madeline, Beau's mother.

Beau carried a heaping plate to the umbrella table where Jax and Matt were sitting with Marie and Lucas. They made a place for him and Jax poured him a cup of coffee. Beau frowned at his sisters. He didn't understand how they could jump into marriage so easily. Especially Jax. Not only had she witnessed the breakup of their parents' marriage, but she'd gone through a bad marriage herself. Yet here she was, gazing into Matt Taggart's eyes, married and deeply in love again, and positive that this time it would end happily ever after. Where had she found such a deep well of optimism? How could she ignore all the evidence that marriage was a battleground where sooner or later nice people got badly wounded?

"Beau...oh, Beau? Earth calling Beau Delacroix."

When he looked up, Marie was snapping her fingers and grinning at him. "Lucas and I are going to see the new Spielberg movie tonight. Would you and Holly like to join us?"

Considering how they had parted on the phone last night, he doubted that Holly wanted to see him right now. "Not tonight, but thanks."

"That reminds me," Matt said, tearing his gaze from Jax's face. "Jax is showing Pretty Lady on Thursday in Baton Rouge. We wondered if you and Holly would like to make a day of it. We could attend the show, then catch a bite afterward at a little place Jax and I discovered. We think you two might like it as much as we do. Best blackened redfish you ever tasted."

"It sounds wonderful, but I think we'll have to take a rain check."

"I knew he'd say that," Jax said, nudging Matt in the ribs with her elbow. "For the next three weeks Beau's going to be practically living in Hot Shot's stall. Worrying about things like shipping fever, pulled muscles, lost irons, tying up, washing out." She smiled at Beau. "None of which is going to happen to Hot Shot."

"From your lips to God's ears," Beau said, returning her smile. But his thoughts were on the startling fact that his family was beginning to view Holly and him as a couple. Marie and Jax hadn't invited him and a date. They had invited him and Holly Gibson. He had a sneaking suspicion that before he left Riverwood today, Shelby and Charly would come up with some invitation that also included Holly.

After he finished eating, he carried a second cup of coffee to the terrace railing and leaned against it, turning a brooding expression in the direction of the farm. It was a full minute before he realized that Jax had joined him.

"Thinking about dry weather and a fast track?" she asked, teasing him. "Or are you missing a certain gorgeous brunette?" She put a hand on his arm. "Why didn't you bring her to brunch? Father wouldn't mind. He's dying to meet Holly."

"How do you do it?" he asked, gazing into gray eyes so like his own.

"Do what?"

"Ignore the fact that marriage is a miserable trap."

Her eyebrows rose and she stared at him. "That's a heavy subject, brother of mine."

"I know what you went through during your first marriage, Jax, and we both saw how hard it was on our parents to dissolve their life together. How can you pretend these things didn't happen?"

"Oh, Beau," she said softly, studying his expression. "Is that your impression of marriage? A bomb with a long fuse? An inevitable failure?"

"How many people can you think of who are happily married?"

"How about Joanna and Logan? Toni and Brody?" She continued with an impressive list, naming couples they knew who had been happily married for many years. "Beau, some marriages go sour, that's a fact of life. But not all do. You aren't Father. And Matt is nothing like my ex, Greg. If you and..." she cleared her throat. "If you get married, your marriage will be unique to you and your wife. It will be what you make of it. If you put your career first, like Father did, then your marriage will suffer. If you stifle your wife and try to make her into something she isn't, then the marriage isn't going to be happy. But if you work at it, and if you set your priorities right...if the marriage is really and truly important to both of you...then it can work. I believe this. Look around you and you'll believe it, too. Stop assuming the glass is half-empty and start noticing that it's half-full."

He pondered Jax's viewpoint throughout the afternoon. In fact, he watched Bear set up for a five-and-a-half-furlong breeze and was too distracted to pay much attention even when Hot Shot flew over the finish in record time.

Bear pounded him on the back. "By God, did you see that? Al asked her for some run and she gave it to him!" Not waiting for Beau, Bear strode toward Al Sellers as the jockey slid out of the irons and released Hot Shot to one of the hot walkers. Bear shook Al's hand and beamed. "We're going to win the Bayou Derby. No one's going to come close to her," he said happily when Beau joined them. "If she performs like this, Hot Shot will take the lead early and finish several lengths ahead of the field!"

Beau knew Hot Shot's time was excellent, but the edge was off his excitement. That's what women did. They insinuated themselves into a man's mind and prevented him from fully concentrating on business. He should have been buzzing with excitement the way Bear was, but he kept thinking about Jax saying something about stifling a woman's interests and then applied that to his disapproval of Holly's interest in vodun. That wasn't all. He had told Holly that he wouldn't be able to see her much during the next three weeks because he'd be getting Hot Shot ready for the Bayou Stakes. Putting *his* interests and *his* career and dreams before his relationship with her. Just as his father had done for so many years.

Insight came with a shock. He was repeating the behaviour of men who had ruined their marriages. If he continued on this path, everything he feared would come true. He wouldn't be able to sustain any relationship, because what he was doing was sending messages that stated loud and clear, I want you to change to please me. And, you are not first on my priority list. My dream and my career come first.

His first instinct was to find the nearest phone and call Holly and tell her what he'd just discovered about himself. But he didn't do that because he didn't know what he would say next.

Logically, he should then say something to demonstrate that he didn't want to change her, that he supported her pursuit of knowledge and her interest in voodoo. And he should tell her that he was confident in Bear's abilities and in the abilities of all the people working their butts off to get Hot Shot ready. Preparing for the Bayou Derby would not affect the amount of time he could spend with her.

But he wasn't sure if he could say those things or give those assurances. It was one thing to recognize his faults, another thing to do something about them. Before he could change, he had to think carefully and make very sure that this was what he wanted, or any changes would be only temporary.

Later in the afternoon, he stepped into Hot Shot's stall, loving the long, gleaming, healthy look of her, and gave her an apple and a chocolate chip cookie, her favorite treats. She held her tail high, always a good sign, and seemed very pleased with herself.

Beau smiled. Winston Churchill had been correct when he'd said, "There's something about the outside of a horse that is good for the inside of a man."

"You did well today," he said, stroking Hot Shot's sleek neck. She turned big brown eyes to look at him. "I've waited my entire life for you, darlin'. We're going to go all the way, you and me." He could visualize it.

Relaxing, he let the familiar dream wash over him, picturing himself and Hot Shot standing inside the winner's circle at Louisville. From the age of about sixteen, he had been mentally rehearsing what he would say to reporters and friends at the moment of victory. There would be cameramen and cheers, champagne and a horseshoe of roses. And a trophy that he would cherish for the rest of his life.

For the first time, he realized there was something missing in his vision.

Someone with whom to share his celebration of dreams come true.

He had never followed his dream beyond the excitement of winning the Derby, hadn't moved past his moment of glory standing in the winner's circle. What happened after the reporters and the cameramen departed? After the champagne had bubbled away and the celebration had faded?

Would he be left standing alone with no one beside him who understood what the moment meant? With no one to nod and smile with when, years later, he said, "Remember when Hot Shot won the Kentucky Derby? Do you remember that day and how happy we were?''

A sigh lifted his chest and he ran a hand over Hot Shot's back. ''Sleep well, honey, you've earned it. Now I need to check in on my other girls.''

He stopped by Ma Chere's stall and stood at the door, talking to her and rubbing her behind the ears the way she liked. Then he straightened his shoulders, thought for a minute and walked toward his car.

He had a suspicion it wouldn't be as easy to cozy up to the third female in his life.

IF HOLLY HADN'T GONE into the kitchen to fix a pitcher of iced tea, she wouldn't have known that Beau was in the vicinity until he rang her doorbell. As it was, she glimpsed him parking the Porsche in front of her house and had a minute to smooth her hair and frown down at her oversized shirt and bare legs before he knocked on the screen door.

''Hi,'' she said, wishing she'd had time to change into a pair of slacks, dab on some lipstick and comb her hair.

''Hi. I brought you a peace offering.''

At least he understood that he needed a peace offering. ''What is it?'' she asked, peering at him through the screen.

Smiling, he held up an apple and a chocolate chip cookie. ''These treats worked with Hot Shot. I hope they'll make you happy, too.''

She couldn't help it, she burst into laughter. Another man might have brought flowers or a box of candy. But those items hadn't occurred to Beau. He'd brought her his horse's favorite treats. Hers too, now that she thought about it. Opening the screen door, she invited him inside and accepted the apple and cookie.

''Thanks. I hope you'll excuse the way I look. I wasn't expecting...'' She spread her hands. ''Well, you know.''

He ran a long, sultry look over her bare feet and legs, then let his gaze travel up the flowing lines of the loose shirt until he reached her eyes. ''You look fabulous to me,'' he said in a husky voice that sent a thrill of excitement down her spine. ''Holly, I came to say that I'm sorry for the way I behaved on the phone last night. I was out of line."

"Yes, you were." She wasn't going to make it too easy for him. "You've bought your way out of trouble," she said, lifting the apple and cookie, "but, Beau, we have to talk about this and try to work it out."

"I agree," he said, following her into the kitchen. She could feel his gaze on the back of her bare thighs as she set aside the apple and cookie and opened the refrigerator door.

"Would you like a glass of iced tea? Or would you prefer something stronger?"

"Iced tea sounds good." He slid onto a stool and propped his arms on the countertop. She could almost hear him thinking before he spoke. "Desiree used to make the best tea I ever tasted." His words hung between them, opening the way.

"She still does," Holly replied. She popped an ice tray over the sink and dropped cubes into two tall glasses, then poured tea from the pitcher. "This is one of her recipes, in fact. It's an herb tea with soothing qualities." She glanced at him from the corner of her eye. "Could you use a little soothing? I sure could."

"I'm not surprised. I'd be upset, too, if I had to defend my dream every time we talked about Delacroix Farms or Hot Shot racing," he said slowly, rolling his glass between his palms. "Yet that's the position I've put you in. Every time you mention going into the swamp or visiting Desiree, I raise some kind of objection." Lifting his head, he met her gaze. "I'm going to try not to do that in the future, Holly. I can't promise that I'll always be successful, because I care about you, and what you're doing worries me. I don't want anything bad to happen to you."

"Nothing bad is going to happen to me, Beau."

"I know you believe that, and probably you're right. But I can't help worrying. Part of my problem, I think, is that all of my life I've been hearing about voodoo. When I was a kid, my friends and I used to scare the daylights out of each other by talking about zombies and people dying from a voodoo spell. Then, every couple of years, rumors would go around—they still do, as a matter of fact—about voodoo cults sacrificing stolen children in blood rituals."

Holly's eyes widened. "That's ridiculous! Surely you don't believe that junk, do you?"

"No," he said flatly. "But I half believed it as a kid. And it's easy to see why. All you have to do is visit the New Orleans cemeteries and even today you'll find chalk markings on many of the tombs."

"I've seen them."

"Some are what you call veves. Others are red crosses or symbols that don't make any sense to me. But they undoubtedly have meaning to the people who sneaked in there and drew them. Someone believes those chalk symbols mean something or have some power. A lot of someones, actually, because there are a lot of symbols. And as you've pointed out, there are boutiques all over the Delta area selling voodoo charms and candles and God knows what all.

"Add to that the occasional reports of a coincidence where someone believes they're cursed and the curse appears to be successful."

"Beau," she asked gently, "what are you trying to say?"

"I guess I'm trying to tell you that your experience and mine are very different. You're coming to voodoo fresh, with a scholarly outlook and without a lot of false information to overcome. That's not the case with me. Voodoo has seeped into my existence and my experience over a lifetime. It's always been there, something dark and mysterious, and occasionally frightening. It's something Louisianians can't ignore as much as we might want to. So we laugh at voodoo or ridicule it or exploit it to make a buck. If you ask, most of us will insist that voodoo died out a century ago." He stared at her. "But we've grown up seeing those symbols chalked on tombs in our cemeteries. And we hear about veves or occasionally stumble across one. Every few years the stupid rumors resurface about the walking dead or drums in the swamp. And we laugh and dismiss it as nonsense. But the truth is, Holly, we aren't sure if it's nonsense or not. We just…aren't sure. Instinct and all those tales from our childhood tell us something frightening and dangerous might be out there, something it's best to ignore and avoid. We don't have to think about this. It's visceral. Automatic."

"Beau Delacroix," she said, finally getting it. "You believe in voodoo."

A flush of color flowed up from his open collar. "I believe there are things best left alone. And, honey, it isn't me making offerings to a house spirit. I'm not going out to the swamp every day to learn how to cast a spell or draw a veve." Reaching across the countertop, he took her hand. "What's worrying me is that it looks like you're being drawn into this step by step, losing your objectivity without your even noticing." Caressing the back of her hand with his fingertips, he gazed into her eyes. "I've begun to worry that you've ceased being an observer and started being a practitioner."

Her first instinct was to take offense and strongly deny the suggestion as being ludicrous. But she caught herself, thinking about planting the mustard seed, dribbling pepper in her purse and shoes, tucking matches in her hair. Only by making an effort did she resist glancing down at the grains of salt sparkled on the kitchen floor.

Gazing into Beau's worried eyes, she suddenly wondered what on earth she had been thinking when she did these things. All that was required for her research was to gather information. Sprinkling salt around her own house didn't teach her anything new. It only made a mess.

Most disturbing of all was the subtext. A person who took measures to ward off a spell believed that a spell had been cast.

Confusion drew her brow into a frown. If one of her patients had reported acting this contrary to his or her nature, she would have been deeply concerned. She needed to think about this. And she would. After the ceremony.

As for believing a spell had been cast against her...well, anyone might succumb to that suspicion if they found a nasty veve on their doorstep, then watched a silver dime turn charcoal-colored in their mouth. But that didn't actually mean that she *believed* it. Putting pepper in her shoes and tossing salt around her house were simply precautions, an experiment to see if...

Raising a hand to her temple, she closed her eyes. She was doing it again. Trying to justify actions she didn't really understand. This kind of thing was so unlike her.

"I'm not telling you all of this to excuse my failure to support you," Beau said. "I'm telling you to explain why I feel the way I do. I can't change the experiences that have influenced my feelings, Holly, but I can change the way I express those feelings. And I'm going to try to do that. Because I do support your dream to write a scholarly book. That's an admirable goal and I hope you succeed in achieving it."

She tried to pull her thoughts from her puzzling behavior and focus on what he was saying. "Just don't fight me every step of the way, Beau. That's all I ask. Don't try to change my goals. If you'll let me follow where my curiosity leads, then we'll be fine. I don't mind you expressing concern, but I resent it when you throw up walls. I don't want to fight you just to be me."

The expression on his face told her that she'd struck some kind of chord. He stared at her, then he stood, came around the counter and took her in his arms, burying his lips in her hair.

"I don't want to change you, Holly. I love you just the way you are."

Her breath hitched in her throat and she stood very still, pressing against him and listening to her heart pound. He'd said he loved her. Tears of joy moistened her eyes.

Easing back, he stared down at her and smiled. "What are you thinking?"

"I want to tell you that I love you, too," she whispered, knowing that her eyes shone with happiness. "But I don't quite know how to do it."

"I can think of a way," he said, grinning wickedly at the front of her shirt and pulling her hips close to his.

"I was thinking about offering you half of my chocolate chip cookie," she murmured huskily, tracing the contour of his lips with her fingertip. "But I like your idea better."

Laughing, he swept her into his arms and carried her through the house to her bedroom.

CHAPTER TWELVE

JACKSON REACHED for the keys in the ignition, but it was too late to peel some rubber and spin out of the parking lot behind PJ's Pizza Place. Huey's thugs had spotted him. Leaning back in his car seat, he gripped the steering wheel with one hand, played with a toothpick with his other hand. Tried to look cool and casual, like his heart wasn't knocking against his rib cage when Huey's boys got out of a long black Lincoln and two of them walked toward him.

He rolled down the window, letting a blast of hot air inside the car, and leaned an elbow outside. "I was looking for you boys," he drawled. Cool as a cucumber. "Want you to carry back a message and tell Huey that I'll have his money soon."

The two thugs who walked up to his car looked like they might have been linebackers on a team up at the federal prison. Big and ugly. They stared at him a second, their pig eyes full of contempt, then one of them dropped a photograph in through the window and stared some more before the two of them walked back to the black Lincoln.

Limp with relief, Jackson watched the car glide out of the parking lot. He'd dodged a bullet. He could hardly believe that they hadn't pulled him out of his car and worked him over. That's what he'd half expected when he watched them coming toward him. That he was on duty, wearing his uniform and sitting in his squad car, wouldn't have deterred them. Huey knew he wouldn't press charges.

When his breathing settled, he picked up the photograph and lifted it from his lap to the light streaming in the window. This time he thought his heart would leap right out of his chest.

Thought he would have a frigging heart attack right there behind PJ's place.

Suddenly he wished they had beaten him up. He would have preferred that a hundred times to having this photograph dropped in his lap.

He rolled up the window, mopped his forehead, then turned the air-conditioning on full blast before he took another look at the picture. It could have been any swamp shack, propped up on stilts, the roof sagging. But it wasn't. That was Flora sitting in the rocking chair out front. And that was Desiree caught midway between the shack and the shed out back.

Swearing, he tore the photograph into confetti.

The photo was intended to scare him and it did. Immediately, his imagination kicked into overdrive and spun out a series of visual horrors that made him sweat despite the cold air flowing out of the vents.

What he ought to do right this minute was hightail it to the shack and warn Ma and Grandma. Tell them to load up the shotgun and keep an eye out for anything suspicious. Shoot first, ask questions later.

But they would want to know why. And sure as hell they would blame him instead of Huey. He chewed on a thumbnail and thought about that.

When push came to shove, the truth was he feared Flora's temper more than he feared Huey's boys. If he told Flora that she was in danger because of him, she'd flay him alive. She'd cook his liver and feed it to him for supper.

Telling her was not a good idea. No, the answer here was to pay Huey the damned money. To do that, he needed Philip.

Reaching for his phone, he called Big Daddy on the firm's private line.

Ten minutes later he entered Philip's office through the private door.

"Make it fast," Philip said, looking up from his desk. "I've got a stack of phone calls to return and my campaign manager is waiting outside with the caterer."

"Giving a party?" Jackson asked, sitting down in the leather chair facing Philip's desk. Someday he, too, was going to own a real leather chair. No one would sit in it except himself.

"In case you've been too busy playing cops and robbers to notice, the election is looming. It's time to start thinking about my victory party."

If Philip was planning a victory party, then something must have changed in the polls. The last time Jackson had checked, Philip was running substantially behind his opponent. Maybe he'd been greasing a few palms that Jackson didn't know about. It wouldn't be the first time a politician had purchased votes.

"Well?" Philip asked coldly. "Why are you taking up my time?"

Jackson shrugged and arranged a smile on his lips. One of those smiles that was almost a smirk. The kind of smile that just suggested, mind you, that he was laughing at Philip deep inside.

"No reason, really. Just wondered if you'd heard what Beau was saying around town..." He let the bait dangle and almost laughed when Philip touched his stupid little bow tie the way he always did when he was annoyed.

"So what is Beau saying that you think I should know about?"

Jackson relaxed, rubbing his fingertips over the buttery soft arms of the chair. "He's saying he can't prove it, but he knows you cheated to win the Delta Stakes. He's saying you're going to lose the Bayou Derby just like you're going to lose the election. He got a big laugh down at the roadhouse when he said that just because you're a horse's ass doesn't mean you know diddly about horses." Pausing, he let the last barb sink in good. "Beau's putting it out all over the state that Hot Shot's going to win the Derby Stakes and leave your horse back in the pack of losers. Says that's where you belong."

Leaning back, he waited for Philip's reaction, and he was pretty sure he knew what it would be. Philip Delacroix hated to lose. And Jackson had just tied the election and the Bayou Derby into one pretty package. If Big Daddy Philip was the least bit worried about the upcoming election, he would swallow the bait, hook, line and sinker. He'd be furious if he believed Beau was out there calling him a loser, making him look bad in the eyes of the voters.

Philip's eyes narrowed and he swore. "That arrogant son of a bitch. Spreading lies and trying to sabotage my campaign."

Jackson shrugged, enjoying himself immensely. "I wouldn't worry about it too much."

It was hard not to laugh as he watched Philip work it out. Even if Philip won the election, if he lost the Bayou Derby, it would appear that Beau had called it correctly. If Philip lost the election *and* the Bayou Derby, he'd be branded a loser big time. Either way, Philip's pride would hit the dirt. And the old man wouldn't stand for that. No siree.

Philip stared at him. "I don't care how you do it, but make sure my horse wins the Derby."

He'd anticipated this and was ready with a response. But he took his time answering, as if he was thinking it over. Finally he shook his head. "You know as well as I do that I can't fix who wins. The last thing you need is for the track officials to run a spit-and-pee test after the race and disqualify your horse. You don't want the whole state screaming fix. A scandal could hurt you bad."

"So what do you suggest?" Philip snapped.

Oh, no, he was too smart to fall into that trap. For all he knew, Philip had his office bugged. He shrugged again. "I just follow orders."

Philip leaned back in his chair and tented his fingers on his chest just beneath the bow tie.

Jackson waited, biting his tongue. He'd said enough. Either Philip would head down the path he had shoved him onto, or he wouldn't.

"Is Hot Shot as fast as I'm hearing?"

"Faster," Jackson said confidently. "Beau's right about that part. Hot Shot's going to win the Bayou Derby as easily as sniffing the breeze. And then ole Beau is going to ride that horse all the way to Kentucky."

"Well, we'll just have to see that that doesn't happen," Philip said with a cold smile. "I've got fifteen grand that says Beau isn't going to win the Derby, and he isn't going to Louisville." He stared at Jackson and lifted an eyebrow.

"Well now, I don't know." He ran a hand down his jaw like

he was thinking it over. "Things have gotten real tight in the racing industry. It's not as easy to arrange things as it used to be. A man's taking a serious risk. Looking at serious time if things go wrong."

"Cut the crap, Jackson. What's it going to take? How much?"

"Fifty ought to get you what you want." Hell, it was worth a try.

Philip's smile became frigid. "Thirty thousand. Not a penny more. If you can't slow Hot Shot for thirty grand, I'll find someone who can."

Relief and elation made his stomach go liquid. But he turned down the corners of his mouth and managed to look disappointed. "Half right now. The rest after the race."

Philip opened a desk drawer and removed an envelope. He counted out a stack of hundreds. "Five thousand now, the rest when I hear that Hot Shot didn't place."

"That's not our agreement. You said you didn't want Hot Shot to win. You didn't say anything about her coming in second or third."

Philip's eyes resembled chips of ice. "Beau's nag doesn't finish in the money, understand? She loses. Period. No trophy. No piece of the purse. A total loss. Work it out."

Frowning, Jackson picked up the money and tucked it in the pocket inside his jacket. This was going to be tougher than he'd figured.

He had almost reached the door leading down to the private entrance when Philip spoke behind him. "I hope you handle this better than you handled getting the deed to Desiree's place. Once the election is over, we're going to have to have a long talk about your work."

"You got your money back." And he was still steamed about it.

"Just make sure you don't screw up this deal."

He was still smarting over that last remark when he slid back into the cruiser and let the air conditioner send a cold stream over his face.

On the other hand, he thought, tapping his fingers on the steering wheel, he'd gotten what he wanted. For the first time it occurred to him that Flora might actually have a real shot at getting old Philip to change his will in their favor. He had just proved that Philip could be manipulated. Flora had always insisted he could be, but Jackson hadn't believed her.

By God. He let himself think about it. Flora might just pull this off. She might just force Philip to acknowledge him as his son and leave him and Flora a pile of Delacroix money.

Spirits soaring, images of soft leather chairs and polo green Porsches lighting the back of his mind, he wheeled the cruiser toward the causeway. The best thing to do was to take the five thousand to Huey before he was tempted to blow off the afternoon and go to the track. But he felt reasonably sure that he could turn the five thousand into at least eight.

Then the stream of air from the cooling system stirred the bits of confetti on the floor of the car and reminded him of the photograph. No, he'd take the money straight to Huey. And this time when he promised that Huey would have the rest of it soon, the statement would be true.

The first part of his plan was firmly in place. Now all he had to do was figure out how to make sure that Beau's Hot Shot came in dead last in the Bayou Derby.

Making sure that happened was going to be a lot harder than jerking Philip around.

THEY STEPPED OUT of the cool movie theater into the warm night and paused on the sidewalk to hold hands and smile at each other. "Your place or mine?" Beau asked gruffly, only half in jest. "Or is it too late? A man hates to make love to a woman who's thinking that tomorrow is a workday instead of concentrating on the moment at hand."

He loved the sound of her laughter and the way her eyes crinkled at the corners when she smiled. He loved the glossy shine in her dark auburn hair and the curve of her lips. He loved the shape of her long legs and the sweet curve of her waist. He loved her intelligence and her sense of humor, loved the expressive way she used her hands, loved the way they saw so many things alike.

Once he had said those three little words aloud, it was as if a dam had burst inside his chest. It amazed him. He couldn't remember why it had once seemed so hard to say "I love you." Now he looked at Holly's radiant face and the words tumbled off his lips as easily as if he had never felt a moment's resistance.

He loved her. And nothing had ever felt this good or this right in his life.

She looked up at him, eyes sparkling. "Thanks for dinner and the film. But if I know you, you're dying to check in on Hot Shot. So...even though it's late, how about your place?"

In the car driving out to the farm, he glanced at the clock on the dashboard. It really was getting late. Six months ago, he would probably have skipped looking in on Hot Shot and driven to his cottage and taken his date straight to bed. But tonight, with Holly, he wouldn't do that. They would stop by Hot Shot's stall, talk for a while, and then he'd drive her back to town.

The surprising and wonderful part of loving her was that sex wasn't as important as just being with her. Making love to her was great, fantastic, but what was even better was knowing that she wasn't going away. There was always tomorrow. For the first time in years, sex was not the primary focus of a brief and largely unsatisfying relationship. He loved Holly and they were building something warm and good, and that changed everything.

After he parked the car, they walked hand in hand toward the barn. "It's almost a full moon," she remarked, squeezing his hand. "Very romantic."

"Thank you for noticing. I arranged that moon just for you."

He left her at the door to Hot Shot's stall long enough to run upstairs to his office and fix them a nightcap. When he returned, he touched his glass to hers and they made a toast to dreams coming true.

"I have something for you."

"What is it?" he asked, giving her an exaggerated leer.

"Not you," she said, smiling. "These are for Hot Shot." Opening her purse, she produced two chocolate chip cookies and fed them to the horse.

It filled his chest with warmth to realize that she'd thought ahead to bring the cookies, that she had guessed they would return to the farm. What had he ever done to deserve this wonderful woman?

They spent another ten minutes with Hot Shot, then looked in on Ma Chere and the other horses before they returned outside and sat on a bench in the moonlight. Beau slipped his arm around her and relaxed when she leaned into him. "I'll take you home after we finish our drinks."

"Honest, I wouldn't be thinking about how late it is..."

"Not during," he said after kissing the top of her head. "But you'd be thinking it immediately afterward. And you'd be tired all day tomorrow."

"One of the things I love most about you is how considerate you are," she murmured, turning to brush a kiss across his lips.

"Be careful with those kisses," he said in a gruff voice, "or I might change my mind and destroy my image as a sensitive nineties guy."

Enjoying the moonlight and holding each other, they talked of nothing in particular for a while. Then they discussed Hot Shot's future and how important it was to win the Bayou Derby.

"Hot Shot is one in a million," he said after he'd bragged about her latest track times. "I knew she was special, but I don't think I really knew just how special until we intensified her training." Excitement infused his voice. "For the first time, the Kentucky Derby is genuinely within reach. It could really happen."

"I hope it does, Beau. You and Hot Shot deserve a chance."

There was something about the tone of her voice... "Holly? Are you having one of your hunches?" He felt a little foolish asking her this. He wasn't superstitious in any area of his life except when it came to racing. Then he was as superstitious as any of the jockeys and grooms. "Tell me what you see?" he asked, hoping he didn't sound as anxious as he suddenly felt.

"I never actually 'see' anything," she said in a voice that sounded uncomfortable. "The hunches are just strong feelings."

"All right. So what are your strong feelings about Hot Shot and the Bayou Derby? Or, more importantly, about Hot Shot and the Kentucky Derby?"

Her body went very still and his anxiety wound another notch tighter. "I wish I hadn't asked," he said, meaning it.

"Please don't jump to a wrong conclusion," she said, sitting up. Turning, she gazed into his eyes. "I don't have a hunch about

Hot Shot one way or the other. That's what's so strange. Usually I can ask a question, then listen to an inner voice that strongly suggests an answer.'' She gave him a quick kiss and an embarrassed smile. "I wasn't going to tell you that I'd tried to get a hunch about the race results. Explaining it makes me feel foolish.''

"Don't feel foolish," he said, smoothing a tendril of hair behind her ear. "I don't care if you have hunches."

"Just as long as I don't start talking about spaceships or little green men, right?'' she asked with an impish smile.

"Right. But about the hunches...what happens when you ask if Hot Shot will win or lose? Do you feel anything at all?" He was new to this kind of thing and not really sure that he believed in premonitions. But everything about Holly fascinated him. He wanted to know every detail about her, wanted her to know that he was trying to be supportive.

She tilted her head, thinking about it. "Nothing happens," she said finally, frowning. Suddenly she smiled and shrugged. "It's like asking a computer a question and the computer comes back and says, That question doesn't compute."

"Fun-ny," he said, returning her smile.

"Seriously, it's as if the question is somehow irrelevant. I know," she said, placing her fingertips across his lips. "It's relevant to us. But not to—what shall I call this?—the hunch part of the brain."

To us. God, he loved her. He eased her back into his arms, enjoying the moonlight and the warm night and the scent of her sexy perfume. He wanted to repay her for making his Derby dream relevant to her, too, so he asked when the voodoo ceremony would be held.

"Thursday night. But, Beau, I absolutely do not want you to even think about coming with me." She paused, then looked up at him. "It would be a terrible breach if I brought along an uninvited guest. The meeting is private and the ceremony itself is considered secret."

"Desiree knows you're going to write about it in your book, doesn't she? It won't be a secret forever. In fact, it isn't a secret now. For twenty dollars, tourists can see a stage show that claims to be an authentic re-enactment of a voodoo ceremony. I can tell you what you're going to see. A bunch of people dancing around a bonfire to the pounding of a few drums. Desiree or Flora or some other woman—it's always a woman—will lead the events and pretend to go into a trance. Then a few others will pretend to go into a trance and they'll say or do rude things to each other. Maybe someone will get a head start on Sunday's dinner by wringing the head of a chicken, just to make things feel authentic.''

She didn't smile. "You're right that voodoo ceremonies have been described in the literature on the subject. But you're wrong that they aren't secret. Each group has its own unique ritual, which is zealously protected. Members are sworn to secrecy, and only the manbos, the priestesses, if you will, may invite guests without seeking prior permission from the group.''

She'd seen through him, of course. He wanted to accompany her just to make certain that nothing unpleasant happened. He didn't think anything would, actually. But traveling in the swamp alone at night simply was not a good idea.

After kissing her, he grinned, trying to lighten the tone of the conversation. "What does one say to a person going off to a voodoo ceremony? Have a good time? Don't drink the disgusting stuff in the communal bowl? Gee, I hope they don't feed you to the alligators?''

She stared at him, then burst into laughter. "Beau Delacroix, you're just impossible!'' Standing, she pulled him to his feet and gave him a kiss that set him on fire from his scalp to his toes and made him wish that it wasn't so late. "Come on, fella, take me home. I've got a tough session tomorrow morning, and I still have to review my files before I go to sleep.''

They drove back to town, easy with each other again, and he walked her to her door and pulled her into his arms. To his amusement, he was careful not to stand on the place where the veve had been drawn.

After he kissed her a dozen times, he gazed into her soft eyes. "Seriously, Holly, you will be careful, won't you?''

She smiled, then rose up on tiptoe and kissed him. "I'll have a good time. I won't drink the disgusting stuff in the communal pot. And I won't let the alligators get me. I'll return safe and sound. Come for breakfast on Friday morning and see for yourself.''

"It's a date." He wanted to ask her to call him before she left and after she returned home, but such a request would rightly have offended her.

During the drive back to his cottage, he considered his dilemma. Knowing that Flora Boudreaux would undoubtedly be at the ceremony concerned him greatly. He couldn't help it; he had an uneasy suspicion that Holly was an innocent about to walk into a lion's den. Although he trusted Desiree, he didn't know how much control she exerted over her daughter. From where he sat, it didn't look as if Flora listened to anyone.

By the time he turned the Porsche into his driveway, he'd made a decision.

No way was he going to send his woman off to a voodoo ceremony alone. If everything went smoothly, Holly would never know he was present. But if something went wrong...

CHAPTER THIRTEEN

DANDY DOG HUNG TWO lanterns at the front of the swamp boat and another at the back. He frowned and handed Holly a flashlight. "Are you absolutely sure there's nothing I can say to talk you out of this?"

The lanterns made her feel secure, but they also tended to make the night seem darker beyond them. Uneasily, Holly wondered if she might be better off with nothing but the full moon.

"I've been coming out here every day for almost a month," she reminded Dandy. "Don't worry, I know the way."

"The swamp looks different at night. If you aren't careful, you can drift down a side flow and never realize you're out of the main channel until you're so lost you don't know which way is up. Look. How about I take you to Desiree's place, then come back and fetch you later?"

She touched his massive arm and shook her head. "As much as I'd like to accept your offer, I can't. But thank you. Besides, I really don't know how long I'll be."

He stared at her for a minute, then he gazed at the full moon, swore and spit on the pier. "I just figured it out. Pardon me for saying so, Dr. Gibson, but you got rocks in your pretty head. Take my advice. Turn around, get in your car and go home. Forget about this stuff."

Turning away from him, Holly climbed down into the swamp boat and picked up the pole. "There's no need to wait for me to return. I'll tie up the boat."

"Me and the missus, we hear those damned drums in the swamp, and we know what they mean. Dr. Gibson, this ain't something you want to mess with. A love potion, a little charm to bring you luck on the riverboats, that's one thing. But this here

is way different. Bad different. You don't wanna go into the
swamp tonight.''

"Bye, Dandy."

Leaning her weight on the pole, she pushed away from the
pier, watching the lights on Dandy's rental shack slide away from
her. Almost immediately a cloud of mosquitoes surrounded her
face and exposed hands, making her thankful that she had remembered to slather on plenty of insect repellant. And more
swiftly than she had anticipated, she rounded a curve and the
darkness closed around her.

At once she accepted that Dandy was correct. The Spanish
moss that appeared so delicate and picturesque by daylight
seemed eerie and ghostlike at night. Splashing noises that she
wouldn't have noticed in the sunlight captured her imagination
now. Alligators? Water moccasins? Some kind of danger that she
didn't know about?

Peering nervously past the lanterns, trying to penetrate the
moonlit shadows beyond, she struggled to identify landmarks she
would have recognized at a glance earlier in the day. She thought
she was still in the main channel, but suddenly she wasn't sure.
Was that the thick cedar where she bore left? Or had she already
poled beyond it?

"This is one of the dumbest things you've done in recent memory," she muttered, waving a hand at the insects trying to inspect
her face at close quarters.

In fact, she had been thinking about her entire research experience during the past two days and had arrived at some troubling
conclusions. While it was true that part of the reason she had
accepted the clinic's offer was the opportunity to observe and
possibly write about vodun, that opportunity had played a minor
role in her decision. The idea had always been there, but it hadn't
come to full fruition until after she moved to Louisiana.

In fact, since she'd arrived in Bayou Beltane, she hadn't set
any speed records diving into the research. She had dropped by
a couple of the touristy voodoo shops down in the Quarter, where
she'd heard Desiree's and Flora's names for the first time, but
she had been more or less content to let things languish from that
point.

That was how things stood until she met Desiree sheerly by happenstance the day Hot Shot colicked. Even then she might not have pursued the research project very aggressively, except that she'd started dating Beau about the same time, and his objections and obvious disapproval had triggered the same stubborn rebellion that her father had brought forth a dozen years ago. And once she started defending her interest and intentions to Beau, her course was set. Actually, she had enjoyed getting back into research and pumping new life into her dream of writing a scholarly book. But even if she hadn't found satisfaction in the work, pride would have prevented her from backing down.

An honest and hard look at what had been happening was sobering. Strange things were occurring to her, the most shocking of which was that Beau's observation had been correct. Somewhere along the way she had ceased to be merely an observer of voodoo and had become a practitioner. Admitting this stunning fact embarrassed her, and she had tried a dozen ways to rationalize setting out an offering to a house spirit, pouring salt around the house and all the rest. But the truth was, there was no acceptable explanation. And with every eerie moment that passed tonight, it was getting harder to justify being here, harder to recall why she had thought it was such a great idea to pole into the swamp alone at night.

And there were the dreams. A chill shudder twitched her shoulders and she frowned. Ever since she and Desiree had fed the python, she'd been having strange and frightening nightmares. Sometimes she dreamed the python was draped around her neck, its weight so heavy on her shoulders that when she awoke, her muscles felt sore. In the dream, the python kissed her cheek with its hissing, darting tongue and she gazed into its eyes and felt herself dissolving, becoming one with the snake. Her body seemed to narrow and elongate, and a sinuous twining power filled the spaces where her limbs had been. Through yellow eyes she saw a bonfire leaping and heard dancers call her name. *Dambala.*

God. What was she doing? She didn't want to remember dreaming that she'd turned into a snake. Especially not now, not tonight.

Almost at once the fire dream filled her thoughts, even though she didn't want to think about that dream, either. It was the same conflagration that she'd been dreaming about since she arrived in Bayou Beltane, but new details had recently appeared.

Now she knew that the blazing building was Beau's barn. And the strange unearthly screams came from horses trapped in burning stalls. Another new element in the fire dreams was Flora Boudreaux's presence. She didn't actually see Flora—all she saw was the flames that beckoned her into the heart of the blaze. But she felt Flora all around her, heard Flora's voice seductively urging her into the fire, and she was powerless to resist. The horror of knowing that she was walking trancelike to her death made her feel sick to her stomach when she jolted awake.

Closing her eyes, Holly blinked rapidly to clear her head. In some way that she didn't understand, it was all tied together. Her hunches, the dreams, her visits to Desiree, the malignancy she sensed in Flora. And the Delacroix. Things were happening in Bayou Beltane and in the swamps, things that had their beginnings in a past that didn't include Holly. But she'd been swept up in it because she loved Beau.

And because she had wanted to understand her hunches. If she was rock-bottom honest with herself, her interest in vodun had deepened as she began to question her "hunches."

Was that why she now found herself in the swamp alone at night, her heart pounding with nervous anxiety? Was it as simple as trying to explain the hunches she'd had all her life?

Distracted by her thoughts, she almost missed seeing the single candle burning in the window of Desiree's shack. It gave her a nasty shock to realize that if she hadn't looked up when she did, she would have continued to pole the boat past the shack—and become hopelessly lost.

Heart pounding, she peered through the shadows that distorted everything familiar, until finally she made out the pier. In the moonlight, she had mistaken the narrow pier for a large log. Even with the light of a full moon, the shack sat in such dense shadow that she hadn't noticed it at all. And the candle burning in the window was placed so deliberately that it could he glimpsed for only a few seconds before a boat in the channel would pass it by.

After tying up at the pier, she extinguished the lanterns on the boat and gave herself a moment to grow accustomed to the darkness. In this section of the swamp, tall cedars and ancient live oaks blocked most of the moonlight. Colors ranged from black to gray to small patches of moon-washed white. Nothing looked familiar. It was almost like stepping into the frightening landscape of a childhood nightmare, where everything known was distorted and twisted into menacing shapes and forms that appeared to advance when one wasn't quite looking.

Resisting the temptation to return to the boat and leave, Holly drew a breath and studied the dark shack. Obviously the meeting was not taking place here. Plucking up her courage, she drew a deep breath and walked around the shack toward the shed behind it, studiously ignoring rustling noises in the undergrowth. And she refused to acknowledge the rush of relief she felt when she spotted a lantern on the ground near an old cedar that had been split by lightning at some time in the past.

Pressing her lips together, she walked toward the lantern and then spotted another, farther along what must be a trail. The light cast by the lanterns was dim and low to the ground, meant to guide whoever would attend the meeting but not intended to be seen from the channel.

By the time Holly reached the second lantern, she picked up the distant sound of drumbeats and rattles. The jarring rhythm reassured her that she wasn't utterly alone; there were people besides herself in the swamp tonight. Feeling better, she picked up her pace, following the lanterns toward the drumbeats until she reached a clearing defined by an earthen floor and a bonfire blazing in the center.

Many of the two dozen people present were black, but not all. The men were bare-chested and wore white cotton pants. Most of the women wore white dresses with colored sashes and had tied their hair up inside knotted bandannas. The difference between their attire and Holly's jeans and denim shirt offered her a distance from the proceedings that she badly needed right now. It helped underscore that she was the observer and they were the participants.

Placing a hand over her pounding chest, she examined the

clearing. A pot steamed over a second, smaller fire, surrounded by bowls of food placed on the ground. Her gaze focused on the carcass of a headless chicken before she swallowed hard and continued her inspection. Three men were on her left at the perimeter of the clearing, beating the drums. Dancers shook the rattles. For a full minute she watched the dancers bending and spinning, then she spotted Flora.

Flora sat on a raised wooden dais, wearing a deep purple dress with a crimson sash and crimson underskirts. Gold hoops swung from her ears and circled her arms and ankles. Reclining in a velvet-draped chair, with firelight flickering on her face and smoothing her features, she looked wild and beautiful, every inch a voodoo queen. Holly couldn't look away from her.

While Holly stood in the shadows watching in fascination, a woman danced up to Flora's platform, chanting in a low voice. She placed a jar of coins beside Flora's feet. Now Holly noticed other offerings at the base of Flora's chair. Flowers, food and additional small jars of coins. But it wasn't Flora whom the woman appealed to when she lifted her arms toward the sky. "Dambala! Hear me, Dambala!"

Finally Holly let herself look at the crate. It sat in front of a draped shrine where thick candles burned in front of pictures of Catholic saints, a skull, a collection of gris-gris, bowls of smoking incense, shells and other items Holly couldn't identify from this distance.

But she recognized the python, and a hot shiver ran down her spine as if someone had dragged their fingernails down her back. The snake was agitated tonight, its head darting back and forth, back and forth, its coils slithering and readjusting. And then, almost as if the python sensed Holly's presence, its head stopped moving and turned toward her as if it were watching her. Waiting. Instantly, Flora was aware of the change in the snake's restlessness and she, too, turned her head sharply and narrowed her eyes on Holly. The corners of her mouth turned down and her dark eyes glittered.

Flora's stare was so malevolent that Holly gasped and stepped backward. She might have fled if Desiree hadn't appeared seemingly out of nowhere and grasped her arm. Standing as straight as the pines on the edge of the clearing, Desiree stared back at the dais. Her stance and her hand on Holly's arm announced to all that Holly was here at her invitation and that she was Holly's protector. Desiree continued to stare at the podium even after Flora leaned to spit over the edge before she turned her attention back to the female supplicant in front of the platform.

"You're going to get a show tonight," Desiree muttered, frowning. She studied Flora and the snake, seemed to think for a minute, then turned her gaze to Holly. "Listen," she said in an urgent voice. "This isn't good. I shouldn't have brought you here."

The drums and rattles and the shuffling feet of the people moving in a slow dance around the bonfire seeped into Holly's body and mind. The strange hypnotic music and thick drifts of incense made it difficult to concentrate; the rhythm of the drums was insistent and primitive, thudding in tandem with her heartbeat. The longer she listened, the more the observer in her seemed to slip away, but not before she understood that the drums dictated the pace of the dancers and the rate of their pulse. When the drumbeats accelerated, so did the dancers, as if they were marionettes controlled by invisible threads wielded by the drummers.

Desiree's fingers dug into her arm. "Listen to me, *chérie!* This is a mistake. Dambala wants you, but you're not ready yet." She released Holly's arm and covered her eyes with a shaking hand. "This is my fault. I wanted Flora to see how strong you are so she would leave you alone. But you're not ready to receive Dambala."

The drums had crawled under her skin and her hips rocked in time to the beat. Across the clearing, the woman who had given Flora the coins screamed and moved back from the platform, twitching and jerking, spinning and bending. The drums slowed then raced, coaxing her deeper into a trance state. She jerked upright as if pulled by an unseen wire, and her eyes popped open. She limped toward a young woman near the fire and squeezed the woman's breast with a leer that was almost mannish. The crowd laughed and chanted, "Papa Legba! Papa Legba!" Someone handed the woman a top hat and a cane and she limped among the dancers shouting obscenities and stroking and slapping both men and women in a vulgar manner.

"She's a wonderful actress," Holly said, laughing with the crowd at the woman's antics.

Desiree stared at her. "She's not acting. The loa rides her. Papa Legba has taken her for his horse."

When Holly glanced at the podium, Flora was watching her with a triumphant expression, as if to say, "See what I can do?"

But it was the python that caught her gaze and held it. The snake's head still pointed in Holly's direction as if it watched her and waited, its head swaying, tongue flicking. Beckoning. Summoning. Calling somewhere deep inside her, just below the thudding of the drums and her heartbeat. Swaying on her feet, she heard a name pulsing deep inside her mind. Dam-*bal*-a. Dam*bal*-a.

One of the dancers whirled past her as the drums accelerated, pounding faster, and the dancer placed a bowl in her hands. "Drink!" And he was gone.

Eyes still locked with the snake's, Holly lifted the bowl to her lips and swallowed a warm and pungent liquid, salty yet sweet. It shocked her when Desiree slapped the bowl out of her hands.

"Go!" Desiree urged in a voice that was half command, half plea. "Holly, this is a mistake. Go while you still can!"

But the drums would not release her. The beckoning voice curling like smoke in her mind summoned her forward, not back. And the clouds of incense and whatever she had drunk from the bowl made her dizzy enough that she didn't think she could follow the path back to the shack and the pier.

"What was in the bowl?" she murmured, placing a hand on Desiree's arm to steady herself. Her head reeled, yet oddly she felt alert, as if her mind had expanded to encompass the night. She was acutely, wonderfully aware of the colors leaping inside the flames. She could hear the trees breathing around them and could sense the tiny heartbeats of small animals watching in the underbrush. Her skin was astonishingly alive in a way she had never felt before, supple and elastic, capable of growing or shrinking. The sensation delighted her and made her believe that she could become taller merely by wishing it, or she could contract until she was the size of...Dambala.

On the podium, Flora had opened the crate, and a bare-chested man lifted Dambala up over his head. The drums rushed to crescendo and the dancers whirled and sweated. Skirts billowed over bare feet. Rivulets of perspiration rolled down naked chests and shining faces. Two dozen voices shouted, "Dambala! Dambala!" Holly, too, gazed at the upraised snake with shining eyes, knowing it as the earthly symbol of the power whose name it bore, and she heard herself whispering, "Dambala!"

But something was wrong on the podium. When the man attempted to drape the python around Flora's shoulders, the snake writhed and lashed its tail. Flora and her assistant exchanged frowning glances and tried again, but the snake opened its jaws and lunged at Flora's face. She drew back, furious and embarrassed by this display of rejection. Whirling, she sent a look of pure hatred toward Holly.

"It's starting to happen," Desiree moaned. "But you're not ready," she whispered over and over. "Run away now, *ma chère*. Dambala doesn't want to, but he'll crush you, hurt you because you can't control your power yet. You're not ready!"

It was like the fire dream. As if her conscious mind floated above her, observing, warning, but no longer in control of her body. Unable to stop herself, Holly walked forward, her hips moving to the drumbeat. On some level she knew when the drummers spotted her and recognized that something was happening. As if they could see inside her, the drummers slowed their rhythm until they matched the pounding of the drums to her heartbeat, caught the beat of her pulse and claimed her. Now the drums controlled her, causing her pulse to race or slow at will.

As if observing from a point above the flames leaping in the bonfire, she watched Flora and her assistant struggle to control the snake. Watched herself moving through the dancers as if she were hypnotized, her gaze locked on the hissing, twisting python.

Dambala called to her, yearned for her as she yearned for him. As she approached the platform, her movements became sinuous and twisting, a parody of the snake. A throaty, hoarse chant whispered past her lips. "Dambala. Dambala. I'm coming."

The python extended the upper part of its body away from the man struggling to hold it, its head straining toward Holly. "Yes," she murmured. "Yes, yes, yes. I long for you, too."

Her bones were contracting, shrinking, her limbs disappearing. The drums pounded in her head, wild and hard and as fast as her racing heart. A wave of heat seared through her body, and with it a feeling of such power as she had never imagined possible. She could have pulled down the platform with one hand. Could have curled her body around a tree limb and slithered upward to watch the dancers from above. She could have reached to the sky and plucked the moon from the heavens.

The man fighting to hold the python sent a stricken look toward Flora, whose face contorted with rage. And then he staggered to the edge of the platform, trying to gain his balance as the snake stretched its weight toward Holly.

The dancers knew they were witnessing something extraordinary, and they opened a path for Holly, clapping and moaning and chanting, "Dam-*bal*-a. Dam-*bal*-a!" Hands darted to touch she who had been summoned. The rattles shook with frenzied urgency.

The man on the platform was no longer in control of the snake; the python's straining weight controlled the man. When the snake dropped its head toward Holly, there was nothing Flora's assistant could do but kneel on the edge of the platform and watch the python glide out of his hands and settle around Holly's shoulders.

Dimly, Holly sensed the weight draping her shoulders, but she felt no discomfort. This was a mantle she had worn in some lost and ancient time. A primal memory stirred, something primitive and dimly sensed but not fully accessible. Raising a hand, she stroked the snake's head, felt the pressure of its body rising against her palm as if returning her caress. A wild, elated pounding surged through her blood, but she no longer knew if it was the drums or her own heartbeat. She gazed into Dambala's yellow eyes and felt herself drifting toward a dark place. Urgent voices whispered deep in her head, the words tumbling over one another, a dozen voices clambering for attention and recognition. Confused, she tried to sort them out. But she couldn't concentrate because she was falling, falling into yellow eyes that beguiled and

ypnotized and drew her inside until she felt herself becoming
ne with the snake. Power surged through her body, and she felt
er strength expand, felt the restless coils and her capacity to
ngulf and crush.

BEAU ARRIVED AT the perimeter of the clearing in time to see
Holly slither and glide through the dancers. Ducking low in the
erns on the marshy ground, he frowned and peered through con-
ealing leaves, trying to figure out what in the hell she was doing.
he looked strange. Her eyes were wide and sultry, fixed on a
nake some man on the platform was wrestling while Flora
creamed at him. Beau didn't give a damn about Flora's snake
roblems, but Holly worried him. A lot.

He'd never seen her move the way she was moving now. Her
ones seemed to have turned liquid, she was that fluid. And
atching her move was the most erotic thing he had ever wit-
essed. Although he wasn't sure if she was aware of what she
as doing, she ran her hands over her hips and breasts as
he might have done to entice and seduce a lover. The way
he walked, the expression in her eyes and on her lips, the way
he touched herself vibrated with raw sex. She was fully dressed,
et she created an illusion that she was naked. The wild music of
rums and rattles, the leaping orange-and-red shadows of the fire,
ie chanting and the dancers, the way she moved and caressed
erself with long, sensual strokes—it all combined in some crazy
ay to create a chimera that heated his blood and stirred some-
ing primitive in his mind.

Beau shook his head hard and tried to make sense out of what
e was witnessing. Despite her trancelike gaze and almost pagan
exuality, no one coerced Holly to glide toward the platform. The
ancers stroked her arm or her shoulder, then spun away from
er with expressions of awe and fearful respect. They didn't push
er, and yet he had a deeply uneasy sense that something pulled
propelled her, something outside herself, but he couldn't spot
hat it might be.

Worse, he didn't know if he should interfere, although every
stinct urged him to do so. Holly wore a peculiar expression and

she moved in that slithery, erotic manner, but she didn't appear to be in danger.

Clenching his jaw and his fists, he swiftly searched the crowd until he found Desiree, standing away from the others beneath the feathery limbs of a tall cedar. Her gaze was riveted on Holly and her teeth were bared as if she were in pain. Instantly Beau understood that whatever was happening, it had moved beyond Desiree's wishes and control.

Snapping his head back toward the platform, he stared at Flora. Rage mottled her features, and she exuded an uncharacteristic attitude of helplessness. She, too, had lost control, and she knew it. Beau stared. Who the hell was in charge here?

The man with the large python sure wasn't. The snake was agitated, giving the guy a hard time. It looked to Beau as if the snake were lunging toward Holly and pulling the man along with him. Surely this wasn't supposed to happen. He'd never attended a voodoo ceremony, not even the productions staged for paying tourists. But he didn't need someone to tell him that the python was the centerpiece of the ceremony or that whoever controlled the snake held the power. It made no sense that the manbo, or whatever Flora called herself, would relinquish the snake to one of her followers. Definitely not to an observer whom she detested.

Something was badly wrong here.

No longer caring if anyone saw him, Beau stood up, fighting to figure out what he was seeing, not sure if he could believe his eyes.

Holly was stroking the snake's head. If the snake had been a cat, it would have been purring, pressing against her, returning her caresses. The drummers had split the cadence into two separate rhythms that were slowly coming together, moving toward one pulsing heartbeat of hypnotic sound. And as the drumming moved toward that one thudding rhythm, Holly and the python shimmered in the firelight and Beau experienced a strange, disturbing hallucination that they were blending, merging, becoming one entity.

"Help her!"

The words cracked through his mind like a lightning strike.

powerful enough to knock him backward a step and startle him to full alertness.

"Get her! Dambala won't mean to, but he'll kill her. She's not ready for this! Go, go!"

Beau clapped his hands to the sides of his head, and his eyes widened in shock. When he could think, he saw Desiree staring at him across the hazy clearing, her gaze narrowed and intense. Her body was taut and trembling, her fists clenched against her chest.

"Help her now!" Her lips did not move, she didn't speak aloud. He couldn't have heard her if she had. The drums and rattles pounded at a frenzied level, building toward a crescendo. The dancers shouted and stamped their feet. Despite the chaos and noise, he heard Desiree's voice resonating deep in his mind. The shock of it paralyzed him for a second, then her words penetrated and all he could think about was that Holly was in danger.

Galvanized, he sprang out of the ferns and raced forward, feeling the heat of the bonfire on his face, throwing himself into the madness of drums and rattles, stamping feet and shouting voices. He flung someone out of his way and reached Holly as she swayed and dropped to her knees. Her eyes were blank, her mouth slack. The python had begun to wrap around her.

He was screaming, but he didn't know it as he gripped the snake's body and ripped it off her. He flung it toward the bonfire, scattering the dancers. Dropping to his knees, he caught Holly as she pitched forward. Frantic, he cradled her in his arms and pressed a hand to her chest to reassure himself that she was breathing. Then he stood and swept her limp body into his arms.

The sudden cessation of the drums was almost as shocking as the noise had been.

Shaking with fury, he stared up at Flora. "If you've harmed her," he said in a hoarse, guttural voice, "if she doesn't recover fully from whatever you did to her here—I'll do everything in my power to destroy you, so help me God! Leave us alone!"

"Don't you threaten me, Beau Delacroix." Flora stood on the edge of the platform, her face crimson with rage. "You'll be sorry that you interfered! You've just made yourself a dangerous enemy!"

"Remember what I said," he snarled. "No more sand drawings. No more gris-gris. You leave us alone, or I swear I'll destroy you."

"Go now," Desiree's voice commanded inside his head.

Above him on the platform, Flora threw out her arms and shouted to the dancers, who stood watching in confusion. "Hear me," she began. "An intruder has offended Dambala!" Beau knew without a doubt that things were about to get dangerous. He felt a prickly tension rise around him and understood that Flora would try to turn her followers against him.

But Flora made a choking noise and broke off midsentence. Her palms flew up to her head and she reeled backward as if she'd been struck. Beau tensed and narrowed his eyes, unsure of what he was seeing. Invisible hands jerked Flora away from the platform edge, spun her and flung her to the floor in front of a velvet-draped chair. That's what he could have sworn he saw.

He didn't stay to see more. Heart pounding, he adjusted Holly in his arms and strode out of the clearing, almost running. Darkness closed around them and he looked about wildly, trying to get his bearings. When he saw a glimmer of light near the ground, he rushed toward it, discovered a lantern and then another. Relief washed over him when he reached the end of the path and recognized the back of Desiree's house.

He carried Holly around to the front and gently placed her on the marshy ground. From here, he couldn't hear any drums, thank God; he heard only the familiar sounds of the water in the channel, the chirp of crickets and the nearby hoot of an owl.

"Holly." Bending over her, he stroked her face. Her skin was so hot that it seemed to burn his fingertips. "Darling girl. Holly?"

Her eyelids fluttered and she looked up at him, her gaze filled with confusion. "Beau?" she whispered, lifting a hand to touch his face. "Beau!" Struggling to sit up, she frowned and looked around, then flung herself in his arms, holding him so tightly he couldn't breathe. "Oh, Beau!"

"Shh." He stroked her back, feeling her shaking in his arms. "It's all right, honey. It's all right now."

"Oh, Beau. Oh, Beau." Her fists closed in his hair and she clung to him. "There were voices in my head. They wanted me to free them, to send them into...I don't know...I... Oh God, I...and the snake!'' A long, violent shudder racked her body. ''I was...the snake was...I was becoming the snake! Beau, I was becoming the snake!''

''I know,'' he said soothingly, stroking her, trying to calm her. That they had experienced the same hallucination scared the hell out of him and made his skin crawl. But he didn't want to think about it right now. He just wanted to get away from here. ''I know, honey, but it's over now. It's over, Holly.''

Whatever had happened tonight, it would not happen to her again. Not while he had a breath left in his body. He didn't care what he had to do. Bring the authorities down on Flora, never leave Holly's side...it didn't matter. This was not going to happen again.

She pushed back in his arms, looking wildly around her as if she feared the snake had pursued them, then her fingers dug into his neck. ''Please. Please take me home. Please, Beau. I have to get away from here.''

Without a word, he stood and picked her up in his arms. His boat was tied in a concealed spot farther along the channel, but he had spotted Dandy's boat when he arrived and he carried her to the pier and helped her climb down the wooden ladder. He dropped down beside her and picked up the pole, pushing the vessel into the main channel. ''Don't think about anything right now, honey, just rest.''

They passed through a bar of moonlight and he saw her head and shoulders slump forward. Her fingers gripped the edge of the seat and she was shaking so badly that he thought he heard her teeth chatter. Damn Flora. And Desiree, too. He ground his teeth together and concentrated on getting Holly out of the swamp as swiftly as he could.

The lights were extinguished and there was no one at Dandy's place when Beau tied the boat to the dock. He would have carried Holly to his car, but she shook her head and walked at his side, holding on to his arm.

''My car...'' she started to say, blinking in confusion.

''We'll come back for it tomorrow.''

Once he had her safely inside the Porsche, he peeled away from

Dandy's place and floored the gas pedal. He'd never been so glad to see the lights of Bayou Beltane as he was tonight.

"What time is it?" Holly asked as he braked in front of her house.

"I don't know. Two o'clock? Maybe three." He walked around the car, helped her step outside. She had left the porch light on and he had no trouble locating the door key she kept hidden under a flowerpot near the white azalea. Inside the door, he turned and drew her into his arms, gently tilting her face up to him. "How are you feeling?"

"Better, I think, but still strange." She gazed into his eyes, and some of the tension flowed out of his shoulders. For the first time since this nightmare began, she looked like herself again, like the Holly he loved. "Later, not now, I want you to tell me how you happened to be there tonight. And thank heaven you were." Her fingers were still trembling lightly when she stroked his face. "But right now, I want a shower. I keep smelling...I don't know what it is, but something that...and I don't want you to leave me. Please say that you won't leave me tonight."

"I won't," he murmured huskily, pulling her close to his body and burying his face in her hair. He kept flashing back to the image of the snake coiling around her, taking it another step and another in his mind until the snake had crushed her. "I love you, Holly. I couldn't bear if it something happened to you."

She wrapped her arms around his neck and pressed against him. "I love you, too. Oh, Beau, I love you so much." They held on to each other, wrapped in a tight embrace, their hearts beating wildly. Then she took his hand and led him into her moonlit bathroom. She turned on the shower, but not the lights, and pushed off her sandals before she stepped into the shower fully clothed. Beau kicked out of his shoes, tossed his wallet and keys into the sink, then followed her.

Moonlight glowed through a frosted glass window, providing just enough light that he saw the satiny glow of her skin as she unbuttoned her wet shirt and let it drop to the floor. For a moment she stood in her bra and jeans, letting hot water cascade over her hair and face. Then she reached for the buttons on his shirt and drew him toward her into the flow of water.

Steam rose around them, pearly in the moonlight streaming through the window glass. When Holly had his shirt off, she combed her fingers through the hair on his chest, then dropped her wet head to his shoulder as he reached behind her and opened her bra clasp. He slid his hands up her back and over her shoulders, catching the straps of her bra and guiding them down her arms. And he gasped when her full breasts pressed against his naked chest.

The soap was right behind her, and he lathered her back as she held on to him, her breath hot on his wet skin. Then she eased away and arched her body so he could run his soapy hands over her glistening breasts and feel the nipples rise hard as stones against his palms.

"Holly," he whispered hoarsely. She was the most beautiful thing he had ever seen. Her hair was wet and sleek, her lashes sooty crescents on her cheeks. Soap bubbles slid down her breasts onto wet jeans that molded her body like a second skin. She was Venus standing in moonlit steam. A vision so ethereal and otherworldly that he touched her throat with a shaking hand to assure himself that she was real.

"I love you," she whispered. "I love you, I love you."

"I've never wanted a woman so much in my life," he said when he could speak past the emotion swelling his throat.

She opened her eyes and gazed at him through the pearlescent steam billowing around them. "Please," she said softly, urgently, her fingers moving on the zipper of her jeans.

When they were naked, she stepped against him and ran the bar of soap over his back and buttocks and thighs, nipping lightly at his shoulder. And when she lifted her mouth, he caught her roughly against him and crushed her lips beneath his in a kiss that shook him to his core. Their frenzied touches and passionate kisses were intensely physical, but it was the emotion running hot and wild between them that ignited them both and made them desperate for each other.

Standing in the needle sting of the shower, he ran his hands over her body, stroking her breasts, her stomach, the soft, feathery darkness between her thighs. And he smothered her moans of pleasure beneath his lips, kissing her with mounting urgency, oblivious to her fingernails digging into his shoulders and back.

When they were both crazy with wanting, wild in their movements against each other, he lifted her and slid her onto him, gasping as her legs circled his buttocks and she pulled him deep inside her. He made love to her in the clouds of moon white steam as he had never made love to a woman before. He wasn't aware of the water spraying over them or the soaked clothing at his feet. His existence narrowed to Holly, only Holly. The satin soapy gloss of her skin and her wet mouth on his. The damp heat of her thighs and legs twined around his hips.

Holly, Holly. He couldn't get enough of her. They stumbled out of the shower, groping for towels then abandoning them, blindly reaching for each other. Swinging her up in his arms, he carried her into the bedroom and they fell on the bed, locked together.

Shortly before dawn, he remembered they had left the shower running and he eased out of bed, careful not to wake her, padded to the bathroom and turned off the water. He wrung out their sopping clothing and threw everything into the dryer, then turned to the sink and splashed cool water on his face and throat.

Straightening, he gazed into the mirror and let the evening's events flood into his mind. The remembered images deeply disturbed and overwhelmed him. But already his mind had begun to cloud the details and blur his memory. Frowning at himself in the glass, he tried to sort out what he had actually seen deep in the swamp. What had been real, and what had he imagined or hallucinated? He wasn't sure anymore. Things he had thought were real when they happened now impressed him as so improbable that his mind must have been playing tricks on him. That conclusion upset him, since he didn't consider himself a fanciful type of man.

Right now, the only thing he was sure about was Holly. He loved her, loved her so much that his chest ached with emotion. He wanted to protect her, cherish her, love her.

"Beau?"

He shook his head, combed his fingers through his hair and returned to the bedroom. Sliding into bed, he guided her head to his shoulder and wrapped his arms protectively around her, holding her close. "Why aren't you sleeping?"

She kissed his chest, then slipped her arm around his waist. "Beau...I...I don't know what happened to me in the swamp. But it was something dark and..."

He smoothed a strand of damp hair off her forehead. "We don't have to talk about it now."

"I'm not sure I'll ever be able to talk about it, not really," she said after a long pause. "But I know this. I'm finished. No more research. And I'm not going to write a book about vodun." She hesitated again, pressing her cheek against his chest. "There's so much that science still has to learn about the mind and how it works. I would like to have made a contribution in that area, but somehow I became vulnerable. I...I got caught up in something that I thought I understood, but I don't. I was frightened last night. Badly frightened. Frightened enough by the vulnerability of my own mind that I know I can't continue with this."

"You won't hear an argument from me," he said, not hiding his relief. He'd been frightened, too.

"There are several possible explanations for what I believed was happening, ranging from mass hysteria to drugs in whatever I drank from the bowl. Or it could have been a hallucinogen in the incense or even a possible fugue state."

He stared at the dawn light pressing at the window. He hadn't drunk from the bowl she mentioned, and he'd had only a brief exposure to the clouds of incense. He hadn't been there long enough to get swept into mass hysteria and he'd never experienced a fugue state in his life and didn't accept that he'd experienced one last night. But he said nothing because he didn't want to frighten her further by casting doubt on the explanations she was struggling to find.

"I guess I don't care how it happened," Holly said at length, her breath warm on his chest. "I just don't want it to ever happen again."

"I'm glad."

They held each other, their fingers gently stroking. Then she tilted her head back to smile at him with soft eyes. "Now, about what happened after we came back here..." Stretching, she kissed his chin and her voice sank to a whisper. "Did I dream that? Or did we really take a shower with our clothes on?"

Smiling, he slid down beside her and gazed into her eyes. "I can't believe this. We share the most erotic experience of my life and you think it was a dream. I'm crushed."

She laughed softly and fit her body into the curves of his. "Maybe if you made love to me again, I'd remember everything. At least the part of last night that I want to remember."

"I think I can do that," he said gruffly before he claimed her mouth.

For the moment, this was all that he wanted to think about, making love to her. He'd think about the rest of it tomorrow. And probably for the rest of his life.

CHAPTER FOURTEEN

BENDING OVER THE BED, Beau kissed Holly's forehead and felt his heart ache with love as she smiled in her sleep. Moving quietly through her house, he slipped outside into the early coolness and left before the neighborhood began to stir. He drove to his cottage, showered and shaved and grabbed a quick breakfast, then he walked toward the barn, stopping to watch a dozen horses grazing in a meadow lit by the morning sun.

The scene was so peacefully normal that it made last night's surrealistic events seem like a distant nightmare. Placing a boot on the bottom rail of the fence, he frowned absently, watching sunlight slide along the sleek coats of the horses. In the clear light of day, he was no longer certain about what he had seen or heard last night. Had he really heard Desiree speaking inside his head? Had he truly imagined that Holly was somehow, impossibly, merging with a snake?

These memories were so incredible, so unbelievable that his mind rejected them. But there were things that *did* make sense even in the bright morning light. Holly had been in danger from the python's crushing coils. He hadn't imagined that. And Flora had wanted the snake to injure or even kill her. He'd seen Flora's face and knew that was true.

Pushing away from the rail, he strode to the barn and upstairs to his office. After arranging for someone to pick up Holly's car from Dandy's Boat Rentals and his boat from the channel near Desiree's, he placed the first call of the day to his sister, Shelby. He caught her at home before she left for the law firm.

"This better be important," Shelby said, yawning in his ear. "What time is it, anyway?"

"Honey, there's something I need you to do for me. I want

you to use the firm's resources to put together a dossier on Flora Boudreaux.'' He stared across the room at a photograph of Hot Shot. He and Bear had a full day planned on the training track. "I want to know everything there is to know about that woman. I don't care what it costs. Put an investigator on it, do whatever you have to do."

"What are you looking for specifically?" Shelby was awake now, her interest piqued.

"I'm looking for anything that can be used against her," Beau said bluntly, his voice hard. "If I wanted to run Flora out of the parish, if I wanted to destroy her, that dossier should tell me how to do it. I want to know what her secrets are, where she's vulnerable, everything."

Shelby whistled softly. "Do you want to tell me what this is about?"

He hesitated. "No." Last night's events were too bizarre to share. He doubted he would ever discuss them with anyone. "Let's just say that I'm sick to death of having my employees frightened by the voodoo signs we keep finding around the farm. I told Flora to cease and desist, and she didn't take it well."

"You must be very sure that it's Flora who's harassing you."

"Who else would it be?" He shrugged. "She told me herself that she's my enemy."

"You know, I have a feeling you're only telling me part of a much bigger story," Shelby said after a minute. She let a brief, hopeful silence develop, then continued speaking when he didn't comment. "Okay, I'll assemble the dossier for you. When do you want to see it?"

"Actually, I don't want to see it. I might be tempted to use it for the wrong reasons. Keep the dossier at the office, and if the time comes that I need it, I'll call you. Just do it, Shelby. And don't let any grass grow under your feet on this."

"Beau? Do you think you'd actually run Flora out of the parish?"

"Oh, yes," he said in a cold voice. "If I have to, I'll use whatever you and the investigator dig up. I'll do whatever I have to do to protect me and mine."

"And yours," Shelby repeated thoughtfully. "Speaking of which," she said with a grin in her voice, "how is Holly?"

Now he smiled. "Holly is...wonderful." An urge to tell someone that he loved her overwhelmed him. The feelings that swelled inside his chest were too powerful to be kept secret. He wanted to shout his feelings from the rooftops. "I love her."

"Beau Delacroix! I've never heard you say that about any woman before! This is wonderful!" Too late it occurred to him that Shelby would hang up from him and call all his sisters to relay this tidbit of family gossip. He sighed, then grinned. So be it. "So, big brother, when's the wedding?"

"Excuse me?" Instantly, his smile faded.

"The wedding, dummy. As the old saying goes, First comes love, then comes marriage, then comes Beau with a baby carriage." She laughed in his ear. "Something like that. I don't believe the old saying actually mentions you by name, but you get the idea."

"You can love someone without marrying them," he insisted, sounding defensive.

"Possibly. But it doesn't usually happen that way. Look, if I don't get off the phone, I'm going to be late for work. Nepotism cuts no ice at the firm. Grandfather expects everyone to arrive on time, all bright eyed and bushy tailed. I'll get things started on Flora's dossier today. Don't give it another thought."

After he poured a cup of coffee, he paced up and down his office thinking about Shelby's comments. And wondering if Holly believed that he had made some kind of permanent commitment when he told her that he loved her.

That had not been his intention. His declaration had been impulsive, not something he had thought through. He'd meant only to express what he was feeling. He hadn't intended to imply that wedding bells were ringing in their future.

Although...

He shook his head angrily. What was he thinking? Marriage was a no-exit highway leading straight to pain. All right, recently he'd had some second thoughts about this conviction. He had to concede Jax's point that happy, good marriages did exist. But the odds still appeared stacked against long-term bliss. And a few doubts didn't mean that his opinion had done an about-face. Besides, Holly was as opposed to marriage as he was.

Wasn't she?

HOLLY AWOKE with a headache severe enough that she called the clinic and instructed the receptionist to cancel her appointments for the day. Even after aspirin brought the headache under control, she didn't consider going in to work. Not today. There were too many knotty issues that she urgently needed to sort out.

After dressing in a pair of jeans and a crisp checkered shirt, she carried a pot of coffee and her cup out to the patio table in her backyard. At home, September signaled the beginning of autumn. A few trees would be starting to turn color on the slopes of the Wyoming Tetons. But in Louisiana, aside from the morning being a little cooler, she hadn't noticed any evidence of autumn changes.

Dropping her head in her hands, she massaged her temples. She felt a long way from home today.

When she could face an examination of last night's events, she drew a deep breath and began with the easiest item to think about. Her proposed book.

She still believed that her profession needed an academic work addressing the mind-altering aspects of fringe religions. To her knowledge, no one had studied vodun from that angle. She was still convinced that her book could have been a success.

But that wouldn't happen now, because she would never write a book about vodun. It wasn't that she lacked a scientific approach or an analytical mind, she assured herself, seeking to bolster her pride a little. The truth was more subtle, and frightening in its implications.

She herself was vulnerable to the mind-altering elements of vodun.

Lifting her face to the morning sun, she closed her eyes and thought about that. For years she had shied away from any association with the paranormal. But in her heart she knew that her "hunches" were anything but normal. Her hunches had proved to be a conduit of sorts that had widened her vulnerability to the hysteria, or whatever it was, inherent in vodun. Because of this, she had lost objectivity in her research. And because her hunches opened some kind of inner door, vodun had reached her on a level that was neither scientific nor scholarly.

Maybe she would write a serious book someday. She hoped so. But the subject would not be vodun. And after thinking about it, she understood that she was all right with this decision. Relieved, in fact.

Deciding to abandon the book made thinking about last night a little easier, because she didn't have to fear a repetition of those frightening events. Her association with Desiree and Flora Boudreaux would end. Thankfully, she would never have to see the snake again.

A deep shudder made her body shake, and she swallowed a rush of panic.

Much of the ceremony remained hazy in her mind and she was glad about that. But she remembered the snake as if those moments were part of a terrifying dream. Something had altered her perception of reality. For a brief, horrifying few minutes, she had utterly believed that she and an ancient power in the form of the python were becoming one. Even now, with the sunshine warm and bright all around her, remembering the way she had felt last night made her go cold inside and caused her fingers to tremble.

Logic insisted that some sort of hallucinogen must have been employed during the ceremony. But...she just wasn't sure, and she never would be. But she was absolutely certain that vodun was dangerous to her. She had been stubbornly wrong, and Beau had been right.

When she thought about Beau, she smiled and the tension that cramped her shoulders and stomach ran out of her body. Beau. That part of last night had been wild and wonderful. There had been erotic moments and intensely tender moments. Moonlit moments with a strange ethereal feel to them, and moments of emotional connection so complete that she had felt as if she and Beau had been together always and would be together until the end of time.

That thought led to the next as she remembered how passionate their declarations of love for each other had been. If she'd had any doubts about the depth of her feelings for Beau, or his for her, last night had dispelled them. So where did that leave them?

Holly got up and wandered around her backyard, pausing to examine the shrubbery and pinch off a withered blossom here and there in the beds of flowers.

How did commitment work between two people who feared marriage? After pondering that question for most of the morning, she straightened her shoulders and returned inside the house, heading directly to the telephone. Pausing, she asked herself if she really wanted to do this, then decided she did. She had to have some answers.

"Holly!" her mother said happily. "What a nice surprise. We haven't heard from you in a while. Your father will be sorry that he missed your call, but he drove into town to buy me some nail polish to match the lipstick I bought yesterday." She laughed. "We're going to Evie and John Slovik's anniversary party to-night."

Holly tried to imagine her father making a twenty-mile round trip to buy her mother a bottle of nail polish. This was a side of her parents' marriage that she'd never noticed before, and it surprised her.

"Mom," she said, wrapping the phone cord around her finger. "I hope this question isn't too rude or too blunt, but...why do you and Pop stay married?"

"What?" Genuine shock infused the word.

"All my life the two of you have been fighting like cats and dogs. You don't seem to even like each other. I've always wondered why you didn't get a divorce, why the two of you stayed together."

"Holly Gibson, you've just shocked the daylights out of me. I need to sit down." Holly heard a chair scrape across the kitchen floor, then her mother came back on the line. "Do you really think your father and I fight all the time? That we should get a divorce? Holly, I can't believe you could think such things."

"I can't believe you think that you don't fight." The conversation was not going at all the way she had expected it would.

"Honey, maybe you're right," her mother said after a lengthy pause. "Maybe we do argue and fuss. But there are all kinds of relationships in this old world. Some folks have to have a smooth bump-free marriage or they think they aren't happy. Other people like the spice of a few arguments, or maybe they just disagree about most things. And maybe that's your Pop and me. But, honey, you have to look deeper than the disagreements. Your Pop and I love each other and we always have.'' Holly heard the smile in her mother's voice. "A man doesn't go off to buy nail polish for a woman he doesn't care about. And I sure wouldn't be happy cooking and cleaning up after a man I didn't care about.''

"I think I need to sit down, too," Holly said, astonished and a little bewildered by what her mother was saying. "Are you claiming that you and Pop have a happy marriage?''

"I'm saying our marriage works for us. There are long stretches when I'd like to bash your father over the head with my skillet. And he probably feels the same way toward me. Then there are long stretches when things are pretty calm around here.'' She hesitated. "The thing is, honey, each couple makes their own kind of marriage. No two are the same. My marriage might not work for you, but it works for...oh, my heavens. Holly, have you been thinking all these years that Pop and I have a terrible marriage?''

"Well, yes. That's how it's looked.''

"Oh, honey, I'm so sorry." Now her mother sounded upset. "We've had our bad moments, but...arguing is just part of who we are. Most of the time, we don't even notice that we're fussing. But please don't think that we don't love each other, because we do. And don't think that we've had a bad marriage, because we haven't. From our point of view we have a successful marriage and a good life. Oh, Holly. I wish we'd talked about this before. Your Pop and I can argue and get into a shouting match about what time it is. And the arguing and the shouting don't mean a thing. It's just how we are." Frustration sounded in her voice. "I wish I could explain things as well as you do, then you'd understand.''

There came a time in a person's life when she suddenly saw her parents not as parents, but as people. And this was the moment for Holly. If Harlan and Lucy Gibson had sought her counseling services, after two sessions she would have spotted that both were argumentative and that was their way of communicating. She would also have seen that the underlying marriage was strong and enduring. If they had requested her assistance, she would have sent them off with a list of rules for constructive arguing and perhaps some material about handling anger. She would not have considered them representative of all marriages.

The abrupt insight took her breath away. It staggered her to realize that most of her life she had had a totally wrong perception of her parents' marriage. She'd been blind to the most important point: her parents' marriage worked for them. And wasn't that what counted? Not how the marriage appeared to outsiders but how it worked for the couple themselves.

After thinking about the conversation with her mother for several hours, and recalling memories that she now examined with fresh insight, Holly laughed out loud. Maybe she hadn't grown up within a marriage that matched her idea of happiness, but she'd grown up within a successful marriage. She just hadn't recognized it.

She suspected her new knowledge would have a far-reaching effect on her thinking and would give her much to ponder in the coming weeks.

But right now, she had one more thing to do before she could put last night out of her mind and devote herself fully to the positive things in her life and to exploring her relationship with Beau.

She had to visit Desiree one more time.

JACKSON LISTENED impatiently to the argument raging between his ma and his grandma, waiting for a moment to interrupt and get his ma off to himself. Nursing a cold beer, he followed the shouting and yelling long enough to discover they were fighting about the same old thing. Which of them was the most powerful manbo. Apparently Flora blamed Desiree for humiliating her at one of the swamp ceremonies, and the fight also had something to do with Desiree's protégé, Holly Gibson. Now, there was one for the books. Dr. Holly Gibson attending a voodoo ceremony deep in the swamp. Jackson hadn't attended a ceremony since he was a teenager, but he'd have gone if he had known Holly would be there. He'd like to have seen her face when Flora started working her show with the python.

"I don't have all day to wait around," he said irritably. "I'm on duty." He looked at Flora and jerked his head toward the screen door. "I need to talk to you privately."

Flora stood beside the wood stove, hands on her hips, her face dark with anger. "I'm warning you, boy. I'm in no mood to talk about money, so don't even ask." She glared at her mother. "Thanks to her, I've lost my following and I'll have to start all over. My credibility is ruined and it's her damned fault. I told you it was a mistake to let that woman attend the ceremony, but would you listen? Oh, no. You prefer a stranger to your own daughter!"

"That's not true and you know it," Desiree said. She looked exhausted. "Holly Gibson could be the most powerful manbo these swamps have seen in fifty years. And I'm bringing her along, step by step. But you don't care about the faith. All you care about is yourself and what you can get, not what you can give. That's the problem with you, Flora. You were born grabbing, and you've never stopped."

"See?" Flora screamed. "See how she talks to me?"

Jackson had heard it all before. He made a show of looking at his wristwatch. "Are you going to give me five minutes of your precious time?" he asked sarcastically. "I need your help."

Flora sent Desiree a nasty look of triumph. "At least somebody around here thinks I have something to give." Tossing her head, she flounced past Jackson and out the screen door, banging it hard behind her.

"It's not my fault that Dambala chose Holly. She wasn't ready and that is my fault. But how was I supposed to know that Dambala would pick last night?"

"Grandma, I don't have time for this," he said, hearing Flora stamping around on the porch.

"And you don't care about anything unless it has to do with you." Desiree said sadly. "There's a lot of your mama in you, Jackson."

No way was he going to get into an argument with Desiree. "I'll see you on Sunday for supper," he said on his way out the door. Flora was sitting in one of the rockers, glaring at the muddy water in the channel and rocking back and forth like she was trying to break the chair.

"Me and Desiree are going to have a showdown," Flora said as he sat in the rocker next to her. "She just can't stand it that I took her place. She wants to be up there running the show. It just kills her that it's me calling the shots and not her. She'd rather have some white-bread stranger working Dambala instead of me, that's how spiteful she is!"

"Ma, I gotta talk to you. This is important. Damn it, I need some help."

"You always need something. None of you ever think about me!"

"Philip's horse has got to win the Bayou Derby."

She stopped rocking and whipped her head around to stare at him. "Now, where's your brain, boy? Why should I help that old bastard if I don't have to?"

"Don't give me that. You've been helping him all along, just like I have. When he wants to put a scare into someone, he asks you to go do some hoodoo, and you do it."

"I do it for you. You know I'm trying to get Philip to change his will. But I sure as hell don't intend to help him out just outta the goodness of my heart. So whatever you're thinking, the answer is no!" She started rocking furiously again.

Leaning forward, he clasped his hands between his knees. "Ma, listen. I've thought about this and there's no way to guarantee that Philip's horse will win the Derby. It isn't as easy to fix a race as it used to be. But Philip's horse should win easily if Beau Delacroix's horse, Hot Shot, isn't in the race. If that happens, then Philip will pay me thirty grand, and I can get Huey off my back." He thought about the photograph of the shack and ground his teeth together. He didn't know how much time he had before something ugly happened, but he suspected the clock was ticking. "Now, help me figure how to work this out."

The rocker slowed and he could see her shifting gears and thinking about what he'd just said. "What do you want from me?"

He shrugged. "I don't know. Maybe you could put a hoodoo

on Beau's horse or something. You made her colic once, or so you claimed. Couldn't you make that happen again right before the race?''

''What you really want is not so much for Philip's horse to win, but for Beau's horse to lose. Now, that's pretty interesting.'' Reaching down beside her, she picked up a fan and waved it in front of her face. Jackson spotted a tiny thoughtful smile at the corner of her lips. He'd seen that smile many times before and it always signaled trouble for someone.

He didn't understand why Beau's losing the race would interest her so much, but it did, and now he saw how to play this. ''It's time that arrogant Beau Delacroix was taught a lesson in humility,'' he said, testing the waters. Flora nodded vigorously.

He saw her smile settle in place and he started to relax. Philip's thirty grand was as good as in his pocket. ''What are you thinking?'' he asked.

''I'm thinking about killing two birds with one stone,'' she said in a dreamy voice. ''But you got to do your part. When we get this all set up, I want you to break into Holly Gibson's house and I want you to stir the contents of a certain packet into her coffee can.''

A frown puckered his brow. ''Holly Gibson?'' He shrugged. ''Makes no nevermind to me. I don't care if you settle a score there, so long as we get Beau's horse.''

''She keeps her coffee in a glass jar beside her coffeepot. You stir my packet into the top third.''

''Now, how would you know that she keeps her coffee in a glass jar beside the coffeepot?'' There were times when Fora seemed downright spooky. She knew things that she had no way of knowing. Unless she'd broken into Holly's house. That was possible, of course, but it impressed him as unlikely.

''That's none of your business,'' she said smugly. ''Despite what *she* says—'' she tossed her head toward the screen door, indicating Desiree ''—I have powers. Strong powers.''

Things were moving in the direction he wanted. ''What I need to know is how stirring some powder into Holly Gibson's coffee is going to make Hot Shot lose the Bayou Derby.''

Flora's laugh made the hair stand up on the back of his neck.

"Hot Shot isn't going to lose the race. Hot Shot isn't going to be in the race to start with."

"And how are you going to manage that?"

"Not me, son, you. How are *you* going to manage that? I'm not going to do all the work for you."

"All right," he said, wetting his lips. For thirty grand and the chance to get out from under Huey's threats, he was willing to do whatever it took. "What am I supposed to do?"

"Fire," she said in that same dreamy voice, smiling at the sunlight on the water.

Jackson sat up straight, staring at her. Fire. Hot damn, why hadn't he thought of that? After a minute, he slapped his thigh and laughed. "Hot Shot can't run if she's fried meat. Ma, you got some kind of brilliant mind on you."

"You put out the word that your ma predicts Beau is going to suffer some bad luck, a real setback. I might as well get some press outta this." She relaxed in the rocking chair and fanned her throat. "My credibility needs a boost."

He grinned, loving it. "Are you going to start the fire? Or is that my job?"

"Don't be an idiot." She rolled her eyes. "You've got access to arrest records, don't you? Seems to me like you shouldn't have much trouble locating someone with experience in this kind of thing."

She was right, of course. In fact, now that she'd pointed him in the right direction, he could think of two suspected arsonists in the area. One of them should have been in jail now—everyone on the force knew he'd set at least two serious fires—but no one could prove he was guilty. Arson itself was easy to prove, but it was almost impossible to discover who lit the match. A slow grin curved his lips.

He left the shack a happy man, whistling as he poled his boat through the channel. It was his boat, and he kept it tied to a private pier owned by the family, not too far from Dandy Dog's place. He was walking to his cruiser when he spotted Holly Gibson's car flash by on the swamp road, heading toward Dandy's.

Pushing a hand into his pant pocket, he closed his fingers around the packet Flora had given him. He didn't know what it contained and he didn't want to know. But he did wish he'd paid more attention to the argument between Flora and Desiree. Then he might have had a better idea of why Flora was dragging Holly into the deal about roasting Beau's horse. His ma might still be mad that Holly had counseled Nikki Gideon, but she hadn't mentioned that or Steven's death in a long while.

In the end, he didn't care about Flora's agenda. All he cared about was getting his money.

And it was pleasant to think about Beau getting his comeuppance. The Delacroix barn would go up like a pile of kindling. Along with everything inside it. Like the horses. Best of all, he'd get to personally watch Beau's dreams go up in smoke because the police department routinely responded to fires.

"Is FLORA HERE?" Holly asked through the screen door. She dreaded seeing Flora but wanted to face her and say what she had come to say.

Desiree opened the door and beckoned her inside. "I expected you, *chérie.*" A tray with a pitcher of iced tea and two glasses waited on the table, supporting her statement. "Flora's outside digging herbs. It's probably best that you two not meet just now."

Holly nodded, ashamed of the relief she felt. She sat at the kitchen table across from Desiree and watched the old woman pour the tea. In a way, she would miss this place and the pungent fragrance of drying herbs, old incense and cooking smells. There was knowledge here that she hadn't begun to tap or understand. Secrets that would forever remain hidden.

She tasted the tea, then cleared her throat. "I've come to thank you for all the help you've given me on my research project, and to tell you that I won't be coming again. I've decided not to write my book, after all."

Desiree nodded, turning her glass between her palms. "I know." She lifted her head and looked at Holly, and Holly again experienced the uncomfortable feeling that Desiree saw into her thoughts. "Flora says I let you come to the ceremony because I wanted to humiliate her and turn her followers against her. That's not true. I wanted to test your powers, see them for myself. Maybe

I wanted you to see your power.'' She closed her eyes and swayed on her chair. ''I was wrong. It was too soon.''

''I don't know what happened last night,'' Holly began uncomfortably.

''I'm a foolish old woman who wanted to see one more great voodoo queen before I die.'' Desiree stared into her face. ''That's you,'' she whispered.

''No.''

''It could be. I tried to push years of training into a few weeks, but I was wrong to do that. But we could begin again....''

Holly shook her head and reached to cover Desiree's hand. ''No,'' she said gently. ''On a professional level, I wanted a book from our association. On a personal level, I hoped to understand my hunches. If I misled you in any way, I'm sorry and I apologize. I have no interest and no desire to practice vodun myself.'' She hesitated. ''I don't understand what happened to me last night. I doubt I'll ever know the truth. But, Desiree, it made me understand that I can't continue with this.''

''I'm sorry you were frightened,'' Desiree said earnestly, gripping Holly's hand.

''I was terrified,'' Holly agreed. ''But, Desiree, there were also moments of exhilaration and joy, a moment when I believed I was part of the universe and understood it. And that frightens me most of all. I've explained this to myself by deciding someone drugged me.''

Distress filled Desiree's eyes and she started to speak, but Holly cut her off.

''That's what I want to think, and I'd appreciate it if you would let me believe it.'' She gazed into the old woman's eyes. ''If I went much further with this, I have a hunch that it would destroy me. I think you know this in your heart.''

Sighing, Desiree turned Holly's hand over and lightly traced the lines in her palm. ''Trust your hunches,'' she said quietly. ''They are a gift. I could teach you how to use this gift....''

Holly shook her head. It was too late. ''The hunches aren't important anymore. I can cope with them.'' She drew a deep breath. ''Please tell Flora that I'm no threat to her. I'm not trying to usurp her place with you or with her followers. That possibility never occurred to me. In any case, my involvement with vodun is finished.''

Sadness filled Desiree's eyes. "Flora's not finished with you," she warned in a low voice. "I'll look after you and do what I can. But..." She pressed Holly's hand between her palms. "Remember this, *ma chère*. Your power is strong. If you let me teach you how to use it, you won't need to worry about Flora ever again.''

Holly smiled. "You're persistent. But no." Gently she removed her hand and stood. "You are a remarkable woman, Desiree Boudreaux. I've enjoyed our time together." Stepping around the table, she embraced Desiree and kissed her on the cheek.

Desiree followed her out to the pier and watched Holly climb down the ladder and drop into the swamp boat. "You and Beau," she said with twinkling eyes. "I have a hunch things will work out the way you want them to.''

Holly laughed. "I have a hunch you're right.''

"But only if...''

"If?" Holly asked. "If what?" She didn't like the way the old woman's expression had suddenly altered. Desiree gazed at the cedars across the channel of water, but Holly had an idea she didn't see the limbs or moss. Desiree's eyes widened and her mouth rounded as if she were looking at something terrible and frightening. "Desiree, tell me what you're seeing.''

The old woman gave her head a shake and swallowed, placing one hand on her chest. "Be careful!" she said in a voice tense with urgency. "Be very careful, Holly.''

Suddenly Holly's palms felt slippery around the pole. "Desiree, please tell me what—''

But Desiree hurried away from her, rushing toward the house without looking back.

CHAPTER FIFTEEN

THE NEXT TEN DAYS were the happiest that Holly could remember. Freed from her daily visits to the swamp and the hours of recording notes for a book that would never be, she finished her workday by driving out to Delacroix Farms to help out wherever she could. Afterward, she and Beau would grab a bite to eat or meet another couple for dinner.

They had been inundated by invitations from Beau's family. It was as if every one of the Delacroix had heard that Beau had a very special lady and wanted to celebrate this event. Aunts, uncles, cousins, sisters and brothers-in-law...everyone insisted on meeting Holly and refused to take no for an answer.

"Who are we seeing tonight?" she asked Beau as he walked off the training track and leaned on the fence rail beside her. "Our social schedule is so crowded that it's all starting to blur." She grinned and pressed her shoulder against his. "Your family is wonderful, Beau."

"But?" he said, laughing and dropping an arm around her shoulders.

"But there's so many of them. A bit overwhelming for us only-child types."

"It's overwhelming for me, too. I haven't seen this much of my family in ages. They all want to have a look at you and get to know you."

"Pressure, pressure, pressure."

He laughed. "No one would guess it. You've charmed the socks off everyone in the family. My father adores you, my sisters think you're wonderful. My grandfather is including you in his Christmas plans. My mother even asked about you in her most recent letter. We can safely say that you have conquered the

Delacroix. Especially this one," he added in a gruff voice, taking her into his arms.

Smiling, she pressed her face against his shoulder, inhaling the good clean sweat of male labor and horseflesh. "You know what I'd really like? I'd like to order a pizza and eat it in bed. Just you and me tonight. No friends or family."

"Great idea. And we can do it because I've announced to the family that enough is enough." He adjusted her hips against his, letting her feel his arousal. "I'm spending every day working with Hot Shot, getting her ready, and spending every night doing the town with relatives instead of catching up on my paperwork or being alone with you." He nuzzled her neck. "That has to change. At least until after the Derby. Until then, there's only two ladies I'd like to spend time with. You and Hot Shot."

Arms around each other's waists, they turned and watched Hot Shot in the paddock. "Look how high she's holding her tail," Beau commented. "She's alert, eager and ready to run." His arm tightened around Holly's waist and excitement resonated in his voice. "Hot Shot is going to win the Bayou Derby, Holly, I feel it in my bones. And she's going to go on and win the Kentucky Derby, too! We've never had a horse like this. She's a born competitor." He gazed at Hot Shot with deep affection. "She's going to take us all the way. Hot Shot is going to make Delacroix Farms famous."

"I hope so," Holly echoed after a minute.

Beau looked down at her. "Did I hear a hesitation? Do you have a hunch about this?"

She knew how hard he'd been working and how gut-deep important the Bayou Derby was to him. The dreams of Beau's lifetime were riding on Hot Shot.

"You're going to win the Kentucky Derby," she stated firmly, not looking at him. Her hunch was so strong on this point that she didn't doubt it. What she didn't tell him was that she couldn't nail down the timing of her impression. When she gazed at Hot Shot and tried to visualize her flying over the finish line, she couldn't see it. Yet when she looked at Beau and attempted to see him standing in the winner's circle at Louisville, the image came to her at once, clear and sharp and true.

Beau gave the rebel yell, a shout of happy triumph, then hugged her close. "There's nothing like having your own personal crystal ball," he said, grinning. "Honey, if you're right about us winning the Kentucky Derby, I'll take you on a round-the-world cruise!"

She wrapped her arms around his waist and gazed up at him. "I love you, Beau, so much I want you to have all of your dreams."

"Does that include you? You're one of my dreams," he said in a husky voice, looking deeply into her eyes.

"I'm yours for as long as you like," she whispered. "I'll be here until you say it's over."

He continued to gaze into her eyes, and a look she'd never seen before clouded his expression. If she had tried to describe it, she would have said he was uncharacteristically sober at that moment. Speculation was reflected in his expression. A touch of anxiety. Hesitation. And love. He looked at her with love, and that was the emotion she concentrated on.

"We need to talk, Holly. We need to discuss where you and I are going. Maybe some things have changed since we first talked about relationships...."

Her heart skipped a beat. She couldn't know for certain what he referred to, but she could guess. Was it possible that Beau had also been rethinking his opposition to marriage?

"I'm ready to talk any time you are, big guy," she said lightly.

"This is going to be one of those serious relationship talks," he said, also keeping his voice light. "But until the race is over, half of my brain is going to be with that lady over there. The discussion I have in mind requires full attention from both of us, so I'd prefer to postpone it until after the Bayou Derby. But the minute we carry off the blue ribbon, you and I need to talk about cabbages and kings. And some other stuff."

"It's your meeting," Holly said with a smile and a shrug. "You set the time, the place and the agenda, and I'll be there."

He kissed the tip of her nose. "I think you can guess the agenda, can't you?"

Her gaze locked with his. "Yes."

"Think about it, okay?"

"I have been." She drew a breath, wanting to tell him about

the conversation with her mother but knowing this wasn't the right time. "Meanwhile, whose bed are we going to leave pizza crumbs in? Yours or mine?"

Beau laughed and hooked her arm around his. They headed toward the barn. "We stayed at my place last night. I imagine you'd like to check in at your place. Give me a minute to pick up some paperwork, then we'll drive back to your house."

"So I get the pizza crumbs." She drew his arm close to her body. "Beau? It scares me to be this happy. Sometimes I feel like pinching myself to see if I'm awake."

Swinging her around in front of him, he pulled her close and kissed her so deeply that she felt as if her bones were turning to liquid. "Does that feel like a dream?" he asked hoarsely.

"That felt like a promise," she whispered.

"Count on it, darlin'."

BEAU DIDN'T KNOW what had awakened him, but he couldn't get back to sleep. Lifting his head from the pillow, he checked the luminous dial on the bedside clock and then stretched out again, smiling. Holly drank coffee right up until the moment she turned out the bedroom light and closed her eyes. He didn't drink coffee after dinner, yet he was the one awake at four in the morning. He might as well have joined her and had a cup.

Wide awake he lay in the darkness thinking about Hot Shot and the Bayou Derby and Kentucky Derby and everything he had to do today. And Holly. Always he thought about Holly, no matter what else he was doing.

Usually he wasn't a man plagued by indecision, and it irritated him to feel himself swinging back and forth as to where his relationship with Holly was heading. Some nights, like now, with her head on his shoulder and his arms wrapped around her, he knew he never again wanted to wake up without her in bed beside him. That sounded suspiciously like a lifetime commitment. At other times, he thought about marriage and a hole opened in his chest.

Holly groaned softly and tensed in his arms, then rolled away from him. Her body twitched and her feet moved. A shudder ran over her. She must be having a bad dream, Beau thought. Leaning over her, he smoothed the strap of her nightgown and gently stroked her shoulder until her expression relaxed and she quieted.

For several minutes he watched her sleeping, loving the look of her, the scent of her, everything about her. Then he decided that perhaps his restlessness was causing her bad dreams, so he eased out of bed and went into her kitchen to pour a glass of juice. It was still dark outside and peacefully quiet. Now that he'd accepted he wasn't going to get back to sleep, this seemed like a perfect time to grab a couple of uninterrupted hours to catch up on the paperwork he'd been putting off for a week.

Returning to the bedroom, he pulled on his jeans and managed to find his briefcase in the darkness, then took it back to the kitchen and spread his papers over the table. He put a pot of coffee on to brew, then sat down and opened a ledger sheet in front of him. He'd been working about fifteen minutes when he heard a noise and looked up as Holly glided past him on bare feet.

"Honey?" he said in surprise. "Did I wake you?"

She didn't acknowledge him, didn't pause. Moving with slow, purposeful steps, a strange, dreamy half smile on her lips, she walked to her purse on the countertop and opened it. She fished out her car keys, then opened the door to the garage and stepped inside, letting the door close behind her.

Paralyzed by astonishment, Beau sat at the table staring at the garage door and waiting for her to come back. It never occurred to him that she wasn't going to return until he heard the garage door rise and then the engine of her car.

Jumping up, he crossed the kitchen in four strides and threw open the door to the garage in time to see her backing into the street. "Holly? Holly!" By the time he ran across the grass, she was already pulling away from the curb. "Holly!"

For an instant, he stood on the sidewalk, dumbstruck, staring at the taillights of her car moving down Magnolia Street. He couldn't believe it. Where on earth was she going at four-thirty in the morning, barefoot and dressed in her nightgown? Without her purse or her driver's license.

And with that strange trancelike expression on her face.

My God. He'd seen that look before and not that long ago.

Whirling, he ran back into the house, thrust his feet into his shoes and grabbed his car keys.

At this hour of the morning, there wasn't much traffic and he caught up to her on Main Street. Pulling into the lane next to her, he honked his horn and rolled down the window on the passenger side, shouting to her.

She didn't look at him, didn't appear to hear the blasts of the horn or his shouts. She drove with both hands on the wheel, her eyes straight ahead, a ghostly smile on her lips.

Frantically, Beau pounded on the horn to no avail. Was she sleepwalking? Dazed? Frustrated, he pulled in behind her, praying that she wouldn't have an accident and injure herself. He was so worried that he didn't immediately notice that she'd turned onto the road leading to the farm.

DRUMBEATS SOUNDED in her head, flirting with the cadence of her heartbeat. And voices called to her, urging her to hurry, hurry. Which she did. She was flying, feeling a cool breeze in her hair and against her bare shoulders, watching trees flash by on both sides of her. She flew close to the ground, but had she wanted to, she knew she could have soared high into the sky and touched the stars. The sensation of flight was exhilarating, joyful, as was seeing color with an intensity that throbbed with life. The trees flying past were a dozen shades of vibrant green, and the asphalt was shining gray and white and striped in bars of soothing faded yellow. Twin beams of light appeared behind her, bluish white with nuances of yellow, and a huge orange light lit the sky in front of her. The colors fascinated her, they were so beautiful.

BEAU SPOTTED THE FIERY glow above the treetops as soon as they left the lights of town behind. Initially he thought he was seeing the first hint of dawn. Then his heart hit his stomach as he realized it was too early. Leaning over the wheel and staring hard out of the windshield, he fumbled to grab his cell phone out of the holder. His hands were shaking and he missed the number on the first try. On the second try, he punched in 911. Probably only seconds passed before his call was answered, but it seemed that he waited a year.

And during that year he had to decide whether to fly past Holly and get to the farm as quickly as the Porsche would carry him. Or stay with her.

"This is 911, how may I help you?"

"This is Beau Delacroix. Get the fire department out to the farm right now. I think my barn is burning."

She was driving fast, so he stayed behind her until she turned into the parking lot. Hitting the gas, he accelerated past her, bumped over the curbing and drove up the footpath as close to the barn as he could get.

When he stumbled out of the car door, he could feel heat on his face. He should have heard alarms ringing like klaxons, but there was only the hungry crackling sound of the flames. Heart pounding, he looked around and spotted a large stone. Whipping off his belt, he tied the stone to his car horn. Immediately a window opened on the second story of the barn. Bear poked his head out then quickly ducked back inside. Lights came on in the grooms' quarters and along the row of cottages.

As if everything were happening at once, he heard a long panicked whinny erupting from inside the barn. Then all he could think about was Hot Shot. And the other horses trapped in their stalls. Shielding his face from the heat, he raced forward.

THE FIRE DREW HER like a child to a Christmas tree. Hurrying up the footpath, Holly reached a car, its door hanging open, the horn blaring, but she didn't stop until she passed it and stood before the blazing barn. Face radiant with delight, she lifted her head toward the flames leaping along the barn roof. Their beauty took her breath away. Red and yellow and orange danced in fiery splendor. Fingers of crimson reached for the sky, breathing trails of gold before falling back to the roof. Orange arms spread to embrace the eaves. The colors whispered to her, alive, hissing and crackling. *Dambala. Dambala.*

When she lowered her eyes, she could see through the barn, down the aisle of stalls on this side. This end of the barn wasn't burning yet, but the far end was a wall of flame so beautiful that it made her chest ache to see it. Near the base of the fire was a shadowy door that swung open as she watched. The drums and the whispering voices seemed to be coming from inside the fiery door, calling her, summoning her. Everything she had ever wanted or wished for lay inside that door. Dambala waited for her there.

"I'm coming," she whispered.

Stepping forward, she walked into the burning barn, into a firestorm of swirling, falling scraps of flaming ash.

"GET THE HORSES OUT of the north end first!" Beau screamed. People had appeared and were running all around him now. Someone had called Jax and Matt. He saw people he didn't know. Most were only black silhouettes against the roaring sheet of flame engulfing the north end of the barn. Smoke was beginning to thicken in the aisle.

Noise filled his ears. The roar of the flames. Shouts and confused instructions. The shrieking of horses trapped in stalls filling with smoke. Rafters crashed down onto the second floor right above his head. Gray-white smoke leaked through the floorboards of his office and swirled into the aisle below. A small explosion occurred in the tack room and flames shot out of the door.

Suddenly Jax was standing before him, tears streaming down her sooty cheeks. "We're going to lose it all." He saw her lips move, otherwise he wouldn't have known what she said. The noise of screaming horses kicking their stalls and the fury of the fire were too great. "My God, Jax," he cried. "You shouldn't be here. You're pregnant!"

Jax nodded as her fingers fumbled at the belt she wore around her hips. She thrust it into his hands. "I can't do it."

In the time it took for Beau to glance down at the gun belt she'd pushed into his hands, she had disappeared out of the burning barn. As he strapped the belt around his waist, he thanked God for her presence of mind in thinking to grab the gun. If one of the horses injured itself and went down in its stall, he would shoot it before he would let it die in the flames. If he had to do that, a piece of himself would also die.

Every cell in his body screamed at him to rescue Hot Shot. But logic shouted that he had to get the horses who were closest to the flames out first. He saw figures running, struggling to force the horses out of the stalls and into the aisle, but the animals reared and plunged and kicked at the stall walls, wild eyes rolling in terror, fighting the people who were desperately trying to save them.

And then he saw Holly.

To his horror, she had walked into the barn, her nightgown billowing around her bare feet, her eyes fastened in fascination on the wall of flames racing toward them. Her face was rapturous, as if she were approaching a lover.

For one terrible, paralyzing instant he could not move. Behind him, Hot Shot screamed and crashed against the walls of her stall. In front of him, Holly moved steadily through the smoke and swirls of flame, walking in a trance toward the hellish conflagration engulfing the end of the barn. Fear gripped his heart, then he bolted toward her.

A cloud of smoke billowed in front of him and a sharp voice sounded deep in his head, shocking him badly. "Stop. You can carry her outside, but she'll come right back. You fight your fight and let her fight hers."

"Get out of my head!" Screaming Holly's name, he flailed at the smoke, spotted her for an instant, then lost her.

THE HYPNOTIC DRUMS were in sync with her heartbeat now, controlling her. She wasn't aware of the bits of flaming ash burning her bare shoulders or scorching holes in her nightgown, wasn't aware of the intense heat on her face and skin or the charred smell of her hair as sparks fell into the tumbled strands. But she heard the voices calling her into the lovely flames. She heard Flora urging her forward and offering the fire as a gift. Flora's seductive voice seemed closer than the others, like honey in her ear, pushing her forward into flames that were so alive they reached her, tried to embrace her. And she wanted to stroke them. Yearned to catch the flames in her hands and laugh as they danced through her fingers like brightly colored butterflies.

Unseen fingers gripped her shoulders and almost knocked her to the steaming dirt floor of the aisle. She stumbled and blinked, her concentration momentarily broken.

Desiree's voice ricocheted in her head. "You've got to fight back! I can't do it for you. Fight, Holly! Fight or you'll die!"

Confused, she looked around her, peering into the thick smoke. Then she turned her eyes back to the flames. They were closer now. She could almost see through the door. Behind it, Dambala waited to wrap her in his embrace, waited to offer her the universe.

"Flora's nearby. You sense her. Find her and fight!" Urgency and fear shook Desiree's voice. Holly lifted her hands to cover her ears. "Gather your power. Pull it in, hold it, then send it out! Do this, *chérie* or you'll die in the fire. Do it now!"

For an instant, Desiree's voice cleared the drums from her mind and she heard the horses screaming and kicking at the walls of their stalls. Something or someone ran past her in the smoke. A large chunk of burning wood fell through the ceiling in a shower of flame.

"My God! It's the dream!"

Terrified, she spun in a circle, slapping at bits of ash clinging to her nightgown and burning through. When she heard her name, she jerked her head up and spotted Beau. He was pounding his fists against a haze of smoke as if it were a solid wall between them.

"Hot Shot," she screamed. The fire had almost reached Hot Shot's stall. Fingers of flame flickered along the wood door. "Beau! Save Hot Shot!"

But she realized he wouldn't go to Hot Shot until he saw her safely out of the barn. Spinning on bare feet, she whirled with every intention of running outside. But she hadn't taken three steps before she heard the drums again. And Flora's hypnotic voice blending with the voice of Dambala, wooing her back to the flames.

Her mind screamed at her body to run, but her legs would not move.

HE ALMOST WEPT with relief when her eyes fluttered and he saw her awaken. Horror followed confusion as her awareness returned. But she'd halted. And he thanked God for it, because he couldn't reach her. Either he had lost his mind to panic or an invisible wall separated him from her. He couldn't smash through it, couldn't move forward no matter how hard he struggled. The smoke parted and he saw Holly's terrified gaze swing toward him. She pointed and mouthed Hot Shot's name, then she whirled and ran toward safety.

Only then did he turn and race for Hot Shot's stall, praying he could get her out in time.

IT WAS LIKE TRYING to move through a waist-deep sea of hot molasses. Stopping, choking on the smoke, gasping, Holly clapped her hands over her ears to try to smother the seduction of the drums and the whispering voices that beckoned beguilingly from the flames.

"No," she whispered. Dimly, she was aware of Desiree, but Flora's voice was the stronger. "Please! Help me!" She appealed to Desiree, to anyone.

"The flames want you," Flora's voice murmured in her ear, so clear that she could have believed Flora stood beside her. "They're so lovely, so beautiful. Turn around and look at them."

Holly snapped her head up—and saw Flora standing outside the barn. Her heart stopped then raced ahead frantically. Although it was impossible—they stood at least twenty yards apart from each other—she felt Flora's hands on her shoulders, turning her back into the flames.

"No!" But she was turning around. She couldn't stop herself.

Oh, God. A lifetime lay before her. Beau and love and laughter. Children. There was nothing in the flames but fiery destruction and death. If she were to have Beau and a life with him, then she had to fight the evil that whispered in her ear, but she didn't know how. There was no one to help her, no one who could understand what was happening. She had to fight for her mind and her life and she had to do it alone and feeling helpless.

Her eyes closed and her shoulders slumped, and she concentrated as never before, summoning every ounce of willpower to fight her way out of the molasses that sucked and tugged at her legs. Invisible fingers continued to turn her back toward the fire, and she let them guide her around as a strange electric heat filled the pit of her stomach and spread through her chest and down her limbs. But she didn't stop when she faced the roaring flames. Drawing on an inner strength, she pressed against the forces controlling her and continued turning in a full circle until she faced Flora again. Sensing Flora's surprise gave her a sudden infusion of additional power, even as Flora recovered and tried again to force her into the fire.

"No!" she screamed, sending her outrage toward Flora with the force of a blow.

Flora's hands flew to her temples and her eyes widened in shock and fury. Holly seized the moment and the weakening of the forces against her to struggle forward, then she stopped with a half sob of frustration when the air thickened around her and seemed to push her back. Images whirled in front of her eyes. Baron Samdi's grinning skull leered at her, as real as Flora's presence. Dambala coiled at her feet. The drums beat a frenzied rhythm inside her head.

She couldn't fight this. Sobbing, gasping for breath, she dropped to her knees and clasped her hands over her ears. The forces arrayed against her were too powerful and she didn't understand them.

Deep inside she heard Flora's hiss of triumph. It was a physical thing as well as a sound, a scraping pain that traveled along her bones. Hot wind lifted her to her feet and spun her to face the flames and the fiery end of everything that was real and precious in her life.

She stumbled toward the blaze and searing heat, weeping helplessly, her will trapped inside a body that wouldn't obey her. And then she saw Beau through a haze of swirling smoke.

He'd gotten a bridle on Hot Shot, but she was plunging and rearing in the aisle, nostrils flaring, eyes rolling wildly. Her hooves came down hard, missing Beau by a fraction of an inch, then she reared again. Man and horse battled in the smoke, flames crackling around them.

Beau. She would never hold him again, would never bear his children or grow old with him. She wouldn't see him win the Kentucky Derby. Pain knifed through Holly's body, and she gasped with horror and sorrow at all she was about to lose.

Beau. His name rang in her mind. *Beau.* She saw the moments they had shared and the moments they would never share. *Beau.*

Throwing back her head, she screamed, "No!" The word tore out of her throat in a long howl of anguish and grief. "No!"

Bending over, shaking hands gripping her knees, her teeth clenched, she summoned control, letting her fury give her strength. Beau's name sang in her mind, and she repeated it like a mantra that would fuel her power to fight.

Heat curled in the pit of her stomach and exploded through her body. She felt an electric tingle shoot down her arms and legs, felt her chest swell and her muscles tighten. An unseen force pressed at her back and she slapped it away with her mind. Breathing hard, she felt the power gathering, filling her body. But she didn't stand up straight until she felt lightning sizzling inside her, flashing and cracking around her.

Then she turned like a discus thrower and hurled the power vibrating her body.

Flora bent over double, clutching her stomach, shock and sudden fear leaping to her eyes.

Holly pushed forward and the molasses dissolved at her first step. Fury shook her body as she made her way toward the entrance of the barn. Reaching with her mind, she jerked Flora upright and spun her around. Flora's teeth pulled back from her lips and she screamed something, then Holly felt a dark force rushing toward her. She caught the evil with her mind and flung it back. Flora dropped to her knees and clutched her chest. Her eyes rolled in her head.

A terrible rage strengthened Holly's power. Flora might not have struck the match that ignited the blazing barn, but Holly knew she was responsible. She knew horses and men would be injured tonight. Knew that Hot Shot would never run in the Kentucky Derby. She knew that she and Beau had come within minutes of losing each other.

Again and again she struck at Flora, taking a terrible dark pleasure in the woman's terror and her efforts to escape. She let Flora crawl to her feet, and then she gathered the power of her mind and in one tremendous effort hurled it with all her will and strength and watched Flora's clothing burst into flames.

As instantly as the fire engulfed Flora's body, it was doused. "No, child," Desiree's voice warned deep in her mind. "Let it go now. Flora will never bother you again. Now she knows who is the strongest."

For an instant Holly met Flora's terrified eyes and knew that she had won. Then she closed her eyelids and felt the power draining out of her into the ground. Her knees crumpled and she dropped on all fours, gasping and shaking. When she could lift her head, she realized that people and animals were all around her, running, shouting, rearing, stamping. She would have sworn that she and Flora were the only two people near the blazing barn, but the chaos around her told her that couldn't have been true.

There was no time to think about it. Strong arms lifted her, then half carried, half dragged her away from the fiery entrance to the barn. Less than a minute later, what was left of the roof crashed into the stall area and a ball of fire leaped into the sky.

"Holly, Holly." Beau held her so tightly that she couldn't breathe, but she didn't care.

She clung to him, weeping, gasping his name, running her hands over his singed hair, his sooty face, the burns in the shoulders of his shirt, while he did the same to her. "You're alive! Thank God you got out!"

"When I saw you walking into the blaze..." He buried his face in her hair and pressed her tightly against his trembling body. "I couldn't reach you. It was like...like..."

"It's all right, we're both alive and it's all right. Did Hot Shot get out? And Ma Chere?"

"There's a dozen horses running loose on the property." He closed his eyes. "Hot Shot...but I don't know about Ma Chere. I think I saw Bear with her, but..."

Holding on to each other, they watched the firemen battle the blaze. But it was a fight for containment. The barn was engulfed in flame and would burn to the ground.

They stood in exhausted and shocked silence inside a group that included Bear, Jax, Matt and several of the grooms. All of them were burned in several places and covered with soot, their eyes reddened by smoke and the struggle to hold back tears.

Shortly after dawn, Justin arrived with coffee and pastries for everyone. Townspeople appeared to help round up the horses and offer what assistance they could. Veterinarians came from New Orleans and Slidell to help Matt examine the animals and treat burns and smoke inhalation and lacerations. Two doctors and an emergency crew arrived to provide medical aid for those who had fought to save the horses. Fire trucks, police cruisers and emergency vehicles crowded the parking lot.

Holly felt the burns on her arms and shoulders now. The medical crew treated the small burns with ointment and wrapped her right ankle. Until the doctor saw her, she hadn't realized she'd been injured. Her hair and one of her eyebrows were singed, and there was a severe burn just below one elbow. But she was alive.

Someone gave her an oversized shirt to wear over her nightgown, and someone else curved her fingers around a mug of coffee. The sun was well above the horizon by the time she left the medical area and looked around for Beau.

She spotted him conferring with a knot of men that included the fire chief, Jake Trahan, Jackson Boudreaux, Bear, Justin and others whom she didn't recognize. When she scanned the area, she decided half the population of Bayou Beltane was here. Needing to be alone, she carried her coffee to the foaling shed and sat on the ground behind it, staring at nothing and trying to make sense of everything that had happened since she went to sleep cuddled against Beau. Was it only last night? Mere hours ago? That didn't seem possible. Eventually, she became aware that someone had sat down beside her.

"I had to stop you," Desiree said quietly, her gaze on the pasture and the men trying to coax frightened animals to the bridles in their hands. "I know you. If you had hurt Flora, you would have punished yourself for the rest of your life."

"Thank you," Holly whispered, dropping her head. Shame made her fingers shake. "I wanted to hurt her." It was the worst, most horrifying truth of her life. Though there was no justification to excuse what she had wanted to do, she still said, "Flora would have killed me. That's what she intended to do." A deep shudder racked her body. If she hadn't seen Beau when she had... If seeing him hadn't given her the strength to fight back...

"Flora won't bother you again," Desiree said firmly. "She

knows now." Turning her head, she gazed at the burn ointment shining on Holly's throat. "She's no match for you."

Holly recognized the subtext. Clasping her coffee cup in both hands, she shook her head. "No one should be able to do what Flora did and what I did. I don't want that kind of power, Desiree. It terrifies me."

They sat in silence for several minutes, then Desiree reached for her hand and placed a packet in her palm and curled her fingers over it. "This is for you and Beau. Sprinkle this powder in his coffee and yours. You and Beau will have good luck and a happy life."

After Desiree left her, Holly stayed where she was on the ground, watching the men chase the horses in the pasture. She finished her coffee and gazed into the empty cup. And a strong impression filled her mind, a hunch, telling her to dispose of the coffee beside her brewer. It was the first thing she would do when she returned to her house. What this meant, she didn't know, but she would do it.

Then she drew a deep breath, dropped her head in her hands and wept until no more tears came.

SHE SAID SHE COULD DRIVE, but Beau insisted that one of the townspeople take Holly home. At noon, his father insisted that he take a break, go to his cottage and shower and change clothes. He hadn't noticed the bandage on his forehead until he started to shave. At some point he must have received medical attention, but he didn't remember it. A quick inventory revealed several small burns where falling ash had scorched through his clothing. The worst burns were on his forehead, the tops of his ears and on his hands. Both hands received third-degree burns and hurt like hell now that he'd noticed.

Staring in the mirror at the bandage on his forehead, he started to shake and a wave of weakness swept through his body. He had to grip the sides of the sink to remain standing.

He kept remembering Holly walking into the blaze, kept seeing her in his mind. The same feelings of horror and loss and fear shook him now. If anything had happened to her...

Lifting his head, he stared at himself in the mirror.

If something terrible had happened to her...

BY LATE AFTERNOON, all the horses had been corralled, and everyone had departed. Holly found Beau leaning against the fence railing, a bottle of beer in his hand, staring at the smoking ruins of the barn. He dropped an arm around her shoulders when she joined him. "What are you doing?" she asked, trying to read his expression.

"A couple of hundred years ago, the famous Globe Theatre burned down in London. A spectator spotted the Globe's owner in the crowd watching the blaze and asked what he was doing there. I can't recall his name, but he said, 'Can't a man warm himself in front of his own fire?'" He pulled her close to him. "I'm warming myself beside my fire."

Holly smiled and drew him closer. "How are Hot Shot and Ma Chere?"

He hesitated so long that her heart sank and she knew the news was bad. "Ma Chere has a deep laceration on her flank, but she'll recover."

"And Hot Shot?" Holly asked in a whisper.

His arm tightened convulsively around her shoulder. "Matt says Hot Shot suffered lung damage from the smoke," he said finally. There was another pause before he could speak. "Hot Shot will never race again."

Tears filled Holly's eyes and she turned her face into his chest, holding on to him. "I'm so sorry, Beau. So very sorry."

He held her tightly wrapped in his arms for several minutes and Holly didn't embarrass him by looking at his face. "Matt isn't sure—only time will tell—but we may be able to breed her. Hot shot will give us a champion yet."

The image that leapt into her mind was so real that for a moment she thought it *was* real. She saw Hot Shot nuzzling a sleek roan foal with a blaze on his forehead. And she saw something else. Three crowns shimmering above the foal's head. Suddenly Holly smiled, tears glistening in her eyes. Hot Shot's daughter wouldn't just win the Derby, she would take the triple crown. The foal would become one of the most famous horses in the racing world.

"What are you thinking?" Beau asked, lifting her chin and studying her expression. "You're having one of your hunches, aren't you?"

"Oh, Beau," she said softly, gazing into his eyes. "There are wonderful things ahead."

"Tell me," he said, kissing her lightly on the lips.

"No," she replied after a moment of hesitation. "I don't want to spoil a fantastic surprise for you." The decision felt right. She wouldn't diminish his joy by predicting it.

"Holly...what happened in there?" He gestured toward the smoke drifting up from blackened embers. "I think I can guess because I spotted Flora just after the fire engines arrived. But I want to hear about it from you."

"I'll tell you everything," she said hesitantly, touching her fingertips to his lips. "But not now." Turning, she leaned against his chest and pulled his arms around her waist, watching the wisps of smoke rising from the barn and then dissipating in the air. "That's the best site," she said after a minute. "But the new barn should be larger." Squinting, she considered the lay of the land. "I think our house should go over there." Raising a hand, she pointed, then peeked up at him. "What do you think?"

He grinned down at her. "I've been considering that, too. But I think our house should go over there." He pointed to a wooded site. "We'll need a large trophy room, of course. We're going to rebuild in a big way and we'll need a place to display all our trophies."

She turned in his arms and encircled his neck. "And we'll need a big nursery."

"And a study for you to write in."

"With enough space for an extra desk for you to use when you bring work home."

They gazed into each other's eyes, smiling.

"We'll make it work, Holly. Divorce isn't going to be an option for us."

"If we have differences, we'll just keep fighting and thrashing them out until we find a solution. And we will." He kissed her then and she felt his love engulfing her. Her heart soared and tears of happiness swam in her eyes.

"We'll rebuild it all. You and me. Together we can do anything."

"Mr. Delacroix," she said, leaning back in his arms. "Do you realize that we've just decided to get married, raise a family and build the best damned horse farm in Louisiana?"

He laughed and pulled her hard against his body. "Yes, ma'am, I do. You've crushed my resistance, beaten me into submission and wrapped me around your little finger. And you know something, darlin'? I love it. I'm going to spend the rest of my life trying to make you as happy as you make me."

Arm in arm, they walked to inspect the site of the house they would build, excited to begin, eager to embrace the wonderful life ahead of them. When Holly put a hand in her pocket, she found the packet Desiree had given her. Holding it in her palm, she gazed at it a minute, then opened the flap and scattered the powder into the breeze.

"What was that?"

"Nothing important."

Turning to face him, her face radiant, she lifted her lips for his kiss. She didn't need a good-luck charm to bring her happiness. She had Beau.

DELTA JUSTICE

continues with

FRENCH TWIST

by Margot Dalton

Ten years ago, Madeline Belanger made the
painful decision to leave Bayou Beltane and start
a new life. But now somebody was threatening
her family—and Madeline has come back to do
something about it. If only she could avoid
Justin, her ex-husband, her first love, the man she
couldn't seem to forget....

Available in June

Here's a preview!

DELTA JUSTICE

FRENCH TWIST

JUSTIN WORE JEANS and an old leather jacket. He lounged with his hands in his pockets, gazing into the shadows with a brooding air.

Breathless and alarmed, Madeline turned, hoping to retreat the way she'd come, but the dogs had already seen her and mounted a chorus of noisy greetings. Justin got up to peer along the path, smiling when he realized who was approaching.

"Madeline," he said, moving toward her. "What a nice surprise."

"Really," she said dryly, hesitating under the spreading live oak.

This had to be more than coincidence, she realized. There was only one path leading from Mary's house to Riverwood. Justin had obviously known she and Charles would be passing this way when they returned from the big house.

The dogs tumbled around her feet, excited, but too well trained to jump. She bent to touch their silky ears, trying to regain her composure. Then she stood erect and shifted on her feet, feeling ridiculously uncomfortable. All at once she was a teenager again, shy and awkward, not even knowing what to do with her hands. Finally she stuffed them in her pockets and tried to look nonchalant.

"How's Shelby?" she asked.

"Feeling a little better. I think a good night's sleep will help a lot."

"I'll call in the morning and check on her before I go to Philip's office."

"Are you sure you want to do that alone?" Justin asked.

"Quite sure." Madeline began to edge along the path, moving

away from him. "And now I suppose I should be going, because I—"

He gestured to the flat rock he'd been sitting on. "Madeline, stay here for a minute and talk with me. It's such a beautiful evening."

She hesitated. It seemed graceless to refuse, but she was afraid of being alone with him, particularly in this setting where the twilight felt so caressing, and the shadows were deepening all around them.

"At this time of the evening I feel young again," Justin said, gazing at the dense shrubbery bordering the path. "I feel like all those years haven't passed by, and that anything could happen—all sorts of wonderful things, just waiting out there in the shadows. Do you know what I mean?"

Madeline understood exactly. But at the same time, she was so surprised to hear him express such an emotion that she forgot her awkwardness and stood gazing at him in astonishment. "You've changed, Justin."

He turned quickly to glance at her, his gaze so probing and intent that she felt compelled to return it. His eyes were dark hazel with little specks of green and gold. Seeing them again made her feel suddenly weak and dry-mouthed with emotion.

"How am I different?" he asked.

She looked down at her hands. One of the dogs stirred and sat up, and Madeline reached out nervously to stroke its head.

"You seem more thoughtful than the Justin I remember," she said. "And yet...I don't know. Almost boyish, I guess."

"Boyish?" he echoed, clearly astonished.

Madeline allowed herself a brief smile. "When you were younger, you were really quite pompous," she said gently. "I suppose it was the responsibility of having a family before you were twenty, but you always seemed...very sober and self-absorbed."

"And now I don't?"

She shook her head. "You're different now. There are times when you seem even younger than Beau. Almost reckless."

He gave her one of those rare, shining smiles that transformed his face. Madeline felt a deep stab of pain and looked away quickly.

"I suppose it's partly because—" she began, then fell abruptly silent.

Because of having such a beautiful young lover....

HARLEQUIN SUPERROMANCE®

...there's more to the story!

Superromance. A *big* satisfying read about unforget-
table characters. Each month we offer
four very different stories that range from family
drama to adventure and mystery, from highly emotional stories to romantic comedies—and
much more! Stories about people you'll
believe in and care about. Stories too
compelling to put down....

Our authors are among today's *best* romance writ-
ers. You'll find familiar names and
talented newcomers. Many of them are
award winners—and you'll see why!

If you want the biggest and best
in romance fiction, you'll get it
from Superromance!

Available wherever Harlequin books are sold.

Look us up on-line at: http://www.romance.net

HS-GEN

Harlequin® Historical

From rugged lawmen and
valiant knights to defiant heiresses
and spirited frontierswomen,
Harlequin Historicals will
capture your imagination with
their dramatic scope, passion
and adventure.

Harlequin Historicals...
they're too good to miss!

HHGENR

HARLEQUIN PRESENTS®

HARLEQUIN PRESENTS
men you won't be able to resist
falling in love with...

HARLEQUIN PRESENTS
women who have feelings
just like your own...

HARLEQUIN PRESENTS
powerful passion in
exotic international settings...

HARLEQUIN PRESENTS
intense, dramatic stories that will keep you
turning to the very last page...

HARLEQUIN PRESENTS
The world's bestselling romance series!

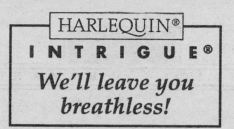

LOOK FOR OUR FOUR FABULOUS MEN!

Each month some of today's bestselling authors bring
four new fabulous men to Harlequin American Romance.
Whether they're rebel ranchers, millionaire power brokers
or sexy single dads, they're all gallant princes—and
they're all ready to sweep you into lighthearted fantasies
and contemporary fairy tales where anything is possible
and where all your dreams come true!

You don't even have to make a wish…
Harlequin American Romance will grant your every desire!

Look for Harlequin American Romance
wherever Harlequin books are sold!

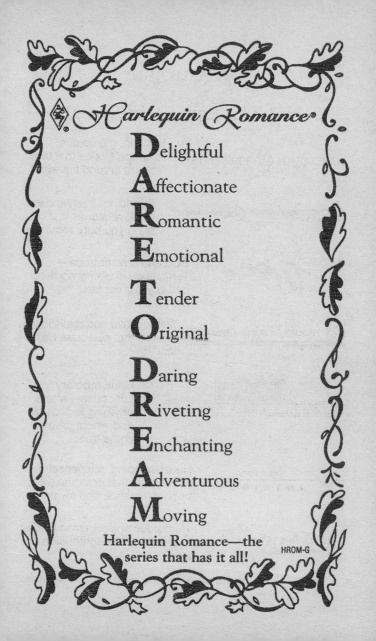

Harlequin Romance®

Delightful

Affectionate

Romantic

Emotional

Tender

Original

Daring

Riveting

Enchanting

Adventurous

Moving

Harlequin Romance—the
series that has it all!

HROM-G

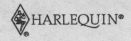 **HARLEQUIN®**

Not The Same Old Story!

 **PRESENTS®**
Exciting, glamorous romance stories that take readers around the world.

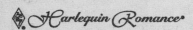
Sparkling, fresh and tender love stories that bring you pure romance.

Bold and adventurous—Temptation is strong women, bad boys, great sex!

 **HARLEQUIN SUPERROMANCE®**
Provocative and realistic stories that celebrate life and love.

Contemporary fairy tales—where anything is possible and where dreams come true.

Heart-stopping, suspenseful adventures that combine the best of romance and mystery.

Humorous and romantic stories that capture the lighter side of love.